Pressed Pennies

by

Steven Manchester

Cover Art by Stephanie Grossi

For the beautiful women in my life:
Paula, Carissa, Isabella, Mom, Darlene & Jenny

Early Praise and Reviews of Manchester's *Pressed Pennies*

"Steven Manchester's *Pressed Pennies* evokes a world still present in memory -- the 70's & 80's. The abiding sense of family as a crucible fostering love, alienation, fear, pain and, ultimately, healing is at the heart of this wondrous tale. There is the alchemy of pennies on the railroad tracks, flattened and crushed but containing wishes like wishes wished on stars, forever. For it is the wish, the intention, that seals the fate. Love is all around -- for young and old alike. There are many chances to set right what goes wrong with people. And, Manchester's characters do. They create families that are as myriad and diverse as snowflakes on the wind. But it is love that is called to soothe all wounds and bless all new beginnings."

-Maureen O'Donnell, *Brown University*

Pressed Pennies is a story of true feeling, childhood wishes, and real life. Steven Manchester has the ability to portray the lives of characters in a way that captures the reader and makes us truly want to know what the outcome is. His text is full of raw emotion, realistic and likable characters, and intricately detailed scenes that will leave your mouth watering for raspberry ice cream.

To quote character Richard Giles, "Good writers make people think, while great writers make their readers feel." Steven Manchester is a great writer."

- Heather Froeschl, *Quilldipper.com*

The characters will have you crying, laughing and cheering them on as you become enmeshed in their day to day dramas. The women who read this book will fall in love with Bill as I did as he courts Eunice to make her his own. Theirs was a love that transcended life and made the thought of death nothing to fear.

I enjoyed reading this book, turning page after page long into the early morning hours. I enjoyed the rollercoaster of emotions I felt as I became enmeshed in the lives of each family. *Pressed Pennies* is one of those feel-good reads that I recommend to everyone looking for renewal in their beliefs that love does make a difference."

- Jozette Aaron, *DeSilva's News*
(Canada)

"In the spring of 1978, young Richard falls in love with Abby. Unfortunately, the financial misfortunes of Richard's widower father force them to move away. The action fast forwards twenty years and Richard and Abby meet again. They both have been through failed relationships and are wary. Abby and Richard have to not only deal with emotional baggage of the past, but Abby's daughter, Paige, has not dealt well with her parent's divorce and shows extreme hostility toward all of Richard's overtures to establish a relationship.

Although most of the novel revolves around Richard and Abby, there are two other tales of couples developed and interwoven into the plot. Eunice and Bill are senior citizens who find true love in their "golden years". Grant and Carmen are an example of love that can sour and poison lives. All the characters are well developed and come alive in the compelling third person narrative.

The author compares his novel and style to Nicholas Sparks. This is a fair assessment as the storyline is one that is tender, sweet and more geared toward female readers. It takes a talented storyteller to appeal to the opposite gender and Mr. Manchester surely has that gift. He adds his own exceptional voice with gentle poetry that he weaves directly into the story and still maintains an excellent flow and pace.

The novel also addresses the theme of change in society for both good and evil and how we have often traded modern "must-haves" for the simple pleasures of the not so distant past. A bittersweet tone underlies much of the narrative. Most of all, PRESSED PENNIES is a tale of love and second chances and affirms that love can come at any stage of life if we are just open. This is a book that is sure to warm your heart.

Mr Manchester has written other books and the reader can discover more about him at www.Stevenmanchester.com"

- **Roberta Austin**, *The Compulsive Reader* (GA)

Acknowledgments

First and forever, Jesus Christ- my Lord and Savior.
With Him, all things are possible.

Paula- the absolute love of my life.
My sons, Evan and Jacob, and daughter, Isabella, who share the best part of my heart.
Carissa- my friend and constant source of inspiration.
Mom and Dad, Billy, Randy, Darlene, Jenny, Philip- my beloved family.
My mentor and dear friend, Russell N. McCarthy.
Keith Drab, my friend and editor on this project.
Terri Denson, Don DiMarco, Polly Labonte, Mary McDonald, Peter Zieger, Donna Russo Morin, Dawn Wheeler – whose early critiques turned *Pressed Pennies* into a much better read.
And Robert Denson III - my determined, compassionate agent, and wonderful friend. His belief in my writing has made all the difference in the world.

In no particular order:
Dan and Carol Calis, Rob and Julie Letendre, Don and Tracy DiMarco, Patrick J. Barry, Mark Grocholski, Barry M. McKee, Matt and Cheryl Olivier, Lou Matos, Nelson and Tina Julius, Brad and Lisa Cowen, Lynn Stanton, Al and Sandi Correiro, Manny and Shelley Bernardo, Tom and Ana Thompson, Paul and Tonia Patricio, The DeSousa Family, "The Dream Team" of Operation Desert Storm, My brothers at SECC, Anita, Cathy, Coley, Fred and friends at SSB, and all those my poor memory has failed…

My life has been richly blessed for having known each one of you!

"Love knows no age limit, follows no timetable
and once it finds you, all you can do is count your blessings."

- Eunice Giles Stryker

Prologue

Rick Giles wrote:

In the evolution of the 80's child, though life began as wholesome and innocent, technology quickly took over. Suddenly, two parents needed to leave the home and work. Day care, fast food and a list of coveted luxuries replaced family suppers, tree forts and long talks in porch swings.

Question: Did the American family have to be traded in to experience the American dream – was the world better back then, or is it better now; today?

Love can happen at any time in life – adolescence, adulthood or even in the winter of life.

Question: If living each moment to the fullest produces a life worth living, does it really matter when?

Some profess that the world is a small place and, whether we believe it or not we're all connected.

Question: If this is true, can any of us ever be truly alone?

In an era of divorce and single-parenthood, there are many trying issues associated with living in a non-traditional family.

Question: In such a time, how do we raise our children with respect while peacefully co-existing?

How do we make the whole thing work?

I wish I knew.

Chapter 1

Spring 1978

"**I** don't give a damn what the neighbors think!" Butch Gerwitz screeched. His words were so slurred they sounded alien. As he struggled to free himself from his worn recliner, several empty beer bottles careened across the floor and crashed into the wall. Instinctively, Claire, his wife, scurried out of his path. Butch staggered to the front door and threw open the screen. "YOU HEAR ME, YOU HYPOCRITES," he roared. "I DON'T CARE WHAT YOU THINK OF THIS FAMILY!"

Tattooed and normally unshaven, Butch Gerwitz was a heavy drinker with an equally heavy hand. And drunk or sober, he instilled fear in everybody around him. Though he'd nearly made it as a professional bowler, his abuse of alcohol determined that he'd be better suited as the caretaker of a run-down nursing home. Rage couldn't begin to describe his attitude. In the days when physical discipline was common practice, he used it more commonly than most.

Claire grabbed his arm. "Please, Butch...don't." Her plea came out as more of a pathetic whimper than a spousal request.

He started to raise his hand, but she cowered before he could complete the vicious gesture. "If you think I'm gonna let that daughter of yours become a tramp like you..." He hissed every syllable through gritted teeth, while his eyes changed from angry to murderous. "Then you got another thing comin'!"

She didn't dare a reply.

Just above the combat zone known as the family room, Abby Gerwitz closed her eyes and fought back a hurricane of dark emotions. "Don't you dare cry," she whispered to herself. "Don't you dare give him that." It was no use. The first teardrop rolled down her cheek and splashed into her miserable childhood. Like most nights, though, just beyond the sobs and sniffles the world turned quiet and black.

At daybreak, steam rose from a ground fresh with dew. Birds chirped, the wind sang in the trees and for a moment there was silence; a new start filled with hope.

While a single dog's bark warned those still sleeping, lights from a milkman's truck rumbled up Freedom Avenue. Warm blankets were pulled tight under chins to ward off the dawn. A moment later, footsteps and the clank of glass bottles offered the day's first greeting.

In a pair of worn penny loafers, Jim Giles stepped into the neighborhood bakery and offered the baker a grin. "Mornin'," he said.

The paunchy, white-haired man returned a nod. It was as if they shared a secret unknown to those who slept in and wasted the most perfect moments of the day. Early morning was truly the most beautiful and serene.

Abby peered out her bedroom window to find Richard Giles staring at her. Within seconds, though, she felt her face blush. He was looking at a robin red breast that had landed between their houses to search out the season's first breakfast. Feeling silly, she hurried to get dressed. Another New England winter had come to an end, and the first day of April vacation had finally arrived.

The creak of rusty hinges preceded the slam of screen doors. From their front porches, Abby and Richard looked at each other and smiled. The air was cold to the touch, pure and refreshing. Abby drew in a deep breath and glanced toward the pink coral sky. In the solitude of the morning, even God felt close. She looked back at Richard and smiled again. As long as they were outside, it was another day to explore and dream and play in a world that was safe and good, promising new experiences and endless possibilities.

Richard Giles wore a winning smile with dimples that made the girls stare, though his eyes were his most prominent feature. Like two mood rings, they changed different shades of blue and green depending on his demeanor. An unruly mop of blonde hair, a face full of freckles and a constant ring of dirt around his neck finished off the rough package. He was an All-American boy. He'd started a rock & roll album collection, adored a Jack Russell terrier named *Roy* and loved bacon and eggs at any meal.

Abby's hair flowed like curls of chocolate and her eyes were so dark they shined like two marbles of coal. She was a tad on the chubby side and had received the cruel nickname *Pork Chop* from her father. She deplored the name, but absolutely loved her cat, *Mrs. Pringle.* She collected rare coins and preferred macaroni & cheese over any other dish.

Since the first grade – when he'd saved her from the wrath of a hissing squirrel – Richard Giles and Abby Gerwitz were inseparable.

The sun had just peeked over the brim of the world to face a dark, shadowy horizon. Flowers turned their faces toward its welcomed warmth. Slight breezes played ping-pong with the distinct smells of decaying leaves and wet earth; a reminder that the world was coming to life again amid the sweet aromas of pancakes and coffee.

Animals stretched out and began another day of fending for their young. Cars started and pulled out of their respective driveways – dads off to work to put food on tables and shoes on feet.

Richard waited until Abby's Dad's Plymouth Duster was completely out of sight before he headed over. As she waited, Abby sat in her porch swing and sucked in a lung full of air. She loved that swing—the creak of the chain; the slow easy ride. It was like sitting in Mama's lap. And according to her Ma, the swing was their confessional where they could open their hearts and tell all, good or bad. Abby pumped her legs once, and took in the quiet surroundings.

Perhaps it was she and Richard's pre-adolescent perspective that made the neighborhood seem enormous.

Freedom Ave was a quaint strip of cozy cottages adorned in manicured hedges and squares of fresh-cut lawns. Ancient oak and maple trees lined the sidewalk, causing the concrete to buckle and ripple at each base – proving that Mother Nature's roots were stronger than any man-made materials. White picket fences and black tar driveways created aesthetic boundaries, while gas lit lanterns illuminated the walks in front of each home. It was the kind of place where faith became reality every day.

Abby met her best friend on the wet grass. After a frigid season of waiting, the world was all theirs again – that is until the streetlights came on in a few hours and it was time to go in for supper. Abby cleared her throat. "Sorry about all that racket last night."

Richard waved off her apology. "Don't give it another thought. You can't help how your Dad acts. Everybody knows that." For a brief moment, he rested his hand on her shoulder. "It's not your fault."

Abby nodded and began to breathe again. Richard was an amazing friend. Since they'd met in first grade, she'd trusted him completely. This wasn't something that needed to be earned. Rather, it was a given from day one and he'd never once let her regret it. Besides her Ma, he was the only person in the world with whom she felt comfortable enough to tell anything. He never judged.

Richard hated the awkward silence and smashed it to pieces. "Let's get our bikes and wake up the rest of the gang," he said. The mountains of snow had finally thawed and he'd never felt so excited.

Abby nodded. "I'll race you," she said, and was already at a full sprint toward the shed before he could jump.

Laughing, he started for his own back yard. It was time to test out their spring legs.

Atop their steel ponies, Abby and Richard's first stop was at Tracy Martel's house located directly across the street. As they approached, Abby waved. Tracy was already waiting, seated on the new purple bike she'd gotten for Christmas.

Tracy was the world's biggest worrywart. She was overly sensitive and excessively concerned with everyone else's feelings. Ironically, she was also the opposite of her older sister and parents. Phil and Joan, as they preferred to be called, were true children of the 60's and insisted that the neighborhood kids call them by their first names. Richard remembered his Dad's firm tone. "I better never hear those names from your mouth," he warned. Even Abby's Mom didn't think it was respectful and asked that Abby avoid them.

While free love, peace, and rebellion toward any established administration that flexed its authority over another were their mottos, young Tracy lived in a state of constant fear. It was bizarre. Neither genetics nor environment seemed to play a part in her makeup, and everyone questioned where she came from.

Richard and Abby slowed down, but never actually stopped. Within seconds, the three rode abreast down Freedom Ave – Tracy frantic in her attempt to stay aligned.

Vinny Bono's house was the next stop. Freedom Ave was divided by a sharp curve in the middle and Vinny lived on the other side of that bend. It was a plain, one-story ranch with all the character of a mud hut.
Richard knocked on the door. A moment later, the kitchen light came on and Vinny stuck his head out. "Ready to ride?" asked Richard.

Vinny gestured for his friend to be quiet, stepped out onto the stoop and slowly closed the door behind him. Abby chuckled. It was always the same story with Vinny. He was so animated that he should have come with his own theme song. His parents were both teachers, 'know-it-alls' intent on molding the world. Their patronizing, condescending ways had been passed down to their only offspring. Everything about Vinny spelled drama. He was a constant debater, the devil's true advocate, but he was also a coward – which made him more tolerable. Each one of his snooty insults and meaningless arguments were easily remedied by the simple threat of physical violence.

"Keep it down," whispered Vinny, "My parents don't get to sleep in too often. They'd have my neck if…"

Richard grabbed Abby and headed back to Tracy and their parked bikes. "Sure, Einstein," he said. "If you're hungry, or want me to beat you up, meet us back at my house. Grandma's already got the bacon on and it's been awhile since I slapped you around."

The last stop was a little Cape at the end of the street. From the welcome sign and lawn ornaments in front to the tree fort out back, it was the perfect picture of happy, middle class America. Anyone who lived within twenty miles of Freedom Ave and wasn't in a coma knew it was only a picture. When the world was watching, the Wright family smiled and waved as if they were marching in some invisible parade. When the front door slammed closed, the sharpest, most disturbing arguments spilled from behind heavily insulated walls. At the Wright house, it was another Vietnam.

Young Grant Wright was waiting for the gang. Liquid blue eyes, jet-black hair, a dimple in his chin and two perfect rows of white teeth made most girls in town want to claim him as their own. Grant's smile, however, didn't have the same effect on Abby. She'd been around him long enough to catch a glimpse of his insides and they weren't pretty. Even with all his hidden insecurities, Grant's self-absorbed arrogance turned her stomach. He didn't see it that way, though. The chubby girl's disinterest was nothing more than a challenge.

"Hi, Beautiful," he said to Abby.

"Hi, Sexy," Richard answered.

The gang laughed.

"You guys eat?" asked Grant, and then pointed toward his mother standing behind the screen door. "My Mom says she'll…"

"Richard's Grandma has already started making us breakfast," said Tracy. "It would be rude if we didn't get over there."

"Blah, blah, blah," Grant said. "Whatever," and he took off toward the back of the house to grab his bike. His Mom waved once and closed the door.

As they peddled toward breakfast, Richard turned to Grant. "Where's your Dad been?" he asked. "We haven't seen him…"

"He's been working a lot," Grant interrupted. With a shrug, he stood up on his pedals and pumped hard – pulling away from the gang. Each of them took chase.

Several yards into the race, Richard's ball cap flew off his head and jammed itself into the spokes of his rear tire. His bike came to a screeching halt, nearly catapulting him over the handlebars. While the rest of the gang swung back to see if he was okay, Richard jumped off the bike and surveyed the damage. "Shoot," he said and wrestled his favorite cap free from the iron shredder.

Abby's heart raced with worry. Grant nearly fell off his bike from laughter.

Jim Giles was finishing his croissant over the morning news when the Freedom Ave gang appeared on the horizon and headed straight at him. He dropped the paper in his lap and grabbed his coffee. There was no better sight in the world, and no bigger sign that spring had finally arrived.

Each bicycle was tricked out with handlebar streamers; baseball cards in tire spokes and personalized license plates. Richard and Vinny each rode chopper-style bikes with the shifter on the crossbar, while Grant wheeled an expensive ten-speed. The girls sat on yellow and pink banana seats – Tracy, a new one, Abby's torn from its previous owner and patched with reflective stickers.

Jim stood and stepped to the edge of the porch with his coffee in hand. His sidekick, Roy, joined him. The dog's tail started wagging as soon as he spotted the kids.

It was amazing how each bicycle had grown with the kids. From bells and lights to storage bags that hung behind the seats, every birthday and Christmas that passed had dressed the two-wheelers more. In time, each bike became unique to the personality of its owner. Jim shook his head and chuckled. For now, it was their only means of freedom.

The kids patted Roy's head.

"Aren't you a motley looking crew," Jim said.

Everyone smiled.

"You guys aren't going to be getting into any trouble this vacation week, right?"

"No, Sir, Mr. Giles," Tracy blurted.

Abby and Richard shook their heads.

Vinny took a step closer. "If we do," he said, "then you can bet that it'll be Grant who starts it."

Grant half-lunged at the rat when Richard put out his hand to stop him.

"Have fun," Jim chuckled, "but be good."

They nodded all the way to the kitchen, Vinny a few safe paces behind Grant.

Everyone loved to hang out at Richard's house. It was the coolest place on earth. His Mom had passed away in a tragic car accident when he was young and his father and grandmother were raising him. Individually, they were both a bit eccentric. Collectively, though, they provided the most nurturing and loving environment the kids had ever known. Mr. Giles was the quiet one. Grandma was everything else.

She wore her gray hair in a long braid, with crow's feet at the corners of soft green eyes. By the easy way she lived her life, one would have never known she was too old to be a product of the 60's. She was way ahead of her

7

time. Though well read and intelligent, she was also very practical. She was compassionate and smart, but never pompous. Preferring people to anything trivial, she had an incredible affinity for children and bonded easily with them. She was a gifted cook, enjoyed all types of music, and lived for sunsets curled up under a blanket with a good book. In warm weather, she walked around in loose fitting clothes, with sandals on her painted toes. When it was cold, heavy sweaters and a cup of hot tea were a given. She was a Renaissance woman, a new age mix with enough tradition to be called Grandma.

As the gang swarmed the table, *Penny Lane* by the Beatles played softly in the background.

Richard passed Grandma at the stove and threw his torn ball cap into the trash.

Her gentle hand stopped him. "What are you doing?" she asked. Isn't that your favorite cap?"

"Yeah," he answered, "but it's ruined."

Grandma shook her head, retrieved the hat and studied it. "Nonsense," she said, "I can repair it. Don't be penny wise and pound foolish." People from Grandma's generation never threw anything out. They fixed everything – radios, lamps, shoes, clothes.

Richard and his friends, on the other hand, were prone to believe that people who threw things out showed the greatest signs of affluence. They could easily replace whatever was missing. They could always buy more.

"Don't ever throw anything out unless you absolutely have to," Grandma advised, "those who save things and mend them are so much better off – so much wealthier."

The gang listened, never realizing she was talking about so much more than material objects.

Besides another of Grandma's priceless lessons, a banquet of favorites awaited them. Eggs, bacon, pancakes and a big bowl of macaroni & cheese, made special for Abby, were devoured within minutes. It was still enough time for Grandma to ask questions, give answers and make each of them know they were loved. With John Lennon's classic lyrics playing sublimely in the background, she offered an attentive ear, a caring heart and then wrapped the whole thing up with a pat for each bum.

As a hurricane of children blew out of the room, Richard kissed the kind woman. "Thanks, Grandma."

She returned the kiss. "You're welcome," she said and took a seat at the kitchen table. Shaking her head, she reached into her pocket, took out a piece of crunchy bacon that she'd saved for Roy and threw it to him. The dog inhaled his treat. "Ahh," she sighed, "the joys of youth."

As they headed back into the wild, Jim grabbed Richard on the porch. "Remember our afternoon obligation," he whispered, "be back by four."

Richard nodded and then noticed that Abby was waiting for him on the front lawn. She looked perplexed. He descended the stairs and created a few yards of distance before he turned to her. "Today is my parent's wedding anniversary. I told my Dad I wanted to go with him to the cemetery."

She nodded once before they jumped on their bikes to catch up with the other three.

It was almost five when Jim and Richard arrived at the cemetery. With the exception of two elderly women, the place was devoid of life. Jim approached his wife's headstone. Each year, he remembered his beloved with a bunch of fresh-cut flowers and a brand new poem. He placed the flowers at the base of the gravestone. "Happy Anniversary, Hon," he whispered and immediately retreated into silent prayer.

As he shared his deepest feelings and heartfelt wishes for eternal peace, the vivid details of the night that Molly died returned to him…

He'd just returned home from work and was excited about the weekend. They'd planned to take Richard to the city for his first visit to the aquarium. Curiously, Molly's bright yellow Beetle wasn't sitting in the driveway. That was odd. She always waited for him at the door when he returned home from a miserable day at the prison. He stepped into the house and checked the kitchen table for a note. There was none. He'd just picked up the telephone to call his mother's house when he spotted the black and white police cruiser pull into Molly's normal spot in the driveway. His stomach sank. Something was wrong. He hurried to the door. Randy Philips, a veteran officer and long-time friend, looked ready for tears. He approached the porch shaking his head. Jim felt his knees start to give. As he steadied himself, Randy cleared his throat. "Molly's been rushed to the hospital, Jim. She was struck by a drunk driver and…" Jim rushed past the man and didn't take a full breath until he was at the hospital.

But he was too late. Molly's body had been broken beyond repair, her mind already beginning a sequence of shutting down one circuit after the next. Although her heart beat for three more days, Jim's beloved passed away that night. She died to the rhythm of her husband's broken heart.

Richard knelt on the cool ground and offered his own prayer. He felt sadness for the loss of his mother, but looking up he felt an equal amount of gratitude for having been blessed with his Dad. The mixed emotions surprised him. He was young when his Mom had passed away. His memories of her were now more like a set of feelings than actual pictures in his mind. He vaguely remembered how their relationship ended; a black dress hanging on his parent's bedroom door, his Dad's awful sobs, a table covered in casserole dishes and then finally the arrival of his wonderful Grandma. He'd been too young to realize the permanence of his Mom's premature departure.

Jim pulled a paper from his jacket pocket and cleared his throat. It was time to offer up his tribute of love:

"Poor Man

A poor man I've been called by most,
with gains enough to live.
But wealth, my love, is like a ghost –
for me there's more to give:

the moon and stars that paint the night,
a bubble bath with wine,
dinner served by candlelight,
the promise of my time

fresh-cut flowers from the wild,
the freedom to be you,
a constant mirror for your smile,
the giggles when your blue

dancing to the tap of rain,
each sunset sharing tears,
a faithful heart that beats your name,
strong hugs to soothe your fears

an ear to catch your silent screams,
long kisses, soft and sweet,
songs that bring peace to your dreams,
massages for your feet.

Though the list goes on I do confess,
as a poor man I shall live.
Yet without man's gold I have been blessed
for the world is mine to give."

He kissed his forefinger and placed it upon her headstone. "I'll be seein' ya, Molly," he whispered.

Richard absorbed each word. He admired his father's love and the man's effortless courage to express it. "I could never be with another woman," his Dad said as they walked back to the car, "It would feel too much like betrayal." Richard loved that about his Dad. He loved everything about his Dad.

With a baldhead and a dimpled smile, Jim Giles was a soft-spoken, even-tempered man whose presence commanded respect from everyone Richard knew. Besides being very much in love with his deceased wife, he enjoyed the finer things in life: The occasional cigar, a snifter of good brandy and a challenging game of chess. He read the newspaper religiously each morning before heading off to his job at the prison, and he never went anywhere without Roy.

Dusk was finally upon them when Jim steered onto Freedom Ave. Richard squirmed with excitement. Evenings on Freedom Ave were magical.

The sun hung on the horizon, offering just enough time to savor the memories of the day and just enough light to memorize the surroundings before the darkness crept in. While the squirrels and birds retired to their respective trees, the neighborhood gang retired to their respective tables for supper. After grace, meals like chicken and dumplings were washed down with tall glasses of cold milk.

Though taken for granted, no matter what was going on in the world, there were two guarantees on Freedom Ave:

Families sat together at the dinner table for the day's final meal. Most had to come with something to share; the best or worst things that had happened to them that day. Jim Giles, the prison guard, was the only one who never mentioned the worst.

The second given was scheduled bedtimes. Structure was a must, and though the kids were years away from appreciating it, these two simple routines provided the greatest sense of security.

After dinner, one screen door after the other flew open and slammed shut, announcing the last surge of youthful energy. Long shadows were cast on everything and the same world was now submerged in mystery. Thrilling games of manhunt were played before the streetlights came on. The darkness always made them feel like they ran faster.

Though the gang awaited Richard's return on the Giles front lawn, a night of adventure was not to be. As he and his Dad pulled into their driveway, Abby's father swung his Plymouth Duster in at the same time.

It took a moment before Butch Gerwitz staggered out of his car and made it to his porch. Leaning on a banister, he scanned the neighborhood. "ABBY," he screamed, "GET IN THIS HOUSE NOW, GIRL!" The gang looked at each other and cringed. But there was no choice. Abby had to go. She looked at Richard.

He nodded that he understood. "I'll be seein' ya," he said.

"Yeah," Tracy said, "we'll see ya tomorrow." Grant and Vinny agreed.

She nodded twice and went in to face another vulgar night of the drunk's cruelty.

Abby sneaked past her Dad and dismissing dinner, hurried upstairs to her bedroom window. As her friends melted into the shadows of the neighborhood, she set her eyes upon the gray sky. "I wish I could escape," she whispered, and then spotted Richard looking up at her. She swallowed hard. "I wish…"

Chapter 2

After the brief school break, Richard Giles stepped back into Mrs. Parsons' class.

She was a heavy-set woman with kind eyes and a raspy voice, and from the moment she met Richard there was no doubt that she cared very deeply for him. It didn't take long for him to fall in love with her, as well. She was the perfect teacher who listened with concern, and was quick with praise or encouragement. "What a wonderful poem," she'd whisper, or "I know someday you'll make me very proud." And God, how he wanted to! They all did. Richard soon learned that the saintly woman was equally quick with the truth. It was the greatest lesson he could have ever learned.

He was walking home from school when he spotted three neighborhood bullies waiting. His heart jumped into his throat. "Oh, God," he muttered and picked up the pace. The Benoit brothers were frighteningly tough, but nothing compared to their Amazon sister who had worn a cast on her right arm for as long Richard could remember. His nemesis, Roland Benoit, was swollen with the courage provided by his sneering siblings. With a dry mouth and sweaty palms, Richard forced his rubbery legs to flee but it was no use. Roland cut him off and without a word, threw one shot at Richard before his brother and sister jumped in. Richard went down and curled up into the fetal position. The Benoit's pounced and inflicted their damage.

Bleeding and ashamed, Richard returned home to hide his battle scars from his proud father. He even made Grandma promise not to tell.

"It better never happen again," she said.

As the weeks rolled by, the thought of the Benoit's loomed over Richard like a five-ton anvil. The memory of the unanswered beating, however, hurt so much more than the lingering cuts and bruises.

Richard was at morning recess when grinning Roland Benoit approached. He was alone. Richard started to tremble.

"Ready for another beatin'?" Roland barked, loud enough to insure Richard's public humiliation.

Richard swallowed hard, amazed at how small the world had just become. With Abby looking on, though, it was time to redeem his honor and he knew it. Though a circle of excited spectators awaited the blood sport, before long it was only he and Roland Benoit. Everything else became darkness.

Roland started with the name-calling. "Chicken."

"You're the chicken," Richard countered.

"How 'bout I punch your head in?" Roland threatened.

"How 'bout I punch yours in?" Richard matched, his knees quivering and a string of sweat beads forming across his forehead like a cruel crown. Everything seemed to be happening in slow motion. He could hear his heart beating hard in his ears. His breathing was quick. For the sake of saving face he knew he wasn't going to cower. While their peers cheered them on, Richard felt like he was going to vomit. It was a living nightmare. Roland was still grinning. Richard couldn't take it anymore. As the crowd began to chant, panic made him lunge.

There was a brief scuffle and in one strange, syrupy moment, Richard had Roland on the ground. Richard looked down and to his surprise he'd pinned his enemy. Roland stared him straight in the eyes. He looked scared. With the bully's arms pinned behind him, Richard went to work.

With each blow, he ignored Roland's girlish pleas for mercy and cut up his face like a skilled surgeon. And with each blow, he felt his fear lighten. A flurry later, the invisible demon that had haunted him was completely gone. Richard Giles had traversed a rite of passage. He was now a man – in his mind, anyway.

While the crowd chanted for more blood, Richard leaned into Roland's swollen face and screamed, "Who's the boss now?" Before his nemesis could answer, Richard worked his fists again like two deadly pistons. He never let up until he realized that Mrs. Parsons was trying to pull them apart. He let go right away.

The crowd erupted in cheers. The vicious beating was a victory for anyone who ever feared Roland Benoit. Everyone celebrated – everyone but Mrs. Parsons and Abby. Both of them looked completely disgusted and it made Richard's stomach queasy. Mrs. Parsons grabbed his ear and forced him to look down at Roland. The frightened boy had folded himself into the fetal position and was crying. "I hope you're proud of yourself, Mr. Giles," she said.

While his hands ached something awful, a sea of emotions raged inside Richard. The angry mob was no longer cheering for him. Abby's face looked contorted in pain. He felt confused. He looked up at Mrs. Parsons and the disappointment in her face broke his heart in two. He'd never felt so awful his whole life. She shook her head, disgustedly. "I thought you were better than this," she said. "I really thought you were a bigger person." At that moment, something inside of Richard went into eclipse.

He was escorted to the Vice Principal's office where he received the strict punishment deserving of any violent schoolboy; a severe reprimand coupled with a three-day suspension. His aching body was then carted home where he suffered his father's wrath. Collectively, and even if multiplied a thousand times, none of this could have ever compared to the pain he suffered from looking into Mrs. Parson's disappointed face. She was the nicest person he knew and he'd let her down. In turn, he'd let himself down.

Days later, when he'd drummed up enough courage to approach Mrs. Parsons, he promised, "I'm sorry for what I did…and I'm going to prove it."

With a simple nod, she accepted his apologetic vow and watched him walk back to his desk.

Though Richard had to avoid several potential fights, the remainder of the year passed without further trouble. On his last day of school, Mrs. Parsons gave him a hug. "I expect big things from you, Mr. Giles," she whispered, "so don't let either of us down, okay?"

He nodded, contritely. It was strange how violence played such an unforgettable role even in childhood. Abby's Dad and the Benoit brothers, however, weren't the only ugliness on Freedom Ave.

R & S Variety sat on the corner and was the last stop on the street. If you weren't used to the place, the tiny convenience store could prove to be a spooky experience. For the neighborhood kids, though, it served as one of the wonderful terrors of childhood; the very place where you got your fix for a throbbing sweet tooth. It wasn't even noon when Abby, Richard and the gang stepped in for the day's first fix. "I hate this place," Tracy muttered.

R & S stood for Reynolds and Sedgeband. Mr. Reynolds, however, died only six months after the store had opened in 1954. Some claimed that Old Man Sedgeband had murdered him and buried him beneath the knotty floor planks. By the time the neighborhood gang discovered the place two decades later, it was so gray and gloomy that Old Man Sedgeband had obviously been condemned to spend his every waking moment in purgatory.

Outside, a Coca Cola machine and an ice machine stood guard on either side of the front door, while a large, padlocked Sunbeam Bread bin – with a young girl who looked like Lucille Ball painted on the front – sat on the side of the small, brick building. Bundles of newspapers were dropped off there for Richard and two other paperboys to collect. The distributor was a smart man. It didn't take long for the boys to learn that if they didn't get to their packages in a timely manner each afternoon then Old Man Sedgeband was going to skim a few off the top and cut into their humble profits.

A heavy door swung open to reveal an unforgettable piece childhood, its front window stickered in two generations of advertisement and memories. Once inside, the gang's eyes took a few moments to adjust to the darkness and pipe smoke. The store's windows were so filthy that only a few rays of sunlight were able to jam their way past the streaks in the glass. Before a single foot stepped over the worn threshold, a brass bell warned Mr. Sedgeband that an intruder was lurking about. The temporary blindness only helped in the store's clever defenses.

"Top of the seventh," the invisible radio announcer called out, "Red Sox up by two."

"Hello, Mr. Sedgeband," Tracy said, nervously.

The old man looked at her with a mix of apathy and contempt, but never replied.

Old Man Sedgeband was a frightening soul. With hair that should have sat atop his head protruding from a pair of cauliflower ears, he wore glasses thicker than a fish tank. He smelled of spearmint and mothballs, wore long-sleeve flannel shirts year round and walked with an old scarred cane.

According to Richard's Grandma, though, "He once chased a would-be shoplifter a quarter mile and nearly caught him before the boy jumped a fence and got away." As the old man hobbled back to his store, Richard's Grandma – who'd been reading on her porch where she'd witnessed the whole thing – began to applaud at the phony actor's speedy attempt. Sedgeband huffed and puffed, and scurried back to his little shop of horrors. "Don't let his sloppy appearance or that run-down store give you the wrong impression," Grandma added. "That old man is loaded with money and is only looking to add to it."

"And the pitch," the radio announcer called out again, "swung on and missed, making the count full for Rice."

With his arms crossed, the crusty codger smoked his pipe without ever touching it, filling his shop with billows of bluish smoke. He looked at the kids, but didn't smile. He never did. He was a miserable man who spoke in grunts – only when he needed to – and threatened to swing his cane at those who dared to pose a question. Richard, Abby and the others supposed it was because he'd been deafened from all the hair in his ears. Their parents, however, knew it was because the criminal was guilty of cheating everyone and tried to quell any accusations by standing behind a curtain of intimidation. Try to match his deceitful ways, though, and you were in trouble. Behind his thick glasses, a pair of giant pupils scanned like a Coast Guard searchlight, shadowing every move. Anyone who entered his store was a suspect; a potential thief. For a lame, blind man who couldn't hear,

R&S Variety enjoyed better protection than Fort Knox.

Atop three stacked milk crates, Sedgeband sat behind the glass case he used as a counter. Like most days, while he smoked his pipe and listened to the Boston Red Sox on a stuttering transistor radio, he played checkers with Oscar, the neighborhood mute.

"And the payoff," the radio announcer said, "hit deep to center. It's going…"

Everyone froze and held their breath.

"Going…GONE!" he yelled and the crowd erupted. "Another home run for Jim Rice."

While the gang quietly celebrated, Sedgeband shook his head. "They're still gonna lose," he groaned, while Oscar nodded – insanely.

At no more than thirty years of age, Oscar was a simpleton with a pronounced twitch and a twisted grin. With the exception of a few odd jobs he performed around the store, he worked as often as he spoke. Though they played game after game of checkers, he and the old man never exchanged a single word. This suited Old Man Sedgeband just fine.

Within that wonderful glass case beneath those marathon checker games, though, boxes of penny candy awaited an owner: Mary Janes, root beer barrels, Swedish Fish, Squirrels, Bit O' Honey, sour balls, licorice, fireballs and squares of bubble gum. The candy necklaces and Wacky Packy stickers were a few cents more. The entire display made their mouths water.

Vinny was the first to place a small handful of pennies on the counter. Sedgeband's catfish eyes abandoned his checker game and counted the money twice before his gnarled index finger swept it up and threw it into the open cash register. With a cough, he snapped open a tiny, brown paper bag, held it in one hand and waited to fill the order with the other. "Come on, what'll it be?" he growled, "I ain't got all day."

Oscar nodded like some mad bobble head.

Vinny's voice was nervous. "Can I have five fireballs, ten Swedish fish and…"

"…and three root beer barrels," Grant finished.

Vinny nodded. "Please?"

Sedgeband went slow, painfully slow, and recounted to ensure that he hadn't cheated himself. (Once, when the old man had a touch of the flu, Grant swore that he'd gotten two extra sour balls. The neighborhood celebrated for weeks.)

Beyond the candy case, old plank floorboards led to outdated displays that offered even more outdated goods. The short stacks of cans and bottles were covered in several seasons of dust. The magazine rack was ancient, though it hardly mattered when it came to the comic books. A toy selection included paddle balls, jacks, yoyos, and whiffle ball bats. For last minute gifts, you could choose from nail clippers, plastic combs (no one bought them because they looked used), nylons, playing cards, or corncob pipes. The one-shelf pharmacy offered feminine supplies and condoms, causing embarrassed giggles. There was also aspirin, band-aids and rubbing alcohol. For Tracy's parents, Sedgeband carried rolling papers and cheap wine. For Abby's Dad, he was kind enough to stock quarts of Narragansett, Schaeffer and Schlitz beer. Butch Gerwitz paid the store's light bill and then some.

Sedgeband also took bets on the weekly pool, four numbers drawn each Friday – posted in the paper. Surprisingly, he paid the winners. They were rare.

For the neighborhood gang, as the years had passed, YooHoo's eventually gave way to Slush Puppie's. This didn't last long, though. Old Man Sedgeband skimped on the syrup and a cup of ice for fifty cents just didn't cut it. Half-filled bags of stale popcorn and nuts sat unsold. A full ice cream cooler housed Nutty Buddys, ice cream sandwiches, strawberry shortcakes, creamsicles and fudgsicles. If it wasn't the candy case, the gang invested their allowance in the ice cream cooler.

Bread, milk and eggs were the only fresh items in the store. Sedgeband was too cheap to rotate stock on anything else. Getting at the milk and eggs, however, was always a challenge. Sedgeband's scruffy mutt, Jed, liked to lie stretched out in front of the coolers.

Richard had to shove the ox aside to get at the only two items on Grandma's list. "Come on, Boy. Move." Jed didn't complain. He just low-crawled back when Richard was done shopping.

For years and for no more than the sake of convenience, Sedgeband was able to make his living selling milk, bread and cigarettes. His charming personality wouldn't allow for more. Most folks didn't mind driving the three extra miles to the A & P to avoid giving him their business. In time, though, he'd devised a plan to change all that.

Old Man Sedgeband announced that he was opening tabs for the adults in the neighborhood. Though the shrewd businessman charged interest (always calculated in his favor), causing many arguments to take place when a debt was settled – Sedgeband threatened to cut off the tab if it wasn't paid in full. Most folks refused to return until they needed something and had no choice but to step back into the old-timer's extortion ring. It was an ingenious scam. He knew everyone's business, and would allow kids to run cigarettes and other items home to their parents. No one liked him, but when they didn't have to see his scowling face he did a pretty fair volume. And their children provided the free home delivery, to boot. For those same neighborhood kids, though, it was strictly a cash and carry business.

While Vinny popped a candy into his gob, Richard put a half-gallon of milk and a dozen eggs on the corner of the counter. "On my Grandma's tab," he said.

The old man surveyed the items, nodded and then scribbled the tally into a green, spiral notebook. After double-checking the figures, he placed the goods into a paper bag and returned to his checker game as though five regular customers no longer stood before him.

"While the Red Sox take the field," the radio announcer said, "a word from our sponsors…"

With his admiration for Sedgeband carefully concealed, Richard turned to his friends. "Let's go," he said, and led them back into the afternoon sun.

They weren't ten steps from the store when Grant stopped. "Check this out," he said.

They all looked back at him.

He reached into his pocket and pulled out a pink rubber ball. "And it's still hot," he bragged, holding it up for his fiends to see.

Richard shook his head. "You're such an idiot," he said and continued on. The rest followed, leaving Grant to enjoy the thrill of the daring heist all by his lonesome.

Fortunately, the summer promised more exciting things to do than spend every nickel they made with Old Man Sedgeband, or take part in Grant's childish cries for attention.

Chapter 3

As was the case with most New England seasons, spring lasted three winks and surrendered to summer. And what a magical summer it was in 1978!

Thanks to the young entrepreneur Richard Giles, rolled newspapers covered in dew peppered the neighborhood's front lawns. As the sun crested the horizon, sprinklers created rainbows amid bursts of sunlight, while barking dogs chased chipmunks as far as their leashes would allow. Oaks and maples provided all the shade needed, promising an exquisite pageant of color in the fall. Each tree was home to families of busy squirrels and sturdy bird's nests; home to hammocks and forts, a place to climb. For the boys, playing soldier and surviving war took place within twisted branches, while the girls played out the damsel in distress scenario. It was a place to think, to grieve and in some cases even fall in love. A tire swing hung from the giant willow tree in Abby's back yard, and the gang giggled from the tickle in their bellies. Life was so innocent and joyous.

Each morning, Richard waited for Abby's Dad to leave before he met her out front. On the days the old man stayed home to nurse a hangover, the hours that usually whipped by became eternal.

On the blessed days that Mr. Gewirtz managed to make it to work, though, Abby, Richard and the gang rode their bicycles up and down Freedom Ave for miles. Some of those days, Richard, Grant and Vinny agreed to jump rope in order to get the girls into some heated games of baseball. It was a tough game to play with only three people, so they needed the bodies. And besides, Vinny ran the bases like maple syrup in December. Hopscotch, however, was completely out of the question.

One night the gang converged on Richard's house to camp out in the Giles back yard. With Grandma waiting on them, they roughed the great outdoors in the soft lap of luxury.

Once the sun disappeared, with the help of a dim flashlight they took turns telling spooky stories. No matter how stupid or immature the tale, everything sounded terrifying in the dark. Most stories included R&S Variety and Old Lady Chouinard's place, the creepy house at the end of the street. As they "oohed" and "aahed," the smell of pipe tobacco wafted on warm breezes. The creaky sounds of rocking chairs sang a constant tune and swarms of flying insects, attracted to the fluorescent blue bug zappers, buzzed around until hypnosis took hold and they were led to their crackling demise.

While the girls, tucked safely in their flannel cocoons, screamed in delight, Richard spun a tale that had his own hair standing on end. "Old Man Sedgeband – better known as The Liver and Onions Man – smelled fear on his next victim and his mouth watered," Richard said. "He waited in the shadows for hours and just when…"

Something outside groaned once and pushed the side of the tent.

"Eeeek!" Everyone screamed – Vinny the loudest.

As fear turned to panic, Roy jumped through the front flap of the tent, wagging his tail. Jim Giles stuck his head in and laughed. "Sorry, guys. I couldn't help myself."

"Leave those children alone," Grandma called out, Barry White's silky voice trailing behind her.

Jim Giles winked at the kids. "Goodnight, guys."

Their breathing returned to normal just in time for the flashlight to go dead. "Goodnight, Little Richard," Grant joked.

"Goodnight, John-Boy," Richard replied.

To the drift and drone of distant neighborhood voices, they laughed themselves to sleep.

On weekend nights, the gang received unanimous permission to sit on the porch steps of one home or the other, and this alternated each week. Abby's porch had a set of wind chimes that sang in the breeze and a porch swing that creaked late into the warm nights, or until the light came on and Butch Gerwitz's sedated head popped out to investigate what the whispering was all about.

It was the same throughout the neighborhood. Each porch was a refuge; a haven from the world. Whether used as a safe-zone during games of tag and hide-and-seek, or for matters of much more importance, its arms were opened wide and waiting to welcome its children home. And it didn't matter how old those children had become, or how tough they thought they'd gotten – everybody had to return when the streetlights came on.

The porch was the place where the big things were discussed, life and death; the only place that was completely open to its neighbors. Except for Abby and her Mom's whispers, no real secrets were told or kept there. That was the wonder of the front porch. Like it or not, it forced people to share.

While radio and television noise played in the background, conversations carried themselves through screen doors. Men played cards – mostly pitch – while women gossiped in hushed tones. And each of these subtle details was a necessary piece to the puzzle that painted the picture of childhood.

"Hurry. It's on!" Jim Giles announced, and the neighborhood rushed into their houses to watch the Andy Griffith Show. It seemed so ironic. All they had to do was step back onto their front porches to find themselves right smack in the middle of Mayberry, U.S.A.

These were the days when parents controlled the week's viewing schedule, and kids were used as remote controls. Hogan's Heroes, McHales's Navy and Hee-Haw were favorites at the Gewirtz house. Tracy's Mom and Dad preferred Lawrence Welk, The Mac Davis Show and The Walton's. Grant's Dad worshipped Paul Lynn and Redd Foxx from Sanford and Son. Archie Bunker was a big hit for most everyone. For the kids, there were The Osmond Specials. For the Moms, there was Englebert Humperdink. And for Richard's Dad, there was radio personality Paul Harvey – "Good Day."

Toward mid-summer, a secret was discovered without anyone leaking it. Puppy or no puppy, Richard and Abby were in love; a feeling that was just too big to wear any one label. With their hearts on their sleeves, it was obvious. Everyone knew it – everyone but them.

Chalk hearts were melting on the sidewalk in front of the Gewirtz house when Abby saw Richard approaching and swept her hand across the masterpiece. He'd been a minute too late and grew jealous. "You like Grant, don't you?"

She shook her head. *If you only knew,* she thought. "I don't like anyone," she said. "You?"

He shook his head. "Nah."

That night, among the chirping crickets and the swoosh of the willow tree dancing with the wind, Richard and Abby sat on the Giles front lawn and watched Tracy's parents smoke some type of sweet smelling tobacco on their front porch. Their silhouettes faced each other and from the soft light that radiated from them, they looked like angels framed in glory and wonder. A moment later, they kissed, making Abby and Richard squirm. If only they had the same courage.

"Gross," Richard mumbled.

Abby agreed, but only because she felt she had to.

Collapsing onto their backs, Richard and Abby gazed up at the sky together and talked openly, sharing truths about themselves and their dreams for their future.

"What do you want to be when you grow up?" Richard asked.

Abby never hesitated. "It doesn't matter."

"Huh?" He was surprised. "You don't want…"

"The stars," she whispered, "I want to walk among the stars."

The summer of '78 was more than anyone could have wished for. While the days were numbered and fleeting, the love was innocent and unconditional. Tragically, it was also a time to learn that the light could not be experienced without the dark; the good without the bad. Dark clouds were gathering above and a heavy downpour was in the forecast.

Claire Gerwitz was a brunette, with tight curls and a thin-lipped smile. Pretty and smart, her sad eyes spoke volumes so she didn't have to. At an early age, she'd married Butch without knowing his many destructive vices. By the time she realized what she'd done, she'd borne the animal a daughter, Abby. From that moment, she chose the role of mother and homemaker, accepting her place in the shadows of life. Butch would have had it no other way. Though they lived on final notices from the utility companies, she was forbidden to work. Even still, in the mornings she was the first in the neighborhood to rise. She'd sit on her porch swing with Mrs. Pringle, the family cat, and hum along with the birds. Most days, she never bothered to change out of her housecoat. There wasn't a good enough reason to get dressed. And there wasn't reason enough to venture beyond the steps of their front porch. Her sole purpose was to get through each day for the sake of her beloved daughter. Her reason for living was to spend as much time with Abby on the porch swing as she could, filling her daughter's heart with strength and her mind with independence.

It was a random Tuesday night, a muggy eve in late July. Everything was right and good – that is until the Plymouth Duster rounded the corner and made its way down Freedom Ave. From the slam of the car door and Butch's heavy footsteps up the walk, the entire neighborhood shuddered. It was fight night at the Gerwitz house.

Butch, a skinny man, with bloodshot eyes and an angry smile, took his place at the head of the kitchen table and then a bite of his supper that had been sitting for an hour. He spit the chicken onto the floor. "This swill is cold!" he roared, and pushed himself to his feet. Snarling at his wife, he picked up the plate. "Look at what I have to come home to every night." With a grunt, he hurled the plate onto the floor where it smashed into pieces.

Though she felt as if she were abandoning her mother, Abby's instincts forced her legs out of the room. From an early age, she understood that her father was an odd-looking man with an ugly soul. She also understood that she and her mother were destined to pay for his sins. Fortunately for her, her mother was willing to make most of the payments.

Abby sat behind her bedroom door, praying. "Please God," she

25

whispered. "Please don't let him…"

POW!

It was a short bout, and when it was over Butch Gewirtz was still the undefeated middleweight champion of the family. Claire had been lucky. He was too tired to go more than one round this time and took it easy on her. She arose from the canvas with nothing more than a black eye.

As tradition dictated, once her Dad passed out in his recliner Abby followed her Ma onto the seat of the porch swing. "Promise me you'll never allow this to happen to you," Claire whispered, her left eye puffy and three shades of purple.

Abby nodded, as she always did, and promised. Claire truly believed that she endured the punishment for Abby's sake, and Abby was thankful for it. But there was also a small part of her that resented her mother for her weakness. It was like her Ma was just waiting to die. There had to be another way.

Claire didn't know one. Instead, she died many deaths because of her love for her daughter.

The next morning, Richard risked knocking on Abby's front door. A few endless minutes elapsed before her Mom cracked it open and whispered through the dirty screen. "Abby's still sleeping, Richard. I'll let her know that you came calling on her when she wakes up." With a pitiful smile, the woman closed the door.

Richard felt ill and needed an explanation about the giant pink elephant under Abby's Mom's eye. As always, Jim Giles was candid. "Abby's Dad is filled with hate," he said, "he's mad with the way life has treated him, so he takes it out on his family. Remember, no matter what life throws our way, we choose how we react. We choose who we are." He ruffled his son's blonde mop. "And if you apply yourself, you can turn nightmares into dreams."

To his surprise, Richard understood and nodded.

"In this world," Jim finished, "you're either a giver or a taker. It's your choice."

Chapter 4

Richard's Dad and Grandma packed a giant cooler and shuffled the neighborhood gang into the car for a full day at Second Beach in Newport. Even Butch Gerwitz didn't object. Either his head was too heavy, or he wasn't prepared to show his face to the world just yet. Packed together like sardines, the kids talked in squeals and giggled in anticipation of the trip. As the draft of tires headed up Freedom Ave, Abby peered out the window to find her Mom standing on the front porch. She was smiling brilliantly and waving after them, clearly excited for her daughter's brief escape. Abby choked back the lump in her throat and joined in the chorus. "...Merrily, merrily, merrily, merrily, life is but a dream."

Grandma had her book and portable radio, Mr. Giles had his newspaper and the kids had the run of the dunes.

There were serious warnings posted at the beach about an infestation of the Portuguese man-of-war, toxic jellyfish that were pretty much invisible to the eye. Once they left their sting, though, a person would know for sure that they were there. And the only way to treat it was to pour household bleach on the infected area. The kids didn't want to find out.

From beautiful young women in their skimpy bikinis to wrinkled old grandmothers in their swimming caps, the beach was packed with vacationers. Sailboats lined the horizon, while an island lighthouse stood guard in the distance. Between the taste of salt air, the sound of the surf and the occasional screech of seagulls, it was heaven on earth.

Before long, the sun's heat became unbearable and everyone headed for the water in search of relief. It was packed and the water felt cold to the touch. Richard took some deep breaths and kept marching. It felt good compared to the oven he'd been baking in.

The tide rocked the mob like a mother with her young. Children were splashing. People laughed. Life was good.

Richard was up to his chest when he felt it. Slowly and quite intentionally, something wrapped itself around his ankle. For a moment, it seemed his heart stopped beating. The most incredible fear made him freeze in place. While the sea creature tightened its grip, Richard managed to swallow the massive lump lodged in his throat. Instinct made him want to scream out. He actually tried, but there wasn't enough air in his lungs to carry the panic. With the next breath, though, out it came. "SHARK!" he shrieked and couldn't believe he'd said it. But it wasn't a shark at all. It was a Portuguese man-of-war and this jellyfish was getting ready to leave its stinger in his leg. With sheer panic swimming in his giant blue eyes, he screamed out again.

This time those around him began staring. From the look on his face they must have realized he wasn't joking. A mass exodus from the water had women and children screaming for their lives. People chugged through the surf with the purpose of self-preservation. It wasn't pretty. Somehow Richard coaxed his legs to do the same.

An entire stretch of beach was invaded with dripping bodies. Even though he exerted every ounce of energy he could muster, Richard was one of the last to make it out. His head spun end-over-end. Three steps later, he collapsed onto the hot sand. He was exhausted, but happy to see Abby rushing over. *Thank God, she's safe*, he thought.

"What is it?" she panted.

"A jelly fish," he said. "A jelly fish wrapped itself around my ankle and..."

By now, a large circle of curious spectators had formed around them. Abby's face showed signs of horror. She was looking at Richard's ankle.

Oh God, he thought, *I'm really hurt!* He pushed himself up on his elbows and looked down the length of his body to discover a blue plastic bag wrapped around his ankle. With his face heating up, he looked back at Abby when the bag unraveled and fell to the sand. It read: *Woolworth's*. A roar of laughter traveled the beach. Richard tried desperately to push his entire body beneath the dune. It was no use. He could feel his face change ten different shades of red.

Abby was mortified, but never said a word. And she never budged. She stayed right by his side.

Richard sat up and looked over at their little campsite. The blankets were still there. The radio was still there. Everyone was standing around him in a circle. He was so humiliated.

No sooner had his father approached than a parade of dark, swollen clouds arrived with him. "Sorry, guys," he said, "We can try it again tomorrow."

Grandma looked up and shook her fortuneteller's head. "I don't know. Looks like we're in for quite a bit of bad weather." She waved Vinny, Tracy and Grant over. "Let's go guys."

Under the scrutiny of a thousand sets of eyes, they packed up to leave. Richard piled the blankets upon himself and trudged through the dunes toward the parking lot. Halfway there, he dropped the gear and looked back. Some people were just starting to get back into the water. Most were still laughing. He shook his head. *Shark*, he thought, *more like a jellyfish.* And he wasn't talking about any sea creature.

Abby never said a word, though. Even when the rest of the gang took the opportunity to get a few laughs at his expense, she never spoke another word about it.

It was collection day, so Richard hurried to R&S Variety for his newspapers. Upon counting the bundle, he discovered he was missing one paper and had to purchase it back from Old Man Sedgeband. He checked the clock and shook his head. He was going to have to make record time before the darkness beat him.

And he did just that until he hit the Chouinard's place.

It was an eerie, old cottage located at the opposite end of the street from R&S Variety. The old spinster walked with a pronounced limp, spoke with a gruff voice and scared Richard so terribly that he dreaded having to go there to deliver the newspaper. If cut open, the kids joked that "the old woman would bleed embalming fluid." It was the absolute worst stop on his route.

The house's gray shingles were weathered and faded, its porch so dilapidated that the floorboards were peeled up on one side resembling a surfer's breaking wave. The windows were filthy, the corners sewn shut in cobwebs. Yellowed, lacey curtains remained closed, concealing all the dark secrets within the house of horrors. It didn't take much of an imagination to picture a toothless woman laughing insanely behind them, peering out from her own personal nightmare. Rows of dirty fieldstones formed the foundation, indicating that the place had been erected long before the turn of the century. The screen door swung in the wind on one hinge, quickening Richard's step and prying open his sweat glands. A black, wrought-iron fence cordoned off a yard choked in crab grass and weeds. The front door was as uninviting as the rusty bulkhead in the rear of the place. And the back yard was even more overgrown than the front. Shrubs and plants grew wildly, forming themselves into the shapes of giant grotesque beasts. It was quite a sight and Richard hated it. From the first time he'd ever set eyes on the place, he absolutely hated it! He would rather not collect on the paper than have to knock at the door. Fortunately, the old hag left a recycled, wrinkled envelope in the milk box on the front porch. It was a true test of courage every Friday when it was time to collect. For anyone looking on, they would have thought young Richard was training for the track team. He was getting quicker with each collection.

After grabbing the money from the envelope, Richard jumped on his bike. In the late breeze, he swore he heard the old lady's screen door crack open. *Oh, God*, he thought and peddled out of the yard like he'd just been shot out of a cannon.

As he was making his getaway, an unfamiliar pick-up truck had rolled through the stop sign and made its way down Freedom Ave, its headlights swerving back and forth like a hunter scanning for prey. Richard heard a motor roar at him and glanced up to see the truck's front grill inches from his face. There was no time to react. He held his breath and waited with squinted eyes.

As he felt the monster bite into him, the air in his lungs was stolen away and he dropped like a bag of bricks. It took a few painful seconds, but when he managed to open his eyes, a pair of headlights bore into his pupils and blinded him. Unlike anything he'd ever experienced, the pain was sharp and throbbing. The headlights quickly turned to two tiny pinpoints before the world turned to black and disappeared.

The squeal of tires had everyone at their windows. Richard had been struck and was lying motionless in the street. Everyone hurried to him. Abby dry-heaved.

A drunken man staggered out of the driver's side of the truck and swayed over him. "Get up, Boy," he slurred, "and get home."

Richard awoke to find his father hovering over him; tears welled up in his frightened eyes. As Richard tried to clear the cobwebs from his aching head, he watched as relief crept back into his father's pale face.

"Stupid kid," the drunken man slurred, "he should'a watched where he was goin'."

The sudden rage in his Dad's face startled Richard. Then, in a state of blurred confusion, he watched as his father beat the drunk driver senseless. As if a switch had been thrown, his Dad's eyes were now void of any emotion, while his hands carved into the man's face like a Thanksgiving bird. Methodically and quite detached, it didn't take long before the correction officer finished his work and turned his attention back to his injured son – the rest of the neighborhood looking on in horror. "Lay still," Jim whispered, his voice calm and collected. "Help will be here soon."

Richard was cut and bruised, his arm clearly broken. While he fought back the tears, he tried to make sense of his father's behavior. He'd never witnessed such a mix of anguish and rage. He searched his Dad's face once more. With a smile, Jim's eyes had returned to love and compassion. Richard was relieved.

Abby trembled from her head to her toes. Besides the show of violence, she realized what Richard meant to her and she wept for them both.

To insure there was no internal bleeding, Richard stayed at the hospital for several endless days. "I was paying attention, Dad, honest," he claimed, "and I saw the truck coming, but I never figured the man wouldn't stop."

The ambulance arrived with two policemen who briefly questioned Jim Giles about his bloody hands. One of the cops nodded and laughed. As the owner of the truck was dragged away in handcuffs, Abby's Dad snickered. "That boy never watches where he's goin'," he called out over his shoulder, and returned to his house for another session of self-medication. In Butch's bloodshot eyes, Richard was at fault. Jim Giles hated him – though not nearly as much as the man's own daughter hated her drunken father.

To insure there was no internal bleeding, Richard stayed at the hospital for several endless days. "I was paying attention, Dad, honest," he claimed, "and I saw the truck coming, but I never figured the man wouldn't stop."

Jim stroked his son's hair and nodded. He didn't dare respond and release the dam of emotion. He was still traumatized over nearly losing another loved one to a drunk driving accident.

Richard knew it was his childish fear of the old lady's house that had made him peddle out into the street. The truth of it ate at him. He silently vowed to never run from anything again. The price was just too high.

Though she wanted nothing more than to sneak into Richard's hospital room and visit him, Abby stayed home and prayed. She loved him more than she'd imagined.

Richard was eventually released to the neighborhood where everyone penned some foolish quote on his bulky white cast.

"You should get all the girls to write their phone numbers on it," Grant suggested.

Richard shook his head and chuckled.

Tracy signed her name under Vinny's. The look in her eyes still spelled trauma. "We thought you were a goner!" she said.

Richard grinned. The cast was like a trophy, a chance to claim some strange bragging rights. For his suffering, he got a new radio with a cassette player from Grandma.

When they cut off the cast, a long scar in the shape of a fishhook, or question mark, was branded on him. This brutal reminder had been carved deep into his forearm for life. "What a great reminder," Jim Giles said, "that the joys in life aren't found in answering the big questions, but rather in searching for them." He patted his son's head. "Fortunately, the quest is never-ending."

After Richard's accident, it seemed silly to hold back anymore. As kids, he and Abby both felt more than either one of them could say, but they were finally willing to try. The very day he returned, Abby slipped him a love note. *Do you want to be my boyfriend? Check yes or no.*

Richard never responded with words. Although it took three consecutive nights with the dull knife he'd borrowed, he snuck out of his house and carved he and Abby's initials into the trunk of her weeping willow; a heart with both their initials in the middle – *4EVA.*

When her Dad sobered up enough to notice it, he was furious. Abby, on the other hand, was swept away by the beautiful gesture and secretly so was her Mom. Butch Gerwitz's anger made it that more precious.

With a fading black eye, Abby's Mom led her to the porch swing. Claire looked at Abby like she had a window to her daughter's soul and smiled. She knew the look. When it came to matters of the heart, age was hardly a factor. "You got it bad for him, don't you?" she asked.

Abby nodded slightly and then lay her head in her mother's lap to dream of Richard.

They sat on the porch swing a little longer that night; Abby with her head in the stars, Claire hypnotized by her daughter's distant eyes.

Chapter 5

"But it's not your fault, Jim," Grandma said in a hushed tone. "You've kept us here as long as you could."

Richard wiggled as close as he could to the stair's banisters without being seen and listened in.

"My son loves this house...his neighborhood friends," Jim replied, the pain in his voice apparent. "And Molly loved this house, too. It was her dream." He paused. "I remember the afternoon they accepted our offer to buy this place. Molly and I jumped up and down so much that the tenants beneath us began yelling for us to stop." There was a longer, more anxious pause. "And now I can't even hold on to the dream that Molly and I shared together. I can't let Richard down like this. How am I going to tell him that we can't afford to stay?"

Instinctively, Richard lunged from the shadows. "We can't afford to what?" he screamed and was still moving toward his father when he realized that he'd just revealed he'd been eavesdropping.

Jim turned to face his son. The look in his face wasn't that of anger, though. It was torment. He kneeled before Richard and grabbed his shoulders. "We have no choice, son. I can't continue to pay off your Mom's hospital bills and the mortgage, so..."

"Why are you doing this to me?" Richard hollered, the reality of his situation creating panic in every inch of him. Tears welled in his eyes. "BUT DAD?"

Jim pulled him close for a hug, but Richard shook violently at the man's touch. With one grunt, he broke free from his dad's grip and ran off to his bedroom. It was the only time he'd ever gotten away with slamming the door behind him.

As he sat in the corner weeping, he would have traded any punishment for this one. "But why?" he wept.

Just beneath Richard's bedroom window, Jim Giles concealed his unbearable sorrow in the darkness. *Why?* he wondered. *Why this, too?* Tears streamed down his cheeks.

Richard's door opened and Grandma stood there, her face kind but firm. "Okay, Kiddo, I think we need to talk."

35

After an unforgettable summer, Abby and the neighborhood gang received the terrible tidings. Richard gathered the gang in his back yard. He felt ready to cry again. "I got some bad news, guys."

"Oh, God," Tracy blurted.

"Yeah?" asked Vinny.

"What now?" Grant asked.

Richard looked at Abby. She was frozen.

"My Dad was promoted, but he has to transfer to another prison." There was a long, painful pause. "We're going to have to move away…next week."

It was a lie. They were moving, sure enough, but Richard's dad hadn't been promoted. The hospital bills from his Mom's accident had finally broken them. It was a matter of money, or more precisely the lack of it. Richard silently vowed that he'd never be put in the same position – ever. *No matter what I have to do*, he swore to himself.

While the rest of his friends hung their heads and complained, Abby burst out crying and hurried for her house.

As a final gift to Richard's friends, Jim Giles announced, "I'm treating you all to Lincoln Park." It was a local amusement park that was famous for its epic Easter Egg hunts and The Comet, the largest and most feared roller coaster on the east coast. The park also had the reputation of hosting some lifelong memories from late spring until early fall.

Abby's Ma decided it was best that her dad didn't know about the excursion. She sneaked her some crumpled bills from their hidden coffee jar intended "for the rainy days," and placed her into the care of Jim Giles who was more than willing to keep the little secret. Abby loved Richard's dad and always wished he were her own.

Jim Giles pulled the station wagon into the front of the park and shut off the ignition. From sheer excitement, the back doors flew open and Richard, Abby, Grant, Tracy and Vinny piled out like a trained circus act. They waited. Jim Giles never opened his door.

Richard ran around to his father's window. "Aren't you comin', Dad?" he asked, still resentful of their upcoming move.

Jim handed his son some money and winked. "This is your day," he said, and then looked at both Richard and Abby. "Stay together, alright?"

They both nodded. "Absolutely," said Richard. "I'll be seein' ya."

"We will," blurted Abby.

Richard's father smiled. "Meet me back here at six," he said, and drove away from the curb.

The gang watched as the wood-paneled wagon disappeared into the distance. They looked at each other and smiled. They'd been set loose for one last hoorah. The world was young and this entire day was going to be their last great adventure together. Past the roller-skating rink and bowling alley out front, they sprinted toward the ticket gate.

Murals of smiling clowns holding balloons and lollipops beckoned them inside. A hand stamp cost $5.50 and allowed them to ride all the rides for the day. Once paid, the land of thrill seekers, big crowds and long lines opened up to them. *That's expensive*, thought Richard, while Grant secretly talked Tracy into paying his fare.

Three steps in and a slew of stimuli nudged them into a frenzy of squeals and high-fives. Flashing lights, carnival sounds and joyous screams filled the park. From popcorn to vomit, the smells were overwhelming. A world of vivid colors – dark reds and yellows and blues – surrounded everything. One look around, and it was clear that romance could blossom here, as well. Richard glanced over at Abby to find her staring at him. Smiling to himself, he turned, waved his friends toward him and ran for the rides. "Come on!"

Everyone took chase.

The Dodgems, or bumper cars, famous for epic traffic jams was their first stop. Electric poles rubbed against the steep grated ceiling, throwing off sparks and the smell of sulfur. Throughout the ride, the operator kept yelling, "Step on the pedal and turn the wheel. Step on the pedal and turn the wheel." Richard targeted Abby and chased her around the slick oval. In the meantime, Vinny, Tracy and Grant hunted him down and smashed him into all four walls. The laughter was contagious and was sure to last the whole day.

Abby's favorite was the Tilt 'O Whirl and all five friends crammed into its rainbow-colored half shell. With a steel bar resting across their lap, they began to spin in circles, while each individual car traveled its own circular track. When the ride hit a certain slant, the momentum had their car whipping around in a rush of uncontrolled madness. Grant sat on one end, Vinny on the other, and depending on the angle, each of them felt the weight of the other riders pressed against him. "Yoohooo!" Everyone laughed until it hurt. They rode it twice more. "I think I'm gonna be sick," Tracy muttered.

While Richard scanned the ground for lost change, the gang worked its way through the park. Hidden speakers spouting the moans and wails of ghouls and mutants soon had them standing before The Monster Ride. "Looks like

Old Lady Chouinard's place," Richard said and everyone agreed. Those who dared to ride were greeted by gaudy, lurking statues of hideous creatures with horns, sharp teeth and insane eyes. Of course, to the older, more discerning eye, the giant plaster of paris knick-knacks were absurd.

Richard led his friends toward the unknown. Tracy wouldn't hear of it. "Come on, Scaredy-Cat," Grant taunted. It didn't matter. No matter how much teasing they heaped on, Grant and Vinny were forced to share a car. Abby had already jumped in with Richard.

From the moment the car hit the double doors and entered pitch darkness, Abby shut her eyes and never opened them. While hideous mannequins waited in the shadows, the car took jerky turns on a squeaky track. "Eeeek," Abby squealed, while Richard did his best not to laugh. Through all the screaming, the smells of the midway wafted in, while several rays of sunlight streamed through the cracks in the old boards. Though these reminded everyone that his or her plight was surreal and quite temporary, it still didn't matter in the belly of the beast. At one point, in a mixture of panic and adoration Abby placed her trembling body against Richard.

He'd never felt such warmth. His whole body tingled and he instinctively tightened his grip. It was almost a hug. A swarm of butterflies fluttered in his guts, but even in the blackness he couldn't bring himself to kiss her. He just couldn't do it.

As the car came crashing through another set of double doors and back into reality, Richard and Abby released each other. Through squinted eyes, they exchanged a grin. The crush was their little secret, and no one had to know.

Waiting by the rail, Tracy gawked at them, smiling. There was no secret.

Majority ruled. It was time to eat. Throughout the park, the choices for lunch were endless: Candy apples, hot dogs, fried dough, spicy Portuguese sausage, cotton candy, french fries, salt water taffy, hamburgers, ice cream dipped in chocolate and then dipped again in fresh peanuts, thick juicy slices of watermelon, and cardboard pizza – all washed down with giant cups of icy cold soda pop. Though they were the perfect ingredients for vomit, the mountain of junk food couldn't have been greasier or served fast enough for them. The costly lunch was barely swallowed, never mind digested. Every second that elapsed, the rides beckoned.

The Carousel was more romantic than thrilling, but Abby helped Tracy browbeat the boys into riding it. "Or Trace and I are done for the day," she threatened.

Hand-painted panels along the outside roof depicted murals of yesteryears, while hundreds of mirrors and clear light bulbs decorated the inside. Though the majestic carousel had lions and tigers mixed in, horses posed in various positions were the coveted prize. As a brass bell sounded the beginning, each of them searched out the grandest horse. Abby hoped Richard would choose the double-seated Chariot. He didn't. He looked at her and then over at Grant and Vinny before he grabbed a horse. A moment later, the sweet notes of a calliope and the beat of a marching band set them off on their course. It was too long and boring for Abby and the guys, but perfect for Tracy.

To redeem his childish sense of honor, Grant pressured Vinny into jumping off the carousel before it came to a complete stop. At a sprint, they headed toward the Flying Cages.

This test of strength and endurance usually catered to adult men. The idea was to stand upright within the cage, and work its weight back and forth by pushing against the padded bars at the front and back. Each time you pushed, the cage climbed higher toward the top in a circular motion. If enough momentum was gained, the riders were able to muscle their weight and the weight of the cage right over the top, and keep going. There was no way Grant and Vinny were ever going to make it to the top. Men twice their size couldn't get the cages to go all the way around. Richard was too smart to try to impress anyone with such a setup for failure. Instead, he, Abby and Tracy took a seat on a nearby bench to do some people watching. Lincoln Park was the perfect melting pot. From every walk of life, people came in droves.

Panting and soaked in sweat, Vinny and Grant returned and offered their excuses, taking turns playing the blame game. "Vinny wasn't even trying," Grant lied.

"Yeah right, Grant," Vinny barked, "you're the one who wanted to quit just as we got started."

No one doubted it and everyone laughed – everyone but Grant. A moment later, they embarked on the rest of their unforgettable adventure.

The Carousel and Flying Cages bought time from facing certain illness, but unfortunately not enough.

The Round Up was a twisted invention designed for the brave of heart. The five of them stood back and watched for a minute.

It looked like a UFO turned sideways, red and yellow lights spinning out of control, human screams escaping from within. Essentially, each rider stood upright while the ride spun in circles so fast that gravity sucked them flush to its steel cage.

"Let's do it!" Grant egged them on.

There was a pause.

"You big chickens," he said.

Everyone – even Tracy – jumped in line, and each was thinking the same thing. Lunch was getting recycled.

Starting at a tilt, the ride lifted vertically until each of their bodies was parallel to the blurry ground beneath them. Richard pulled his wallet from his pocket and held on tight. Two minutes later, the world was one big smudge. *What a mistake!* Before the ride came to a stop, Grant was projectile vomiting. Only the irony of it made the others feel better. Through the queasiness, Tracy's smile returned. "You okay, Grant?" she asked, and the others giggled at her rare display of sarcasm.

Grant could only moan. *I'll get you back*, he thought.

Another vote was taken. "Okay, Grant," Richard said, "even though you don't deserve it, we'll give you a break and play some of the games." The first signs of relief appeared in Grant's handsome face.

The penny arcade beckoned with a game called Fascination. Each player rolled small balls under a plate of glass and into holes to form straight or diagonal lines. Though winners were paid in coupons to be redeemed for prizes or cash, each game cost ten cents and proved much too rich for the gang's young blood. Instead, they settled for skeeball and the newest video games.

While Richard saved his money, Abby gave ten cents to the glass-encased gypsy woman with the crystal ball. A random card spit out. Abby read her fortune. *Love has found you. Hold on tight.* Goosebumps ran over her body when she looked up to find Richard standing behind her, smiling.

"What does it say?" he asked, pointing at the cardboard prediction.

Her face burned red. "Nothing," she answered, and slid the card into her pants pocket. "It's silly."

Richard didn't push it. "The others want to take a picture," he said.

All five of them crammed into the tiny photo booth. It cost one dollar for five photos. Although Grant offered to spring for it, the money actually came out of Vinny's pocket. With wagging tongues and devil's horns, all five shots were taken. Abby divided the souvenir photos evenly, insuring that she got the best copy of Richard.

As they walked out of the arcade, Abby spotted a crank machine that completely removed Abe Lincoln's face by stretching pennies and stamping the words *Lincoln Park* into the center of them. A tingle traveled the length of her spine. As she opened her mouth to share her idea, though, something told her to wait. *It'll be better as a surprise*, she thought.

With fresh and disgusting memories of Grant's lunch, the gang passed The Scambler and waited in line at the Ferris Wheel. The wait wasn't long. From their swaying car, Richard and Abby were able to see all the rides along the midway and looming above them all was the giant roller coaster. To the right, they could also see cars traveling down Route Six, glimpses of the real world and a reminder that six o'clock was quickly approaching.

Once Vinny climbed out of his car, Richard addressed all of them. "You guys ready?" he asked.

They cringed. A few nods later, they faced south and marched the length of the midway – past Kiddie Land with its WhirlyBird helicopters, Mother Goose ride and boats that went round and round in four inches of murky water. The moment of truth had finally arrived.

The Comet, or giant roller coaster, was a rite of passage and the greatest test of courage for children in New England. Standing in the middle of the midway, with the Kiddie Coaster and Mini golf course on the right and the giant coaster on the left, the only real decision of the day needed to be made. "I'll watch the stuffed animals," Tracy said, and plopped down on a green bench with no intention of going anywhere. The rest of them looked at each other. While little kiddies chased each other in circles on The Flying Jets – raising and lowering their planes but never getting an inch closer – the decision was made. The time had come to take the risk and overcome their fear. "Let's do it!"

Abby stepped up to the wooden cutout of a boy who warned that each rider had to be his height to ride. *Drats!* She'd made it. She was finally tall enough. As the gang stepped in line, others filled in behind them. More fear took hold. They were trapped. With sweaty palms, Abby took a few steps closer. As it shot its latest riders up and down its steep hills, the rickety wooden coaster creaked and complained. Each step took Abby deeper into a war that was being waged between her heart and mind. Everything inside her begged her legs to flee. Her pride, however, held on – though just barely. People screamed on the ride. *This is supposed to be fun?* she thought.

Before long, she and the boys stepped up to the final platform's worn boards. She knew thousands, maybe even millions, had passed before them and survived. It was no consolation. Her mind raced, and she recalled her Mom and Richard's dad speak of those who rode the coaster with reverence and respect. She swallowed hard and took another step forward. She wanted that respect.

As they stood before the tracks, the car fired down the home stretch and screeched to a sudden stop. Everyone's faces were white. The passengers climbed out on unsure legs and Abby swallowed hard again. It was time to get aboard. Richard went first and though she followed, she felt like crying. "Good luck," she joked.

"Same to you," he replied and then pulled the safety bar across their laps.

A kind old gentleman wearing a soft hat and chewing on a cigar approached. As he bent to tug on the safety bar, Abby's frightened eyes searched for his help. He winked once and offered a grin that said everything was going to be fine. He walked slowly and with purpose to his podium. With one last look at the cars, he pushed a button that caused the train to belch out a steam of air. He then pulled on a long handle and the cars began to coast forward. As the train of cars rolled past him, his attention was diverted elsewhere. It didn't matter. The ride was now out of his hands. White knuckles threatened to crush the safety bar. It was time for a brief prayer, and the hyperventilating began.

Through a short patch of forest, the cars rounded the first bend. A huge, steel chain grabbed the front car and jerked it violently into control. There was a brief, merciful pause, and then the cars began to ascend slowly toward heaven, the chain clicking off each final moment of life. The sky was blue, with a few marshmallow clouds. Abby's body felt numb. Her mind rushed from primitive panic all the way to surreal acceptance. Perhaps shock had already set in. She gave one quick look toward Richard, her riding companion, and fake smiles were exchanged. At the top, the cars paused briefly again. This time felt cruel.

Abby held her breath. Like a nightmare come true, the car plummeted down the notorious first hill and straight toward the earth. The fall lasted no more than a moment and no less than a lifetime. The hill was longer than expected and lasted well beyond the screams of those who chose to exhale. On empty lungs, they hit bottom and were catapulted back up to an invisible turn. Abby thought they were going right off the track and struggled to roll herself into the fetal position. The bar would not allow it. The turn, however, was just another sick joke from the sadistic designer.

Gravity took over. While the wood boards swayed from the weight of the cars and their uncontrolled momentum, premature questions of life and death were considered. The train of cars then rolled home where the old man was waiting to apply the shrieking brake.

On wobbly knees, they climbed out. Abby was breathing again and smiling to be a survivor. *Yes!* She'd conquered the giant, they all did, and so much more than that. The entire experience was exhilarating, filled with equal amounts of fear and excitement. It was a perfect testament to youth.

Richard turned to Abby. "Go again?"

She nodded. They went four more times.

It was dusk, nearing six, when the park lit up with neon. There were so many flashing lights, they actually generated heat. It was time to leave.

As they waited for Richard's Dad, they peeked into the roller rink and saw a few skaters flying around on the shiny, hardwood floor. *What a great date spot for the winter*, Richard thought, and felt his body convulse. He'd almost forgot he was moving and the reality of it slapped him hard in the face. Just as they closed the door behind them, the *Doubles* light came on and each skater grabbed for a partner's hand. He looked at Abby and felt a terrible sadness.

Abby grabbed his arm. "Let's go see the ballroom before your Dad gets here," she said. "I've always wanted to see it."

He followed her lead.

The Million Dollar Ballroom hosted jazz, swing and orchestra music. Abby peeked through the porthole window at the couples dancing and dreamed of doing the same. Even if she could have talked Richard into it, kids weren't allowed in.

Richard, on the other hand, imagined the place packed for Golden Gloves Boxing, or for the wrestlers like Chief Jay Strongbow, Ivan "Polish Power" Putski, Killer Kowalski, Mr. Fuji, Haystack Calhoun and Andre the Giant.

The ballroom was rectangular with a balcony around the main dance floor. In the center of the floor, a semicircular stage – in the shape of a shell – glistened with a tinsel-like backdrop that ran from the ceiling to the floor. It was a large dome structure, spacious and vast. Colored lights twinkled above the polished dance floor. Every time the door opened, the wondrous sounds of Big Band music escaped. Abby and Richard watched people hold each other close – in a sea of simple elegance – smiling, laughing and twirling in each other's arms. It was luxurious.

Abby turned to Richard and made a silent wish. *I hope we'll dance this same way one day when we're grown.*

Richard looked at her and grinned.

She awaited an explanation for the smile.

He half-punched her arm and then made her chase him all the way back to the roller rink where the station wagon was waiting.

It was well past midnight when Richard finally surrendered to the tossing and turning. Rolling out of bed, he maneuvered past several moving boxes, stepped up to the window and pulled back the curtain. Freedom Ave was deserted and silent. From left to right – as if he were branding the picture into his mind forever – he carefully scanned every detail of the place he could no longer call home. Although one good memory after another played out before him, a sharp pain pricked his heart. No one was watching, so he allowed the tears to flow. Once he'd arrived at the farthest reaches of his vantage point, he forced his swollen eyes to work their way back and absorb more of his past. "Why do we have to leave?" he muttered. "Why?" Before long, his shoulders rocked back and forth to the rhythm of his quiet sobs.

Several yards away, Abby lay in bed and sobbed. *Why?* she asked God in her prayers. *Why do You have to take him from me?*

On the morning that Richard left, Abby's Ma caught her in the 'rainy day' coffee jar fishing around for change. Before she could question it, Abby looked up with torment in her eyes. "It's pouring, Mama," she explained. Claire Gerwitz understood and handed her daughter the pennies she needed.

Abby led the gang down to the railroad tracks and, forfeiting a few Swedish fish and a handful of root beer barrels, gave them each a penny. Under her direction, the five of them formed a circle and made a lifelong pact. "Friends for life!" they vowed and all five pennies were placed on the slick, steel rails. With closed eyes, each made a wish on his or her penny – tiny prayers – and awaited the oncoming train; waiting for the tons of rolling thunder to seal their hopes and dreams within the coins for all eternity.

It took a few anxious minutes. As the train came into view, though, Richard's penny danced off the tracks. He hurried toward it, but there wasn't enough time to recover it. Within seconds, the train plowed by. As Abby, Tracy, Vinny and Grant each picked up their souvenir, Richard complained under his breath. Abe Lincoln's profile remained intact. His penny never got smashed.

"That's gotta be a curse," teased Grant.

Abby stepped between them. "Don't listen to him," she said, "Grant's attitude is the real curse." With a breaking heart, she offered her flattened penny to her best friend.

Richard reluctantly accepted the gift – with Abby's wish compressed inside it. He didn't know what to say. He didn't have the words.

Gray clouds hovered over Freedom Ave. Richard's Dad and Grandma made their goodbyes quick and waited in the overstuffed station wagon for Richard.

Abby and Richard had never said goodbye before. The pain was alien. It hurt something awful. Overwhelmed with emotion, it took both of them a little longer to speak. It was the hardest thing they ever had to do.

Richard wore a mended, black ball cap with the white letters PC embroidered on the front, the brim curled and worn over his eyes.

Through sniffles, Abby finally asked, "We'll stay in touch, right?"

"Yup." Richard was fighting to be strong, and dared not speak more than a word.

Abby lifted the brim of his hat to find a pair of eyes swimming in sadness and love. "Goodbye, Richard," she whimpered.

Richard placed his hand on her shoulder and shook his head. "No. I'll be seein' ya, Abby," he whispered, and with one surge of courage kissed her on the lips.

While Abby tried to catch her breath, he pulled his baseball cap back over his eyes, jumped into the family station wagon and never looked back. One cruel moment later, the Giles family drove away.

As they reached the end of the road, Richard's gaze caught Old Man Sedgeband sitting on the stoop of R&S Variety, smoking his pipe and smiling. *Why not?* Richard thought, *Old Man Sedgeband doesn't have to leave Freedom Ave.* The smart, old coot was financially secure enough to stay forever. Though he was always in a hurry to do nothing and much too concerned with material wealth, Richard considered the small-time mogul to be way ahead of his time. *At least Old Man Sedgeband has what it takes to survive.*

Abby cried with the grief of the bereaved. Some believed she was too young to know true love, but nobody thought to explain that to her heart. It felt as if it were shattered into a thousand pieces. She looked up to find her Ma sitting in the porch swing and hurried to her.

"The world really is a very small place," her mother whispered, "and you'd be surprised at how people's lives can overlap each other's…time and again."

Abby convulsed in her Ma's lap.

"Believe it or not, Sweetie, we're all connected. And you never know what the future might hold."

Though they'd promised to keep in touch, even at their young age Richard and Abby both knew better. Abby mourned straight through Christmas, while life turned out exactly how she'd feared it might. She and Richard never talked and they never wrote. It was tragic that they couldn't share what they would experience and learn in the years to come; everything their adolescence and young adulthood would witness in the 1980's.

Another decade that began as wholesome and innocent would see the birth of true technology. As such, the promise of greater luxuries and comfort was coveted. But what would be traded in return? Two parents working hard to keep up with the Jones's; day care, fast food, incredible stress and dysfunction. Was it a time of progression, or regression? The American family traded in for the American dream?

Far beyond carhops, free love or discos, as teenagers Richard and Abby would be stuck in a time that had great difficulty defining itself. Among the upward swing of technological progress – push button telephones and complicated VCR's – it was a generation struggling to find its voice, its identity.

For Richard, it was a time of Cheryl Tiegs posters and a crush on Kristi McNichol. Mohawks and rattail haircuts seesawed between the Violent Femmes and AC/DC. Jaws, Star Wars and Freddie Kruger were far more entertaining than the after school specials his Dad made him watch. Boom boxes and break dancing preceded colognes like English Leather, High Karate and Polo. A Chevy Nova, acne and a Drive-In movie theater were the perfect ingredients for lost virginity. A Members Only jacket made him feel cool, while Beta tapes replaced Fat Albert and Popeye. Skate boarding, a Bo Derek t-shirt and Converse high tops were a phase just before the leather vest, chain wallet and concert t-shirts. While friends wore turned up collars and different colored Levis, remote controls with wires meant that he no longer had to get up to change the channel. Parachute pants, Smokey and the Bandit's black Trans Am and a Rubik's Cube defined the end of his growing years, as did the Dukes of Hazard, the A-Team and an obsessive game called Asteroids.

For Abby, it was a time of pop rocks, friendship beads and TV dinners on TV trays in front of the TV; better known as the beginning of the end of the American family. Tiger Beat magazines and record players brought on dreams of Flashdance, dancing with Kevin Bacon in Footloose and kissing Chachi from Happy Days. Besides collecting Garbage Pail Kids stickers, the Hardy Boys and Nancy Drew gave her the vocabulary to keep a diary. While The Wizard of Oz played every year on T.V., Friday the 13th scared her so much that she had to watch the movie three more times in the theater. Luvs Baby Soft was the perfume of choice. The Brady Bunch and schoolhouse rock remained viewing favorites. They were the days of English muffin pizzas, banana clips, Charlie's Angels and feathered hair. Soon after, gel bracelets and Dr. Scholl's clogs were worn with hair that defied gravity. Donnie & Marie and the Ice Capades lost their gleam, replaced by new fads like collecting Cabbage Patch Kids, devouring microwave popcorn and beating every level of Pac Man.

The 1980's meant Izod and MTV. Everyone was a "wanna be" Madonna, Duran Duran, Michael Jackson, Cyndi Lauper, or Boy George. The big question was "Where's the beef?" Everyone still knew how to use a rotary phone. Max Headroom was the man. People either knew how, or wanted to be able to Moonwalk. Atari, IntelliVision, TelStar and Coleco were the ultimate gaming systems to own. Leg warmers and headbands alá Pat Benatar were really cool, while Jordache jeans with a flat-handle comb in the back pocket finished off the look. Ferris Bueller's Day Off, Gremlins, The Karate Kid and Porky's were the movies to watch. Live Aid and Van Halen were the concert tickets to score. In Valley girl lingo, it was "like madness." Kool and the Gang celebrated. The J. Geils Band sang about some centerfold. Men At Work talked about living Down Under. Foreigner wanted to know what love was.

And so did Abby.

Chapter 6

Summer 1998

It was a windy, late-summer day. The first of the leaves were preparing to fall when Bill Stryker walked up Crimson Street toward the center of town. His shoulders tucked squarely to the wind, he squinted to navigate his way.

Wrapped in a light throw blanket, Eunice sat on a porch swing, quietly watching the world as it spun in perfect circles.

The distinctive voice of Dean Martin caused Bill to look up. Immediately, he spotted the silhouette of a woman sitting in the shadows of a porch. Tipping his invisible hat to her, he joked, "Good day to fly a kite, eh?"

Eunice leaned forward just enough to reveal her dazzling smile.

Bill felt the warmth of the sun touch his face and his legs stopped moving. He gazed into her kind, green eyes and cleared his throat. "At the risk of appearing too forward, Miss," he said, "I was just on my way to Gray's Ice Cream for one last cone before they close up shop for the season. Can I buy you one?"

She thought for no more than a second before she threw the thin blanket aside, shut off her radio and stood. Gesturing that she'd be a minute, she headed for the door. "Just let me get my sandals."

Ten minutes later, they stood in the small window of Gray's Ice Cream shop. Bill ignored the list of flavors. "I'll have a small sugar cone of black raspberry," he ordered and turned to Eunice.

She was taken aback.

"What is it?" he asked.

"Nothing," she mumbled. She took a step closer to him and grinned. "It's just that…you're my flavor."

He smiled so wide that it felt like his face might break, and then turned back to the girl in the window. "Make that two."

Without any formal announcement, they were dating exclusively. The courtship proved to be both innocent and intense at the same time.

Bill Stryker was witty, kind and down to earth. Distinguished looking, he had broad shoulders and blue eyes. He wore expensive cologne and a magnetic smile. Besides the uncanny ability to watch movies and find their mistakes, his greatest gift to the world was laughter. He had a wonderful way of lightening any situation, reminding people of their common humanity with all its fumbles and failures. "All things in life will pass," he'd say, "and to laugh through the darkness is a gift. A small dose of the giggles is enough medicine to heal whatever ails you." Though he was right, he was also about to discover that when shared with others the gift was even more precious. To the world, Bill Stryker was easily excitable, sweet and considerate. To Eunice, he was romantic, doting and very generous.

And Eunice didn't just love life. She was in love with it and the music that captured each experience. Her motto on love was, "It might very well be the only reason that people exist to begin with. Only in experiencing love – both in knowing how to give as well as receive – do we discover the very essence of humanity." Life was all about karma for her.

For their first formal date, they enjoyed the theater together at the Providence Performing Arts Center and the fine dining on Federal Hill that preceded it. Hand in hand, they strolled along the river during Providence's water fire. Hidden speakers offered the eclectic sounds of primitive chants and tribal drums. Alluring smells of vendor delicacies wafted on unseasonably chilly breezes. Side streets were cordoned off and police officers rerouted traffic. With thousands of pedestrians, the walk along the river moved like warm pudding.

They felt comfortably alone in each other's company, occasionally stopping to share a moment of body heat. As if lovers were sworn to secrecy, other couples offered subtle nods in greeting. Bill and Eunice returned each gesture. As they strolled along, they sneaked swigs of wine from a paper bag like adolescents in love. Steel fire pits sat several feet out of the water, lining the middle of the river every thousand yards, while old, wooden boats filled with thespians dressed in black threw fresh-split cordwood onto each. Like swarms of angry fireflies, a million sparks scurried into the air. Bright orange and red flames licked at the black sky, as strong smells of burnt oak and cedar reminded folks of cozy summer campfires and the free love that could be experienced under a starry sky.

Eunice stopped and wrapped her arms around him. "Thank you for this wonderful experience," she said.

Bill smiled. "I only supplied half of it. Thank you for the other half."

They kissed for the first time and felt as young as they'd ever felt in their lives.

Weeks fit quickly into months, and not one of them passed without Bill either bringing or sending Eunice a bouquet of fresh sunflowers tied in lavender ribbon. Her favorite colors were yellow and purple. Considering that the flowers were only in season a brief time, she marveled over this incredible feat. He was definitely not a penny pincher. "You are the sun upon my face," he'd say. "And I never want you to forget it."

He'd lived long enough to know it was the little things that made all the difference: Flowers on random, rainy Tuesdays. Love notes hidden where she'd surely find them. And the words *I love you* every time he greeted her or they bid farewell. Eunice could have had Alzheimer's and still know Bill loved her. To him, it was the most important thing he needed her to know. The rest was no more than white noise that filled the space around them.

He also went out of his way for those Eunice loved – more evidence of his love for her.

"Do you think we're enough alike?" she asked one day.

He chuckled. "As much as humanly possible, I suppose. It's clear that the Lord put the eyes of a man in his head, while a woman sees more from her heart. I'm just glad He was kind enough to give me the eyesight to understand this, so I could try to see things from your perspective."

She kissed him. "You're learning," she teased, "but you mean SHE was kind enough to give you the eyesight to understand this."

He laughed hard and kissed her back.

As the months unfolded, they shared everything from pet names to Eskimo kisses. Love was meant to be sappy, and lovers shouldn't care what the rest of the world thought.

Time stood still whenever Bill was near Eunice, but when he checked his watch he realized that the world had completed countless rotations without him ever feeling the movement beneath his feet. He walked on air around her. And she magnified all the goodness in him, making him a better man than he'd ever dreamed possible. That was her greatest, most effortless gift. Like a magnet, she drew out the best in him. And the best part was that he knew it.

Eunice had the spontaneity, faith and innocence of a child. She believed the world was good; therefore, it was. She created her own experience, her own reality and anyone caught inside it was blessed. Grace, happiness and peace was bound to rub off and even if it was only felt for the moment, it was felt and known to be possible. Hope was the aftermath of her touch. In her wake, a man could actually drown in a state of utter joy, and Bill was happy to go under. She taught him that love could still exist.

Eunice finally asked, "How much do you love me?"

"There's nothing that could measure it."

"It's that small?"

He nodded. "Yup. As small as all the galaxies in all the universes."

"Liar."

He chuckled. "Thief."

She looked at him.

He grabbed for his heart.

She hugged him.

He then noticed the big, red letters on the alarm clock. They read: 11:11. "Hurry and make a wish," he said.

Eunice closed her eyes and wished that the night would never end.

For Eunice's birthday, Bill did the impossible. He quit smoking. "I'm on the patch," he joked, "500 milligrams fitted like a vest." It was no joke, though. His body couldn't take the abuse any longer. It was the best gift Eunice had ever received.

He couldn't stop eating and quickly started to resemble an aircraft carrier. "I won't be happy until I weigh 400 pounds," he joked, and people laughed along with him. But it was an act. He was more self-conscious of his appearance than he could ever remember. It seemed the bigger he got the more invisible he became to the opposite sex – all but Eunice.

"I don't care," she said. "I don't care about appearances. You're beautiful to me." It really didn't matter to her.

He sighed heavily and tore through the cellophane wrapper on a beautiful pair of cupcakes. It was a taste of heaven and guilt all wrapped up into one little pastry. It was hopeless.

It was a random, autumn night when Bill told his love. "Pack an overnight bag. I have a surprise!"

While they dined on a blue plate special at one of their usual spots, Eunice squirmed with anticipation. *Roger's* was a greasy spoon that promised great food served by good, hard working people, followed by a bowl of some of the best ice cream.

After a short drive to the shore and a walk by the water, Bill said, "I never told you that I love to fish."

Is he taking me fishing? she wondered.

"And there's this boat that I'd love you to see."

She nodded.

"Because of my work, I never had time to fish, but it was my greatest love as a kid. I'm now rediscovering the beauty of the water and would love to share it with you."

Again, Eunice nodded. She imagined a small fishing boat with a loud outboard motor.

As they strolled the docks toward the marina, an attendant spotted

Bill approaching and unlocked the gate. "Good evening, Mr. Stryker," he said, "I made sure that she's ready for you. All hands are on board."

"Thanks, Frank. I appreciate that," answered Bill, and then held the gate open for Eunice.

All hands are on board? thought Eunice. She was confused, and dismissed it as some sort of seamen lingo that she didn't understand.

They approached a small outboard. Bill grabbed her overnight bag, and then helped her aboard.

This seems a little small to spend the night, she thought.

With a smile, Bill fired up the motor. Minutes later, they pulled alongside a yacht so big that it couldn't fit into the marina's largest slip. The name *Can't Buy Me Love* was painted across the ship's stern, and Eunice smiled at the Beatles reference. It was the biggest boat Eunice has ever seen and she laughed at Bill's clever sense of humor.

He never batted an eye.

The ship's Captain awaited them at the ladder. "Good evening, Mr. Stryker," he said, "the crew's on board and ready to shove off when you are."

Eunice couldn't believe her eyes. At 126 feet long and several stories high, the white, steel hulled monster contained five staterooms, along with a captain's cabin, master cabin and four plush guest cabins. Computerized and modernized, it possessed every amenity from satellite telephones and 50" televisions to the galley's double BBQ grill and professional dishwasher. Wrapped in polished mahogany and glass, it was a floating mansion.

With Eunice's mouth still hung open, Bill turned to her. "At a maximum speed of 14 knots, our cruising speed can be maintained at around 12 knots."

Her forehead wrinkled.

He smiled. "It means we can go wherever we want – really fast."

She was still at a loss for words.

"Since we got matters of the heart all figured out, I decided it was time to show you my other side."

One of her eyebrows rose.

"Like it or not," he said, "I'm filthy rich." And through the night, he poured out his soul and shared many intimate details of himself that he absolutely needed her to know. He wasn't proud of them, but he still needed her to know.

"I spent my life amassing a great fortune, or so I believed," he explained. "I was so foolish that once I had all the money I would ever need I actually believed I had everything – except for a wife who truly cared for me, or children who even knew who I was. My days spent with the boys at the club added up to a whole lot of nothing. And that's exactly what I had for most of my life." He placed his hand in hers. "After meeting you, getting to know and love you, I now know that the only thing that matters in life – besides our health – is love." He gave her hand a squeeze. "And if I had to choose between the two, I'd pick love over good health any day."

She squeezed his hand back.

"My wife passed away some years ago and the tragedy of our parting was that we never really knew each other. I'm ashamed to admit it, but she was an incubator and nanny to my children. I didn't have time for her. I provided for my family, but we lived separate lives. By the time we had children, I learned that I didn't have time for them either. We had two daughters, with just as many houses, but we shared nothing."

"And your daughters now?" Eunice asked.

A few moments elapsed before he answered. "I speak to them from time to time; make sure they're taken care of, but I can't really say that we've ever been that close." He shook his sorrowful head. "It's my fault completely."

"Well, we're just going to have to do something about that now, aren't we?"

Bill's brow wrinkled. "I'm not sure they'd…"

"Nonsense," Eunice said, "they're your family – our family – and I'll invite them to spend Christmas with us. Jim will be coming to stay with us, and I'm sure I can get Richard to do the same. It'll be wonderful. Just you wait. It'll be perfect."

He kissed her. "Okay," he said.

"Anymore surprises?" she asked.

He shook his head.

"Good," she said, and kissed him back.

Both R.S.V.P.'s were returned in a matter of days. Bill's eldest daughter, Isabella, wrote Eunice: *I regret that the children and I have a prior obligation, but please send my best to my father.* Emma's reply was even less cordial: *Sorry – not this year.* Eunice shook her head. There was more distance than she'd imagined.

By the third telephone call, Eunice finally got through. Isabella Stryker Napert had the voice of a caring, rational person, but Eunice also detected the aching resentment of a childhood lost. "I don't know," Isabella said, "Emma and I haven't spent Christmas with our father in years. I have my own girls now and as I said, we have plans."

"Please think about it," Eunice pleaded. "If not for yourself, then for your girls – so that they can see where their Mom came from."

"Yeah, money," Isabella blurted.

"True," Eunice said, "and a little more than that."

There was a long pause.

"Your dad would like nothing more than to spend the holidays with his family. He's told me so."

Isabella actually gasped. She couldn't help it.

"And besides, I think it's time that you and I got to know each other."

"Okay," Isabella said. "We'll come."

"And Emma?" Eunice asked.

"You'd better let me take care of that," Isabella said. "When it comes to the anger department, she's even got me beat!"

Eunice sighed. "Thank you."

Someone gave the sleigh bells on Bill and Eunice's front door a shake. "Can you get that?" she called out from the kitchen, and the biggest smile overtook her face. Bill's gift was right on time.

Bill opened the door and felt a shiver travel the length of his spine. The sensation, however, wasn't caused by the frigid air. Each of Isabella's little girls held their Mom's hand, while Auntie Emma balanced a stack of presents and a forced smile. With swollen eyes, Bill pulled his family in from the cold and grabbed the heavy burden from his youngest daughter. "Welcome," he said with a guilty smile. He'd never meant a single word more in his life.

Beyond the awkward greetings, it was a warm holiday reunion. Eunice put out a spread that could have graced the cover of *Country Living* magazine. Though they sat several chairs apart, the intoxicating smells had her son, Jim, and grandson, Richard, at the table long before it was served. The festive sounds of music and children's laughter filled the house. Dinner conversation was nice – polite.

"Can we open our presents now, Grandpa?" Isabella's little one finally asked.

In a flash, Bill was up from the table and running for the tree with two giggling children slung over his shoulders.

While the adults claimed seats around the festively decorated balsam pine, the kids tore through red and green wrapping paper. It sounded like branches falling through a wood chipper.

Bill foraged under the tree and reappeared with two gifts for his love.

With the children's enthusiasm, Eunice shredded the gift-wrap and discovered a set of hand-carved wind chimes.

"I'll help you hang them on the porch in the spring," he whispered in her ear.

"They're beautiful," Eunice squealed, and threw her arms around him.

Isabella and Emma exchanged several looks on the couch. They had never seen their father so happy, so human.

Bill then offered Eunice his second gift. Even the kids couldn't be fooled.

"It's a kite!" they called out.

Eunice pulled back the paper to confirm their suspicions. The wind chimes; the kite – his thoughtful gifts were a clear celebration of the blessed day they'd met. Even with the ridiculous amounts of money he possessed, he'd opted to offer a few simple gifts that proved to Eunice that his heart belonged to her.

"Remember my first words to you on the day we met?" he asked.

She smiled. "Good day to fly a kite, eh?" She kissed him deeply. "You're such a beautiful man, Bill Stryker. And to think that I'd actually given up looking for you."

He returned her sweet kiss. "Let's just thank God you like black raspberry ice cream."

Bill looked around the room and bathed in the glow of his family's smiling faces. Eunice was right. It was never too late to let love prevail.

While Jim and Richard exchanged money cards, Bill turned to Isabella and Emma. "And now for your gifts…" He choked on emotion. "I think you've waited long enough."

They both peered under the tree. There were no presents left.

Bill walked to the couch and plopped down between them. As if they were wings, he spread his arms and wrapped them around his daughters. "I didn't get jewelry for either of you this Christmas."

They each looked past their father and exchanged a surprised glance.

"And you won't be getting money from me."

They both rested their eyes upon him.

He pulled them to him and kissed each of their foreheads. "I hope it's not too late. But I'd like this to be the first Christmas that I give you – me."

It took a few moments for his words to register.

"I'm so sorry for missing out on your lives. I really am." He started to cry. "I just wish…"

Though Isabella hadn't wanted to, she couldn't help it and collapsed into her father's heaving chest. "Oh, Daddy…" she cried. It was the only gift she ever wanted.

Emma was much more reluctant and felt a rage immediately surface. "So it's that easy?" she asked, her tone lethal. "After all these years, that's all you have to say for not being there for us?"

"But I am sorry, Em," he repeated. "I truly am…and I love you both too much to waste another minute."

Emma could only shake her head, while Eunice clasped her hands together and fought back the sniffles. *It's not perfect*, she thought, *but it's a start.*

Though they smiled, Jim and Richard shuffled uneasily in their chairs.

As winter melted into spring, Bill and Eunice's each and every moment were spent discovering a young and budding love. They found a laid back nightclub where they danced away every Saturday. They took long rides, stopped to watch children play Little League, and walked miles of rocky east coast beaches. Together, they captured a hundred sunsets, several jars of fireflies and the love of a lifetime over several cozy campfires. And through it all, they devoured gallons of black raspberry ice cream. Their relationship was comfortable, easy – eternal. On a wrinkled old beach blanket, he finally asked for her hand.

She gave it. "Together forever?" she asked.

"TOGETHER FOREVER!" he confirmed.

She paused. "When did you know I was the one?"

"The moment I saw you."

"No. I mean it. When did you know?"

He grabbed her face. "And I mean it, too. The very moment I saw you and forgot about me." He shook his head. "You don't understand. I feel so peaceful when I'm with you, but at the same time I'm excited. I can't concentrate on anything. You make me laugh, you make me happy and I love you for it. I've been blessed and it's time for me to share it all."

After a long hug, she looked up at him. "Let's go away and do it," she said. "I mean – it's not like our parents will ever complain."

"Not a chance," he snickered.

It was the most beautiful spring afternoon when Bill Stryker and Eunice Giles eloped in the presence of their families on the yacht. With the exception of Emma's scowling puss, the simple ceremony was perfect. For the best man's toast, Eunice's son, Jim, recited his gift:

"Crossroads of Love

Two roads began at separate points
in a time called 'long ago'

To wonder then where they would lead
was a fate for God to know.

Each guided children down their paths
of goodness, hope and love
with nothing but the light that shone
from heaven up above.

The obstacles, the bumps and turns
which stood in both their ways
were merely just a set of tests
that led to better days.

The rains would pass, the winds subside
and with their labor done,
two roads would stop and take the time
to watch the setting sun.

But God had other plans in mind:
Their trips had just begun.
Two roads began at separate points,
but now those roads are one."

During one of the night's many slow songs, Eunice turned to her grandson. "No date, Richard?" she asked with a tone of surprise.

He smiled and kissed her cheek. "No one important enough to share this day with, Grandma," he whispered. She was the only person who still called him Richard.

She grabbed his face and returned his whisper. "She's out there."

He shrugged. "If time allows."

"Getting older only means better choices." She winked. "And second chances."

With that, she and her new husband finished their dance and headed out on the ship's deck to take pictures. As they walked by the hall mirror, they stopped. "Look at us," Bill said, "aren't we the pair to beat a full house?" The wrinkles, crow's feet and paunch midsections could not distract from their glowing smiles. He squeezed her tight. Until Eunice, his heart was known to no one. He peered hard at his reflection. His eyes might have grown old, but his heart felt as young as a morning shower. He and his lovely bride were in the springtime of their love and celebrated the fact with a long, wet kiss.

Richard turned to find his father standing before him. "Nice toast, Dad," he said and then searched for more words that wouldn't come.

Jim nodded, took a step closer and extended his hand for a shake. "Thanks. I wish I could have done more, though."

Me, too, Richard thought, but it had nothing to do with Bill and Grandma. He shook his father's hand. "It was a beautiful poem," he said aloud.

Jim nodded again.

Richard smiled. "I'll be seein' ya, Dad," he said and quickly dismissed himself. The tension between them was unbearable. And besides, there was an enormous yacht to explore. *Bill has obviously done quite well for himself*, Richard thought, and started on his quest.

Chapter 7

Rick returned home from Grandma's wedding to an empty apartment. He looked into the bathroom mirror and stared. Months before, he'd abandoned any hope for his receding hairline and shaved his entire head bald. He now wore a trimmed goatee, and kept himself in top physical condition. Still, life was catching him.

Stripping out of his suit, he jumped into the shower and adjusted the water until it was as hot as he could stand. It was the one thing that could still make him feel. As he had a million times before, he tilted his face under the showerhead and pondered the fateful morning that he and his wife split up nearly nine months before...

Perhaps it was just another example of the times? PC's were exploding onto the American scene and it didn't take long for Rick to gain a VP position within one of the leading software companies and set his sights on the top of the heap. One condo and two BMW's later, the rest of the money was spent on aspirin and antacids. Life was miserable.

Before he realized it, he'd become a high-flying executive, a real Yuppie-type, focused more on climbing ladders of success than tree forts. And Rose, his lovely bride, had become a warm executive to sleep alongside. As far as a long-term commitment in a human relationship, though, the responsibilities of their titles wouldn't allow for it. They had everything – vacation homes, cars – everything but each other.

Rick remembered the hollow sound of wing tips on marble, echoing through their vast home. Everything steel and concrete, even the sky had turned gray that Christmas eve. Rose was out of the country on business, so he'd decided to grab a bite to eat – alone. He checked that the condo alarm was set, popped another antacid and ventured down the street.

There was a row of homeless people sitting in line along the sidewalk. If Rick cared any less, though, he would have been in a coma. He'd actually become Old Man Sedgeband, with good manners.

Two blocks later, he'd just avoided eye contact with a homeless man when he nearly tripped over another. Collapsing to the street, he tore his new leather gloves in an attempt to break his fall. He cursed under his breath, removed his gloves and fired them into a nearby trashcan.

"You should never throw anything out unless you absolutely have to," the homeless man said and fished the gloves out for himself.

Rick stopped fast, while the years of greed and selfishness slammed right into the back of him. They were his Grandma's words and they made him freeze in place.

The only way to be happy is to follow your heart, Richard, he could hear her in his head. *All you need to do is to figure out what's in your heart.*

The hair on his neck stood on end and without ever expecting it, a wave of sorrow crashed over him. *What have I become?* he wondered. But the answer was buried too deep. The one thing he did know was that he'd been unhappy for as long as he could remember.

After offering the homeless man a twenty-dollar bill, Rick turned up his collar and tried to shake off the experience. *I must have walked by this bum a thousand times,* he thought, *why should I care now?* While brushing himself off, he decided to take a good look at the world. His eyes had been on the ground for years.

Smiling faces, framed in woolen scarves and colorful earmuffs, released a chimney of steam into the starry night. Shop windows, adorned in the year's latest clothing styles and ingenious toys, beckoned the masses. The sticky smell of hot cross buns fought with the fumes of rumbling delivery trucks and filthy yellow cabs. Massive strands of garland, strung from lamppost to lamppost, dangled red bowed wreaths at each center. Tiny white lights sparkled from saplings that sprung up from concrete, while the echo of children's laughter traveled the streets. A very old feeling pierced the bitter air: The need to be kind. Up one street and down the next, horse-drawn carriages escorted lovers, each pair buried beneath downy blankets – the nostalgic sound of harness bells clearing their way. Steam escaped manhole covers. Fogged windows concealed goodness behind every pane. In the brisk air, red-cheeked city folks were bundled against the unrelenting cold, carrying packages of sweets and gadgets and dreams-come-true, the stacks of presents tied in white string juggled nicely. Not one set of eyes showed any sign of carrying the world's heavy burdens; people walked with a light step, aware of their wondrous existence. The dark skyline remained mysterious, smoke rising up from rooftops – creating visions of a chimneysweeper working late to feed his young. Parents laughed. Children squealed. Good will was given and accepted by all. And for the first time in years, Rick felt human and alive.

Returning to his condo, he offered his doorman a cash gift. The surprised man accepted, but as Rick walked away he realized that he didn't even know the man's name. The truth of it hurt his heart. *Am I that detached?*

It was nearly a week before Rose returned home to their sterile life, and for the next three nights they fought. Rick needed a change. He needed to find happiness again, and his wife was the most obvious place to begin his quest.

It was going to be another endless night of lost sleep. Rick's hands were tucked behind his pounding head. The arguments had become more vicious, harder to forget. Their internal walls of defense had grown tall and thick. He'd braced himself, knowing the worse was yet to come. He would not have predicted that it would come waving a white flag of surrender. "It's not all about the money," he said, surprised to hear the words coming from his own mouth. "There has to be more."

"Are you ill?" Rose asked.

He felt sick in his heart, but didn't answer.

"What about the trips to Mexico, our summer place? What do you think we've worked so hard for?" she asked.

"But I want more. I need more. I can't take the loneliness anymore – the sorrow," he said, his voice rising in anger. "I need you."

Rose shook her head. Her time was the one thing she couldn't afford to give him.

Months went by, some long months, and Rick's every attempt at making their marriage survive was slain by Rose's other, more important priorities. Counseling was as "out of the question" as the passionate interventions of several couples with whom they socialized. Rose was on the fast track and she wasn't going to let anything slow her down. Rick's depression deepened. Night after night, he toured their lavish condo and was forced to wonder why – for someone who had everything – he felt so empty.

He finally called her cell phone. "Don't you want 'us' anymore?" he asked.

"I do," she admitted, "but the way it's always been – not with you being so needy." She breathed heavy. "I just don't have time for it, Rick."

He swallowed hard and hung up. Their marriage was finished.

Rick spent weeks in mourning, mending his bruised and broken heart. He eventually captured his grief on paper. Sadly, it was the only poem he'd written Rose since the day they'd exchanged vows.

So Long

Caught by the occasional cruelty of fate,
the gentle peace that was once you

is vanished in an angry scream.
A passion: Not dead, but ushered to the opposite extreme.
A relationship: Not ended, but sorrowfully transformed.
Separated by circumstance, one last tear,
exhausted of forgiveness, drips into my now-fragile world.
The impact, silent but deafening,
leaves behind an unfillable void.
My soul- exiled into an invisible solitude.
My heart- left to swim in a volcano of pain.

The rest... a mere charade.

Sulking in the shadows of yesterday,
the night, once my ally,
is now a relentless enemy who seeks to destroy me.
The moon; the only light powerful enough
to illuminate my grief,
reveals the truth that my prideful words
weighed less than the natural course of change.
One beautiful tree has split its trunk in two,
destined to grow in different directions.
Memories, sweet and fleeting, are clinged to,
as a helpless child would its mother.
Instead of comfort

...a reminder of great loss.

Time, once quick and impatient,
now drags its feet- almost cynically.
In the words of those who care to listen,
the pain is understood but never felt,
sealing the desperate isolation of those who lack expression.
The cycle of emotions wanders its path,
leading to a test of faith; a lesson in acceptance.
Hopes and dreams are revisited; renegotiated.
And once completely consumed by the darkness,
I arrive at a shocking realization:
I can never allow myself to become what I fear!
On the rocky roads of life

...I must become a rock climber.

In the forced stillness, I go within-
to finally discover that my needs and expectations
were already satisfied upon the first day I drew breath.

And finally, I am grateful.

He packed and flew south to Barbados for some time to think. He needed to view life from a different perspective; to understand why he hadn't become the considerate man his father had taught him to be.

Each morning, before sunrise, he took a long walk on the beach. The more he thought about his life, though, the more the answers to his dilemma eluded him. By the third day, he decided to clear his mind and just walk.

"Good morning, Mon," a man called out from the shadows beside the docks.

Rick searched the darkness, but could only make out a single silhouette. "Mornin'," he replied and kept walking.

The following morning, the shadow greeted him again.

This time Rick stopped. "Good morning…"

"Vincent," the man said. "Name's Vincent."

Rick nodded and could see that the man was readying his small boat for a day of fishing. "Mornin' Vincent," he said and hurried off.

By the end of his trip, Rick was starting to get enough color on his pasty skin to appear healthy again. In his heart, though, a different story unfolded. He felt so lost and didn't know how – or from whom – to ask for directions.

It was early afternoon when he spotted Vincent – lying lazily in the warm sun – a straw hat drawn over his eyes. A fishing line was tied to the friendly man's big toe, a bobber floating in the turquoise water.

"Vincent, why aren't you out fishing?" Rick asked, startling the man from his daydreams.

"Already been, Mon," he answered, not looking up.

"Then why not go out and make more money?" Rick inquired further.

"For what?"

"To buy more boats."

"Why would I need more boats, Mon?"

"To have others run them, while you reap the profits."

"Why?"

"So you can relax."

Vincent looked up and smiled. "What do you think I'm doin', Mon?"

Rick was stunned. After pondering the lesson for a few moments, he offered a half-wave. "I'll be seein' ya, Vincent."

As Rick finished his walk, he thought about Rose. His heart ached.

65

All they ever had was a starter marriage; a short-lived arrangement that ended in divorce with no children.

He then pondered his time spent in corporate America and realized how much he despised it. At most meetings, he secretly jotted down a list of clichés that were thrown around the room, never adding up to anything being said: "strategic fit, best practice, bottom line, value-added, think outside the box, results-driven, leverage…" He grinned at the foolishness of it all.

He finally remembered the two vows he'd taken as a child; to never run from anything; to make sure he became somebody. He wasn't sure whether he was breaking either, or both. *No, this is different*, he thought. It was too late for his marriage and he knew it. The rest was merely a matter of grieving.

Rick's quest to accumulate wealth had made him near-sighted and he needed to repair his vision before he went completely blind. He needed guidance. It was nearly one in the morning when he landed home and called Grandma.

Bill answered. "She's asleep," he said in his distinctively strained voice. "Anything I can do to help?"

"I just wanted to let her know that I was home, and that I'd be able to start coming over for Sunday dinners again."

Bill sat up. "Oh, she'll be pleased," he said and cleared his throat. "Is that it?"

Rick took a deep breath and rambled on in a wounded voice. He talked about his break with Rose and explained his strange run in with the island fisherman.

As Rick talked into the late hours, Bill did what all good friend's do. He listened.

At the end, Rick asked, simply, "Now what do I do?"

It was Bill's time to talk. "Life is like sledding, Rick. Unless you walk the hill, you'll never feel the tickle in your belly." He snickered. "Sounds to me like you've already figured out the work that it takes to get places in the world. But trust me, my friend, you still have a long way to go toward understanding the payoff. Believe me, I know. I worked hard my whole life and never felt a single tickle until I met your Grandma."

Rick suddenly flashed back to his adventures on Freedom Ave and smiled.

Bill, on the other hand, was just as happy to show Rick the way home. "So, we'll see you Sunday?" he asked.

"I'll be there," Rick said, a sense of relief already working its way into his voice.

As Bill hung up the phone, Eunice smiled and closed her eyes. She'd been listening the whole time.

The following morning, the telephone rang twice, pulling Rick out of his first peaceful dream in months. He picked up the receiver. "Hello?"

The voice was so excited it sounded like gibberish. It was his best friend Danny Francis and he was yelling. "Come over. I got one. I got one!"

Rick jumped out of bed and threw on some clothes. The great hunter had trapped his first prey and needed a hand. "I'll be right there."

Danny was Rick's old college buddy who'd attended school through the GI Bill. By their senior year, he'd gotten his girlfriend, Lois, pregnant and decided to do the right thing by making her his first wife. Things quickly went south. Danny then met Amber, and they had a baby. It was another trip down misery lane. Danny tried to stick it out, but in the end everyone was suffering. It was another painful exit. Several years later, he married Carol; his first real love. The rest of the story was all about his two boys. God, did he love them!

For weeks, Danny had complained, "They chewed through the gutters and are now in my attic, playing in pink insulation like they're at the Discovery Zone. A whole family of them are destroying my house!"

It was a rodent problem and not the average rodent problem. These nasty rats had big fluffy tails, gathered acorns for the winter and looked cute enough to play with. Danny, however, confirmed otherwise. "Those squirrels chewed their way in. Like bats in a belfry we're infested with them."

It was a bit of an exaggeration, but to some degree he was right. A family of squirrels had moved in and despite all the screaming and bad looks from their landlord, they weren't about to go anywhere.

At first, Danny would sit by his bedroom window with his pellet gun, laying in wait to assassinate each one. Even with all his boasting, he was no sniper. He never hit a single one. Driving to and from work, he'd swerve out of his way to smash one with his car. Even with his years of driving experience, he never tagged one. Nearly broken, he finally went out and purchased a trap. It was time to return to the primitive skills of the hunter.

He set the trap, using peanut buttered bread as its bait. The squirrels must have liked it because they stripped the cage clean every night for two weeks. He could almost hear them laughing, as they shared the generous meal. It was a family feud that had gone on far too long. Neither side was budging. Danny needed backup.

Rick arrived in record time.

"Come on in. The water's warm," Danny yelled from his post on the second floor. He was standing on a ladder under the attic door. A proud smile covered his face. Drawing in a deep breath, his face went serious and he offered a solemn nod. "It's really mad," he whispered, "It's been hissing for an hour." He popped open the door to retrieve the trap and cautiously peeked over the rim. With both hands over his head, his upper body quickly disappeared into the attic.

Seconds later, the whole of him reappeared, his sweaty hands dragging a steel trap. He was right. The animal was insanely furious. It bucked and convulsed, screaming in its alien babble.

Rick raised both hands to help ease the trap down. Danny tilted the trap and slowly lowered it. Rick spotted the door open a crack, while a little paw fought desperately to free the rest of itself. "It's opening," Rick warned. "The trap's opening!"

Danny looked down, but by then it was too late. Lowering the trap opened the door a few more inches. It was just enough for the prisoner to bust out. Time slowed to a crawl. As their captive leaped from the cage and made its getaway, Danny jumped down from the ladder. He couldn't believe his eyes. He looked in the cage and then up at Rick. There was blame in his face.

"Forget about it," Rick snickered, "I didn't do it."

But the great hunter was still in shock, disappointed that he'd lost his first prey. "Where'd he go?"

Rick pointed to Danny's sons' room.

Danny hurried over and slammed the door shut. The squirrel was now isolated and contained. Danny's smile returned. "We still have him."

With a baseball bat, a tennis racquet and a blanket as their arsenal, they rushed in. By the second step, they looked at each other and grimaced. With the weapons they carried, they were more likely to kill each other. They slithered back out.

After taking a few minutes to calm down and think, they decided good tactics were needed. They conspired in hushed whispers. Breaking his thought process, Danny turned to Rick and confirmed what his friend already knew. "I gotta get the pellet gun. We're not gonna be able to trap him again." There was a pause. "We're gonna have to take him out."

Rick nodded in agreement. He still remembered the face of an angry squirrel he'd faced in the first grade.

Danny rushed downstairs for the executioner's weapon. There really was no choice. This was war.

He returned and a short poll was taken. Rick was the better shot, so he'd be the triggerman.

Slowly, very slowly, they opened the bedroom door and peeked in. The vicious enemy was nowhere to be seen. They froze to listen. There was nothing, not a peep. They looked at each other and simultaneously nodded. This squirrel had been around for a while. He wasn't about to give away his position.

Danny pushed Rick to the side and slowly went to his knees. At a molasses pace, he bent at the waist to peer under the bed. Inch by painful inch, he folded himself over. Suddenly, he sprang to his feet. With wide eyes, he pointed. "He's under the bed!" He'd tried to whisper, but it came out as a scream. Rick acknowledged the location.

Rick chambered a pellet and pumped the skinny rifle ten times. Insuring that the safety was off, he went down on his knees. It took more than a few seconds before his upper body was completely resting on its elbows. He didn't want to startle the agitated creature. He took a gander. There it was, staring straight at him, a bushy tailed squirrel that looked like a 30-pound monster with massive, razor-sharp teeth. *It's first grade all over again.* Rick thought, and swallowed hard. *Keep focused on the mission. It's either us or the squirrel.*

It took several more minutes before his chest lay flush to the floor. With his eyes peeled on his adversary, he slowly spread his legs into a comfortable prone position. He shouldered the rifle, took a deep breath, and sighted in. He couldn't believe it. In the time he took to justify squeezing the trigger, the squirrel actually took several aggressive steps toward him. He was being challenged. *Steady*, he thought, *steady*. He took one more short breath.

The squirrel jumped, and took off like a bullet. Rick leaped to his feet, panting. Like a professional Jai-alai player, the squirrel flew around the room, using two feet up the walls as its track. Both men stood close together in the middle, watching in shock as the beast circled them – squealing.

Danny shoved his comrade toward the door. By some small miracle, they both made it out.

The slam of the door echoed once when Danny spun on his heels and put his ear to the door. The gesture was overkill. Neighbors two houses over could have heard the blood curdling shrills of the hunted.

"Yup. He's still upset," Rick confirmed.

Thin lipped, Danny snatched the gun from Rick's hands and pumped it a few more times. There was no time to waste. He threw open the door and both men rushed in. As Rick covered the door with the baseball bat, Danny went to one knee and shouldered the rifle. "Cover me," he yelled.

The squirrel never broke stride.

Angrier than scared now, Danny pumped the weapon once more and prepared to pull the trigger. He was determined to end this and if need-be, prepared to disregard the safety of everything in the room; the window, his friend, even himself.

Unaware of how personal the hunt had become, Rick could only insure that the perimeter was secure.

Danny's wife Carol appeared in the doorway. She'd just returned home from grocery shopping when she found her brave hunter preparing to take down his nemesis.

"What do you think you're doing?" she asked.

Startled, Danny glanced up to find his wife cross-armed and gawking. "I'm going to end it," he answered. "This is war."

Carol stepped into the room, looked over at the squirrel and chuckled. "My God," she said, "It's only a baby. You were going to kill a baby squirrel?"

Danny kept his aim. "Baby?" he roared. "This thing's no baby!"

She half-smiled at the ridiculousness of the situation, and proceeded to the window. With one grunt, she opened it and stood back. The squirrel took off at a sprint. Three seconds later, it disappeared into the yard. Danny and Rick looked at each other. Rick smiled. Danny was steaming. He unloaded his pellet gun and stormed past his wife. At the door, he turned. "You've only prolonged the inevitable!" With that, he was gone.

Carol and Rick watched him walk away, and then looked at each other. Instantly, they burst into laughter.

Between chuckles, Rick shrugged. "Gotta love him."

Carol nodded. "From the moment I laid eyes on him," she replied. "And he hasn't stopped making me laugh since." She paused and then turned her attention to Rick. "Danny told you about the party we're throwing the weekend after next, right?"

"I'll be here," he said. "Just as long as you promise not to try to fix me up again."

Carol smirked. "I promise."

Chapter 8

Seated on a rolled carpet, Abby stared at the bare walls like a new patient at the asylum. Once a friendly forest green, the paint was now dingey and faded – except where pictures had witnessed her family go from silent and numb to angry and broken. She shook her head. "What a mess," she muttered. The words traveled through the empty room and echoed down the hall. It was the loneliest, most sorrowful sound. She stood and dusted off her backside. As she reached the door, she looked back once. "Good-bye," she pushed past the lump in her throat. There was silence.

A burly man loaded the final boxes into the moving van and glanced over toward Abby. "That's the last of it," he called out, and then looked toward the horizon. "We should get moving. We're losing light."

She nodded and started for the back yard. It was the moment she'd dreaded most – helping Paige say good-bye.

Beneath the thick gray skeleton of a twisted sycamore tree, her nine-year old was seated in an old tire swing. Abby needed a deep breath to keep the tidal wave of emotion at bay. Since Paige could walk, she'd spent her childhood playing under the beautiful tree. This would be the last time. As she approached, she searched her daughter's porcelain face. Paige was in pain, the kind that needed a lot more than a band-aid and a popsicle. Abby had tried, but there was no way she could have spared Paige this horrid moment. The bitter breakup with Paige's father, Patrick, along with the weasel's abandonment of their daughter left no choice. For eight trying months, she did everything she could to keep the house, but it became too much. *Small price to pay for freedom and peace*, she finally decided. They had to start anew. She crouched before her. "Ready to go?"

The slightest squeal escaped Paige's lungs. She quickly looked away to avoid her mother's gaze.

Abby wrapped her arms around her little girl. "We've talked about this, Babe. It's for the best, remember?"

Paige exhaled deep, but said nothing.

Abby swung the tire around until she was staring straight into Paige's big, brown eyes. "It'll be exciting," she promised, "There's a whole new world just waiting for us out there." With a smile, she stood and extended her hand. "So what do you say – just the two of us. Take my hand and we'll tackle it together, alright?"

Paige grabbed her mother's hand and slid out of the tire swing. A tear traveled the length of her cheek. "But what about this place...our life here? We'll never..."

"Memories," Abby said. "No one can ever take our memories from us." She dropped to her knees and hugged Paige tight. "But it's time to stop living in the past, Babe." She nodded. "I think the time's come to see what's ahead of us."

After a long embrace, Paige wiped her eyes. "Okay," she whimpered. "Let's go then."

Abby pushed the locks of chestnut hair away from Paige's eyes and gazed into her soul. "I breathe for you, ya know," she whispered.

Paige nodded, and the slightest grin forced its way into the corners of her pouty mouth.

Hand in hand, they stepped out of the past and into their future.

On the road, Abby looked over at Paige to find that sometime through Jimmy Buffet's *Margaritaville,* her little girl had fallen asleep. She sighed. It was a good thing. Paige's heart was so big that it was easily broken.

Abby recalled her teacher's recent telephone call. "I thought you should know, Mrs. Soares," the woman said, "We've just started a special ed program in the school. For the purpose of social interaction, many of these challenged kids are being introduced into regular classrooms for a few hours each day. We have an autistic boy, Bobby, who your daughter decided to take under her wing. Anyway, as Paige completed her classroom assignments, Bobby had a tough time keeping up. But the rules are clear: No recess unless each student finishes his or her work. So, Paige volunteered to help out. 'But you'll miss your recess,' I told her. 'That's okay,' Paige said. 'I don't mind.'"

Abby's eyes filled remembering the wonderful report from school. Good grades were one thing. Good behavior was another. But heart could not be measured. Abby couldn't have been any more proud.

Abby emerged from her daydream and glanced into the rear-view mirror. The moving truck was still with them. And so was her crooked nose. Her mind rushed back again – this time to the nightmare that had inspired the move.

No different from a thousand other nights, she and Patrick engaged in a battle that would have made most people cringe. He'd been drinking and became verbally abusive. "You better watch your tongue before I rip it out of your head," he slurred.

She held her ground, as always. "Wow! What a tough guy you are," she said and braced herself for the worse.

The broken nose would have been nothing more than another marital souvenir, but as Abby caught the puddle of blood in her cupped hands she looked up to find Paige watching through the banisters in the staircase. At that very moment, Abby's heart broke clean in half. Even though she hadn't married a jerk, Patrick's idea of love eventually evolved into abuse. In turn, Abby became the opposite of what she'd promised Paige on the morning her angel was born. She'd become Paige's grandmother. She could no longer choke back the old nightmares in her life, and her daughter didn't need to share the same. Drastic changes called for drastic measures. It was time to escape.

Abby worried about her daughter's thoughts once she was grown; what she would think about her parents' breakup. *In the end, I suppose it really won't matter*, she thought, *No matter what the cause, the effect is that she'll grow up without both parents in the same house.* For a moment, she pictured her own father's face and couldn't decide whether that was such a bad thing.

She also contemplated how many single parents brought baggage into their relationship with their children and vowed to avoid the same mistakes. Abby looked back in the mirror and wished she could spare Paige all of the pain. *But maybe that's not the design?* she thought, *Maybe everyone has to learn for themselves?* Paige was a bundle of nerves over her Dad. Abby wanted desperately to ease her child's anxiety, but there was no way she could take it away – no matter how bad she wanted to.

A horn blew, forcing Abby back into her lane; back into the present. She looked over at Paige. Her angel was still out cold. Abby smiled. It hadn't been easy and it took some time, but they'd finally made it out. The family legacy had been severed and the chain of abuse broken forever. Paige was free to grow up in peace now.

Abby pulled the car into the old Cape's steep driveway and exhaled. The first leg of their journey was now complete. She looked into the rear-view again. The moving van pulled in right behind her. As she pulled the keys from the ignition, she noticed the weeping willow tree that bordered their new life.

How sad it looked, its trunk rough and faded; its branches twisted and bent, each fighting for their rightful place. Its roots ran over the ground like a pit of snakes, while its tiny leaves, sagging low, were pulled by the earth's relentless gravity. Yet, it was a survivor. Amid those who stood majestic and strong, clothed in color and fullness, the willow tree had known: The harsh winds and battering rains became the test of all, and while many refused to sway from pride, the willow bent, even danced to adjust, witnessing one beauty after the other break in half, wither, then die. It was a teacher of life. Its appearance, though less than others, lasted long after many had gone. Through acceptance, it did not fight the inevitable, but changed with it. It was the perfect example of forgiveness, perseverance and wisdom. It was the most beautiful of all.

Perhaps it was a mix of nostalgia and intuition, but Abby knew they were exactly where they were supposed to be. She shook Paige. "Wake up, Babe," she whispered, "We're home."

While Paige leaped out of the car to explore this new world, Abby stepped out slowly and stretched her stiff muscles. It was just past dusk. Taking in a lung full of fresh air, she squinted to absorb the quaint, little neighborhood.

Like a massive picket fence in the dim light, an avenue of red maple trees lined the short street. Squares of manicured lawns led to rows of well-kept homes. A warm breeze shook the changing leaves, while a dog barked twice in the distance. Abby listened hard. In spite of her many worries, she smiled. It was quiet and peaceful. It was perfect. As she turned toward the house, the rusty hinges of a front door called out. Abby turned back to see a woman taking in her plants across the street. She waved and yelled, "Hello." The woman looked up, but never spoke a word. Seconds later, she disappeared back behind the door. Abby shrugged and rolled up her sleeves. It was going to be a long night of unpacking.

The following day, Abby and Paige spent most of the sunlit hours unpacking and trying to bring some sort of organization to their chaos. Besides visits from the gas and electric company, the house was hauntingly quiet. Abby searched the boxes for her stereo. Soon, Billy Joel was keeping them company. As the pizza deliveryman rang the doorbell, Abby turned to Paige. "What do you say we call it quits for today?"

From the relief on her daughter's face, she didn't have to ask twice. She and Paige kicked off their shoes and took their dinner to the front porch. Even through the filthy screens, the view was amazing.

It was early autumn in Massachusetts and there was no prettier place on earth. Colored trees of red and green created a feeling of protection, while grimacing pumpkins and waving flags decorated deserted porches. The smell of burnt leaves and chimney smoke wafted on slight breezes. Amid stacks of new-split wood, squirrels busied themselves gathering a winter's nutrition. The days had grown shorter, promising harvest moons and eerie whistling winds. Clotheslines, blue jay feeders and rocking chairs were empty, as this new world prepared for a season of ice and snow. Life seemed so perfect here. Abby had just taken a bite of pizza when an elderly neighbor came walking past. His tiny dog was leashed and dressed in a cute, red sweater.

"Taking you for a walk, is he?" Abby's silhouette teased through the screen.

The man looked up and searched the porch.

Abby and Paige waved.

The man offered a quick wave and hurried along. There was no smile.

"Good-night," Abby called out after him.

The stranger kept his eyes on the sidewalk and never looked back.

Paige turned to her mother. "The people aren't very friendly here, Mom."

Abby threw her arm over Paige's shoulder. "People can be funny, Babe. Sometimes they fear what they don't know. I guess it's our job to remove that fear from them."

Paige smiled. With her Mom's attitude and personality, they were sure to make friends quickly. They locked pinkies.

"Just the two of us," Abby whispered. It had become their new motto.

Paige grinned and closed her eyes.

For a moment there was silence, and then something stirred in the night. It was the willow tree dancing with the wind, the perfect song to sing them to sleep.

The following morning there was a knock at the door.

Excited, Abby answered to find an elderly lady standing on her stoop, the woman's eyes scanning the house like a bloodhound in search of an escapee. "Well, good morning," Abby said. "Won't you come in?"

The woman nodded and stepped onto the screened porch. "I'm Miss Powers. I live with my sister just two houses down from here."

Abby shook the lady's hand. "I'm Abby," she said, "my daughter, Paige, and I just got here last night. Seems like a wonderful neighborhood."

"Tis," Miss Powers confirmed. "And your husband?"

Abby chuckled. "No. We didn't bring him. Paige and I have decided to live happily ever after."

Miss Powers never cracked a grin. Instead, she searched Abby's face, spending a few extra moments at her bent nose.

"Would you like a cup of tea? I could..."

"No – that's fine. I should be getting along. I just wanted to see how you were settling in." And with that, the woman was gone.

Paige emerged from the shadows, wiping the sleep from her eyes. "Who was that?" she yawned.

Abby put her arm around her daughter's shoulder and headed back into the house. "Just the neighborhood reporter."

For the remainder of the week, Abby and Paige did settle in. They checked out Paige's new school, located the grocery store, dry cleaner and hospital. It didn't take Abby long, however, to notice that her waves went unreturned; that her friendly smiles always fell upon wrinkled brows. She didn't have to think hard about the possible reasons.

The more people she set eyes upon, the more it became obvious that Miss Powers worked fast. She and Paige had moved into this perfect, little town without a husband or a father. Their family of two was being labeled, judged unacceptable by those who enjoyed a more traditional home life. Maintaining her smile, she kept on waving.

The first days were long, though – living out of a suitcase and constantly questioning whether she'd made the right choices. Though she'd expected it, there was no real comfort in being free. Instead, there was constant worry. Freedom felt more like a punishment.

Rolling in with the mist of a glorious autumn morning, their first weekend at the new house arrived. With a mug of steaming coffee in hand, Abby retrieved the newspaper from the front lawn when she noticed that their giant apple tree was spitting fruit from its branches. Red-ripe apples had been spread out generously across the front yard. "Hmmm." She hurried for the house. The juicy bounty had given her the idea she'd been searching for.

She and Paige picked nearly two bushels before Abby ran out and bought a handful of gift bags. "Sometimes you can't receive what you haven't already given away," she told Paige.

Paige felt confused.

Abby explained, "If you want people to offer you their friendship, the best way to get it…is to give it to them first."

In the spirit of being good neighbors, Abby and Paige dropped off pecks of apples on the doorstep of each of their new neighbors. As a show of faith, Abby also decided to remain anonymous. If someone wanted to know, it wouldn't be hard to figure out. By late afternoon, every house on the street had a surprise waiting at its front door.

With Sunday morning's first light, the doorbell rang. Abby yawned, threw on an old flowered housecoat and answered the door. She gasped in shock. A half dozen women were standing on her stoop, each holding a baked good. Two of the women held steaming apple pies, another a fresh loaf of warm apple bread. A heavy-set woman held out a huge pan of sweet, cinnamon apple crisp. Her elderly friend palmed two massive jars of applesauce. The last of them balanced a tray of nicely decorated candy apples. They were all smiling.

With the warmest, most innocent smile, the first woman stepped forward and shrugged. "Welcome to the neighborhood."

Abby opened the door wide and gestured that they come in. "Welcome to our home." She turned to find Paige standing there, smiling.

As the women filed into the living room, a feeling of warmth filled the old house. In the midst of their guests, Abby gave Paige a hug. *We're going to be okay*, Abby thought. She just knew it. They were finally home.

"I've already had the pleasure of meeting Miss Powers," Abby teased.

An exchange of smirks traveled through the group. "We know," the bravest of them said. "We've all had to go through it." Each of them chuckled. "The good news is – she won't be back."

Abby laughed.

It was a brief but friendly visit. As the women returned back to their lives, the friendliest of them all, Carol Francis, stopped and leaned into Abby's ear. "Danny and I are having a party next weekend. We'd love for you to come. It's a yearly thing in the neighborhood, a way for the adults to say so long to summer. If you need a babysitter, I know a great one. Just give me a ring." She handed Abby a scrap of paper with her number on it.

Paige followed Abby out to the porch "Are you goin', Mom?"

Abby shrugged. "I don't know about going to any party for adults?" She pondered the possibility. "It might be a nice chance to get to know our neighbors, though."

Paige said nothing, but she didn't like it. Her mother hadn't gone anywhere without her since her parents separated. Even if she'd never admit it, she now relied on her mother's all-consuming devotion. She didn't like the idea at all. *What's next?* she wondered. *Dating?*

Chapter 9

Hunched behind the office partition, Grant Wright overheard the latest man-bashing session and smiled.

"Chivalry is dead," Cathy complained.

Anita chuckled. "Tough commute this morning, or is the dating life starting to get to you?"

"Dating life? What dating life? Guys today only want one thing – and they think that a trip through the drive-thru should be more than enough to get it."

Anita laughed again. "So the commute wasn't bad, huh?" She shook her head. "I'm so glad I don't have to deal with being single anymore."

With a sigh, Cathy fired up her computer and collapsed into another depressing Monday. "All men suck," she mumbled. "I'm done with every one of them. And I can't wait for this summer to be over."

Grant couldn't believe his ears. He'd secretly admired Cathy since she started temping in the company two months before. Her smile, in fact, made his heart skip like a schoolboy. She was beautiful and sexy. *Maybe the guys she's dated have sucked*, Grant thought, *but not all men do. She just needs to be swept off her feet.*

It wasn't ten o'clock when Cathy returned from the fax machine to find a white envelope covering her keyboard. She picked it up. It was sealed and there was no writing on it. She looked around. No one was watching. She tore it open.

Juliette,

I dreamed about you last night. We were together, locked in each other's eyes. You smiled at me and I couldn't help but pull you close and kiss you. You moaned once and the rest of the world disappeared. And then we made love – without ever removing a stitch of clothing. The glances, kisses and touching were so intense. I'd never felt so close to anyone. It was as if I experienced your soul; your very essence far beyond the physical world, and I finally discovered what it means to make true love. And then we undressed...

I dreamed about you last night – without ever closing my eyes.
Romeo

The note had been typed and wasn't signed.

Cathy took in the oxygen she'd forgotten to breathe. The words had touched her soul. She looked around again. The sounds of cogs busy at work filled the giant room. She peered over the partition. "Grant, did you see anyone drop off an envelope at my desk?"

Grant shook his head. "I haven't seen anyone come by here. Why?"

She shrugged. "Oh, nothing. I think someone might have delivered it to my desk by accident." With an angelic smile, she disappeared back behind the portable wall.

Grant swallowed hard. Cathy's eyes shined when she smiled.

The day grew wings and flew by. Cathy asked everyone in the office about the mysterious envelope. No one knew anything. Even Anita – the woman who knew everything that went on at work – was at a loss.

Cathy wasn't two feet from her car when she spotted another white envelope tucked under her windshield wipers. Her heart raced, as she plucked it free. There was no denying it this time. The name *Cathy* had been typed on the front. Her trembling fingers hurried to open the prize.

My Juliette,

I've pictured you and I walking hand-in-hand down a wet cobblestone street in Europe (who cares where). It is just past dusk. The streetlights have come on. We walk past several cafes; past other couples talking and laughing. With a quick look at each other, though, we smile and silently decide not to join them. Instead, we hurry into a shop for a stick of bread, a wedge of cheese, some assorted fruit and a bottle of wine. Hand-in-hand, we hurry back to our little bungalow located just above the busy street, and strip each other of our clothes. Dinner takes place while we make love – the windows to our refuge left open to allow in the breezes and the happy conversations of foreign tongues.

Will you meet me there?

Romeo

She gasped and held the invitation to her chest.

Grant approached the car parked alongside hers. "Hey, did you end up finding out who that envelope belonged to?" he asked.

Cathy's eyes swung up to meet him. "I think so," she whispered. "I'm pretty sure it was meant for me." An excited squeak accompanied the word *me*.

Grant nodded and smiled. "See you in the mornin'," he said and jumped into his classic Ford Mustang. It was all about the thrill of the chase, an ancient game.

"Oh, I'll be here," she whispered, "I'll definitely be here."

Cathy arrived at work earlier than ever, only to find an unaddressed envelope sitting on her keyboard. She looked around. There was no one there, and no evidence that anyone had been there earlier than she. It was strange.

Juliette,

You light a few candles. I pour us each a glass of wine. No TV, just music – some dreamy music that puts a tantric rhythm in our heads. I play with the straps on your camisole as we move together, standing, swaying. Our lips meet, my hands are now in your hair. We pass our wine glasses to the table, barely. I press myself against you and you breathe hard into my ear. We look at each other, but there is no need for words. Minds whirling, hands sweeping, lips touching everywhere, time eludes us as we feel the softness of the carpet on our knees, our backs…

And then we make love without ever losing eye contact.

Romeo

She felt faint. *That's it,* she thought, *I have to know who this is.*

Anita and Cathy spent the entire morning sifting through ambiguous clues and listing possible suspects.

Grant spent the same time sharpening his next arrow. He decided to go for the kill.

Cathy hadn't been away from her desk for five minutes before the next letter appeared. With Anita over her shoulder, she tore into it.

Juliette,

The most important thing to me is to enter into a union with a woman who will become the second half of a whole, someone who will allow me to love her without restraint and love me with the same effortless passion – you.

Romeo

Even Anita broke out in a sweat. As the two shared a moment of breathless silence, Grant walked in behind them and handed Cathy a single rose. "You," he whispered.

Cathy's knees nearly gave out.

Grant Wright was a mysterious man with looks that were extremely kind on the optic nerve. Tall and dark, with chiseled features, liquid blue eyes, and jet-black hair, he had two perfect rows of white teeth. He was well built, bold and charming; the perfect catch. Cathy fell hard.

Several nights a week, they dated. The constant thrills were more than Cathy could have ever imagined possible. During the day, however, they made secret love over email. Each note made Cathy feel like she was floating.

You've rented every room in my head, and left even less space in my heart, he wrote.

I hope I live up to your expectations, she replied.

There's no way you can't live up to them -- because they don't exist, he countered.

If we could have one night together, what would you want to do? she asked.

Turn it into 55 years, he responded, and then turned up the heat:

Juliette,

I constantly fantasize about being with you physically, and I imagine it would not take us long to learn each other's pleasure spots. We begin touching and teasing each other with our fingers...our tongues. We gently caress each other. The heat between us is intense. Kissing passionately, the rest of our clothes shamelessly come off. I tease you until you are on the edge and surrender to me. We then move together in ripples of ecstasy. Sweaty and panting, we hold each other until we can begin again – all night – anything we desire.

Romeo

She wasn't ready and told him so.

His response was perfect. *Don't worry. When I have your heart, the rest will follow.*

She'd never felt this way. He was too good to be true. She wrote, *My heart is already with you. As long as we give ourselves completely to each other, it will be magical.*

He agreed. *I want to make love until the sun decides to pay the world another visit.*

And even with her moral reservations, that night they did just that.

From then on, life became a blur of wonder and ecstasy. She emailed him. *I really think that you are the one I could become one with.*

We have to live in the present in order to get to the future, he replied.

She was surprised by his chilly response.

It didn't take long for things to change.

I've missed you the last few nights, she admitted two days later.

I'm always with you, never any further from you than your mind. Close your eyes for a moment, and there I am – wherever you want me to be.

Just so you know, the man I marry will be the one I share the rest of my life with, all of me, in every way – until my last breath.

There was no response.

It was a Monday night. They were halfway through dinner when Cathy reached across the table and grabbed Grant's hand. "I think a lot about where life's going to go from here, and though I'm not really sure where the next bend in the road is, I know I've been walking around smiling a lot more lately. Thank you for that."

He nodded.

"Where do you think this will lead?" she asked.

He squeezed her hand. "The clock started the moment I saw you."

"You're perfect," she said.

"Not quite." He shrugged. "I'm married."

"WHAT?!" It took a few moments for the first layer of shock to allow the truth in. "But you said all those things," she muttered, "How could…?"

Grant stared her straight in the eye. "I meant every word."

And it hit her. Grant Wright was deceitful and selfish, traits revealed only when the sun went in behind the clouds. Cathy was heartbroken. She was with the wrong Romeo. Rage quickly replaced sorrow. "You piece of garbage," she hissed and stood from the table. "You think you can just play with my heart and…"

Grant rose to meet her. As he tried to quiet her tone with his growing pupils, he reached for her hand. "Cathy, please. We don't have to…"

"NO," she yelled, slapping his hand away. "You mark my words. You're going to get yours!" She tossed her linen napkin in his face and stormed away.

A few awkward moments passed before Grant shook his head for the benefit of those watching the show. "Psycho chick," he muttered loud enough for all to hear, and instantly recruited the support of each male patron in the restaurant. The females, however, continued to burn holes into the yellow stripe on his back.

The following night, Grant met Rick for their weekly game of billiards.

"Whose break?" Rick asked.

"Let's flip for it," Grant said. "I've got heads." He watched his penny spin end-over-end until it landed tails side up. "Damn it! Every time."

"Didn't you wear that sweater to the eighth grade dance?" Rick asked Grant, as he broke the rack of balls with one quick jerk of the wrist.

Grant laughed. "Did you hear the story about the guy who got divorced and was court ordered to pay off his wife with a boatload of money?" he asked.

Rick shook his head and put the eight ball in the side pocket for the win.

As Grant racked another game, he went on. "He used a dump truck to deliver her alimony – in pennies."

Rick's brow wrinkled in disbelief.

"It's true," Grant said, "she brought him back to court, but there was nothing the judge could do. It was legal tender, and the precise amount owed her. Now how perfect is that?"

"It figures that you'd like that story," Rick said, and then smashed the rack of balls to all four corners of the pool table.

Grant smirked. "You're too straight-laced. You were the same way when we were kids."

"Sure, Grant, and if it means anything, you haven't changed either."

Grant started to grin but stopped, unsure whether he'd been paid a compliment or an insult. Rick was right. He hadn't changed at all. He still drove a '74 Mustang, listened to 80's music, dressed in tight clothes and wore his hair long.

Rick chuckled.

"You're right. And I'm never going to change," Grant vowed. "Did I tell you about my latest honey?"

Rick glared at his friend. "Who, your wife?"

Grant eyed up his shot. "Not quite," he said, "I can't help that I'm addicted to romance."

"You mean sex, right?"

With a giant smile, Grant nodded.

Rick couldn't get over it. His childhood buddy was as shallow as a puddle and he still scored big with the ladies. Grant was always tanned, he wore the best clothes and his hair was perfect. Inside, though, his heart was an echo chamber. Grant always used the same lines on women, and he always brought them on the same date: A walk down the beach, wine, poetry, candlelight. "I want to wait," most would say when it was time to get intimate. Grant would smile. "I like you a lot," he'd whisper, "and I really want this to be something you'll never regret." It was pathetic, and it worked every time. One woman even told him, "This was the perfect date." Grant never batted an eye. "It should be," he said, "It's taken me years to perfect it." Rick just couldn't understand. While women rejected scores of sweet-hearted guys, they loved his soul-less friend. At first, Rick supposed that sincerity just didn't go over; that perhaps self-centeredness did. He finally decided, though, that women just loved a challenge. Every one of them wanted to convert the player into a faithful man.

"How can you beat it when everything is fresh and new and no matter what you do – it's for the first time?" Grant asked.

"But it's only a fleeting phase," Rick said, "no more important or

85

exciting than any other phase. From what I've seen, it's a real relationship only if you have to really work at it."

"You're sad," Grant teased, "didn't I teach you anything?"

Rick chuckled and took the stick. "True," he said, "for those addicted to romance – as you call it – the novelty of a relationship is everything. But it's my guess that these people eventually become the lonely ones destined to suffer short, unfulfilling and failed relationships throughout their lives." He sank his shot and looked up at his lifelong friend. "And I'm guessing you're right at the top of that list, my friend."

"Variety is the spice of life," Grant said.

Rick smiled, eyed up the eight ball and sank it right in the side to take another win. "Trust me, Grant, the fire that attracts you in the beginning is the same flame that'll burn you in the end."

Through all the conquests, the excuses, and break-ups, the truth always caught up. In the end, Grant could never be what he wasn't. Even his best lies could only buy him temporary joy.

"Whatever," Grant said. Three seconds later his scowl was replaced by a grin. "What do you say we hook up on Saturday and…"

"Can't," Rick answered, "It's Danny and Carol's annual summer send-off."

"Oh yeah, the one I wasn't invited to."

"Yup. That's the one." Rick worked a grin into his face just to torment his old friend.

"Whatever," Grant said. "Whatever."

Chapter 10

"**I**'m telling you, Rick. I'd rather spend the rest of my life fighting in Iraq than spend another minute not seeing my boys together." Danny fought off the emotion that welled up inside him.

"What does your lawyer say?" Rick asked.

Danny shook his tormented head. "He says I shouldn't push things right now with my boys; instead…look at the big picture." Danny stood to grab two more beers. "The whole thing's been a nightmare."

Rick shook his head. Danny had fathered two sons from two different women. It certainly wasn't what he'd planned, but it was the way his life went. Dillon was nine. Bryan was three. He adored them both, but being powerless with the courts, he hadn't seen his baby boy in over a year. In turn, his two boys, brothers, hadn't seen each other either. Danny suffered terribly from having failed them as a father.

Danny returned with two cold beers and handed one to Rick. "It gets better," Danny said. "Last week, Carol and I were walking through Home Depot when a small voice called, 'Dad?' I never even bothered to look up. But again, the boy's voice called out, 'Dad?' And that's when I turned to find Dillon standing in front of me, alongside some strange man. The wrongness of it actually stole my breath away and nearly bowled me over. The guy caught it and stepped forward. 'I'm Jack,' he said with an extended hand. 'I'm a friend of your ex-wife.' I don't remember shaking his hand, but I guess I did. Talk about feeling so lost…there was my son standing beside a stranger instead of me. After I gave Dillon a kiss, I told him to be a good boy and listen to Jack. My nine-year old son smiled at me and then walked out of the store with a guy I'd never even seen before. Now tell me that's not screwed up?"

As Danny fought back the lump in his throat and walked away, Rick felt his friend's pain. Life just wasn't fair sometimes.

A mix of playful conversation and alcohol quickly lightened the night's mood. Rick was tipping his third beer at the season's final bash when he looked up and saw her. He nearly choked on his drink. She was his age, maybe 30, pretty with an athletic build. Her hair was waves of chestnut, with dark eyes that beautifully matched. She had a mysterious confidence about her and a smile that men would die for. Rick swore she had an aura from her halo to her feet. At that moment, he knew that no matter what it was going to take, he was going to meet her. His mind flooded with questions that would have to be answered: *Who did she know at the party? Who could he gather her background from? Who could introduce them?* As his mind raced, Carol walked over with the beauty.

"Rick, this is Abby Soares," the friendly hostess introduced with a smile. "She's new in town, and I'm betting you two have a lot in common." Carol's smile grew mischievous, and then she walked away. Rick couldn't believe it. His palms were actually sweaty. Abby smelled as sweet as Dutch apple pie.

He glanced up at her. She was wearing the same look of confusion. "You must have a creep for an ex-husband too, then?" Her tone was soft and gentle.

"I do," Rick said, a soft light playing around his eyes. "His name's Rose."

Abby chuckled and took the seat beside her new friend. Her laugh was absolutely contagious.

Rick had bedroom eyes of ocean green, with chiseled features, a goatee and a cleanly shaven head. Medium height and build, he wore a light, sporty cologne and baggy clothes that concealed his fit physique. Abby was surprised to feel such chemistry, causing her face to blush. She looked away.

Rick cracked open a fresh beer and offered it to her. His hands were almost trembling. No one had this effect on him. He was legitimately nervous.

She shook her head. "Thanks, but I don't drink," she said, and then stared straight into his soul. "So, you're divorced, too?"

He smiled. "I am. Seems like the 'in thing' these days."

"Any kids?" she asked, shifting from one hip to the other.

Rick's eyes lit up. "Zachary, the love of my life. He just turned two." He took a swig of beer. "I'm thinking about getting him a bigger tank."

Abby was taken aback.

"Zachary's my fish."

Even through the laughter, Abby couldn't help but stare. Rick wore a great smile, with a pair of adorable dimples. He was quite masculine, but even if he wanted to Abby doubted that he could have masked his sensitive side. Without thinking, she slid closer to him. His presence felt so comfortable, almost familiar.

Rick smiled. "And you – any kids?"

"Paige," Abby answered with the same twinkle in her eyes. "She's nine…just old enough to be furious at the world."

Rick chuckled. "Boy problems?"

Abby shook her head. "No. Daddy problems," she explained. "Her father has chosen a new life and there's not a whole lot of room left for his daughter."

Rick leaned into Abby's face. He smelled as good as he looked. "We're not all like that," he said. "Some men actually care more about their kids than they do themselves." With the same conviction Abby displayed, he pointed toward Danny. "I'm still watching Danny walk through hell for his boys. For him, the separation from his children isn't a choice."

Abby nodded, but quickly changed the subject. "How long have you known Carol?" she asked.

"Too long," Rick answered with a smirk. "Actually, I met Danny in college and met Carol after he returned home from the Gulf War. He was my business partner for a while. He and Carol have been together for almost three years now. She's great. She loves Danny's two boys like they're her own."

"Business partners?"

"I started in software, and then switched over to stocks and bonds – really, really important things like that."

"Still together?" she asked.

"Nope. We've since broken up. I decided that I missed the sunshine a little too much to stay." He thought for a moment. "I write a little now."

"Great," Abby said. She smiled like an angel. "I'd love to see some of your writing."

Rick glowed.

A light drizzle began to fall when Jim and Holly bid their farewell. Rick excused himself from his conversation with Abby and shook his friends' hands. "I'll be seein' ya," he said.

Abby lost her breath. He'd been introduced as Rick, so it threw her. She'd always known him as Richard. She quickly searched his forearm and saw the fishhook scar. "Richard?"

Rick's brow folded. "Rick," he said.

"Not to me," she said. "To me, you'll always be Richard." She stood and embraced him.

A thousand memories flooded his mind. It was she. It was Abby, his childhood love. He searched her eyes. The only thing different was her last name, a bent nose and a slender body. He squeezed her tight. "My God, how are you?"

She pulled away to peer into his eyes. Without a word, she returned to their embrace.

Beneath a wet sky, the rest of the night was spent getting caught up. Though they really didn't know each other as adults, it felt like old times. They'd been so young when they parted and so much had happened since they last spoke. Still, there was a strong connection that carried over from childhood. It was undeniable.

They spoke first about Richard's Grandma and father. "So how are they?" Abby asked. "I've always loved them, you know."

He smiled. "Dad lives in New Hampshire now, working with delinquent kids."

She smiled, her head cocked, so pert. "Did he ever remarry?"

"No. He's never stopped loving my Mom enough to pursue other women. I guess in his own way he still grieves her death."

Abby felt bad, but was also touched by the undying love the man held for his wife. As she daydreamed over such a reality, Rick's voice called her back to the present.

"I think Grandma's right. When my Dad passes, I'm betting that he and my Ma will spend eternity making up for lost time."

Abby nearly cooed at the sweet sentiment. "I'll never forget his dog, Roy," she said.

Rick chuckled. "Believe it or not, he actually has Roy's grandson now – Ray."

She shook her head and laughed. "Roy, and now Ray. What was the dog's name in between?"

"Screw Up."

Abby was sent into a state of hysterics.

Rick shrugged and laughed along with her.

When she'd gained composure, she asked, "And Grandma?"

Rick picked up on the pensiveness. "Still spry and spunky – just a really cool person. You know her motto: 'The body doesn't wear out, it rusts.' She's still listening to her music and raising holy hell."

Abby smiled at the familiar phrase.

"And she got married," Rick said.

"Married?"

"Yep. His name is Bill Stryker and he's perfect for her." With a smile, he shook his head. "She still makes us sit for Sunday dinner." Rick then asked about Abby's parents.

There was a sad pause. "My Mom passed away," Abby said. "From a lack of purpose, I'd say. And I haven't spoken to my father for a few years now." She tried to shake off the pain. "We no longer share a relationship, just some real bad memories. I imagine he's still committing suicide the long way."

"Still drinking?"

"Yup – still doing laps in the bottle."

Rick put down his beer and quickly changed the subject. "Have you heard from any of the old gang?"

Abby's smile returned. "From what I hear, Vinny became an attorney and is living with his wife in Vermont." She thought for a moment. "I don't know how anyone can stand to live with him."

Rick laughed.

"Tracy became a psychologist and moved to Utah."

"Married," Rick asked.

"I think A-sexual."

They both laughed. Rick couldn't stop staring at her cute, pouting lips.

"Actually, I heard she lives with her lesbian lover and goes by the new name Cheyenne."

"You're kidding, right?"

Abby shook her head. She was serious.

"Good for her," Rick said.

Abby's face turned serious. "I haven't heard anything about Grant."

Rick leaned forward. "You're not going to believe this, but the first day I walked into college – there was Grant talking to some pretty, unsuspecting Freshman."

Abby shook her head and chuckled.

"I still see him every Tuesday night. We shoot a little pool and a whole lot of bull."

She was shocked. "How is he?"

"The same. Emotionally amputated. Socially retarded."

As the laughter continued, Rick realized that he had no control over his thoughts or feelings around Abby – just like when they were children. "So much has happened," he said.

A devilish smirk forced its way into the corners of Abby's mouth. "I know," she teased, "even Woolworth's closed."

Rick nearly choked. It was the first time she'd ever mentioned the most embarrassing moment of his life. "That's bad," he said – so pleased she remembered.

"No," she answered, "it's not bad at all. I still think about a lot of the times we shared together."

He looked hard into her eyes and his Adam's apple took forever to travel south. He saw a reflection of everything he could be and knew that was exactly where he belonged. Everything else seemed trivial in comparison. Speaking of the recent past didn't interest him at all – mostly because she hadn't been a part of it.

"Remember in the summers when – every afternoon – the music of Gus's Ice Cream truck would round the corner and have us scrambling into our houses to beg for change?" Rick asked, his eyes growing distant. "Then we'd chase Gus all the way down the street with our pennies."

Abby laughed. "Yup. And even though he knew we were a guaranteed sale, he still loved making us chase his truck." She shook her head at the memory. "And if I remember correctly, 'Smiling Gus' shut down Old Man Sedgeband's popsicle sales from June until August and there was nothing that could have made us happier." Abby giggled. "I also remember the way you used to walk around the neighborhood with your head down, searching for lost change."

Rick grinned. "Find a penny, pick it up and all that day you'll have good luck."

"As long as it's heads up," she added.

He nodded. "Those were definitely the days."

"And that time Grant talked Tracy into a game of show and tell in the woods," Abby said. "I still can't believe she actually went through with it!"

"Yeah, I remember that day. While everyone buzzed about Grant and Tracy's recent discoveries, me and Vinny took Grant's mother's sheets down from the clothesline, made a tent and then caught hell for it."

For a few precious moments, both Rick and Abby returned to the smack of screen doors and the echoes of foolish children running toward the future.

Between the conversation and shared laughter, the entire night seemed to last three seconds. Among other things, Rick learned that Abby was sweet and maternal, smart and playful, but the violent bum who'd abused her and now neglected their daughter had also jaded her.

Abby learned that Richard had grown into a cultured gentleman with a great sense of humor. He, too, viewed life with a cynical eye. Carol was right. They had a lot in common.

Just before eleven o'clock, the clouds opened up and dumped buckets of cool rain on Carol's party. Some took it as a sign to go home. Others darted for the house. Carol, Danny, Abby and Rick, however, never budged. They sat at the round table, talking, laughing and watching as Carol's *circle of friends* candle fought to stay alive. Rick looked over at Abby and watched as sheets of rain illuminated her face. *God, is she beautiful,* he thought.

They were soaked to the bone when they decided to call it a night. Though Rick had quit drinking when he realized Abby had broken her family curse, Carol and Danny were annihilated.

As the rain stopped and the clouds dispersed, Rick walked Abby to her car. He couldn't believe it. Like moonlight through the trees, she'd appeared out of nowhere and touched his soul once again. He was still in love with his first crush. He wanted desperately to kiss her, but decided against it. "Can I call you?" he asked.

She smiled and gave him her number.

"And your email address?"

Abby creased her brow in curiosity.

"I'd like to send you some of my writing."

"Oh, I'd love that," she said. "It's Abby7121@aol.com."

Abby drove home with her head in the clouds and her heart hanging on her drenched sleeve. She couldn't get over how Richard still looked at her. *Maybe I'm not damaged goods after all?* she thought. *Maybe I'm just recycled?*

Rick stood in the middle of the puddled street a few more minutes. It was going to take a little while for the miracle to soak in. His childhood love had rekindled such a fire in his heart, he could almost smell the smoke.

After the short drive home, Abby stepped into the house to find the babysitter sleeping on the couch and Paige sleeping in her bed. Reality hit. This little girl was her obligation. "Don't get carried away," she muttered under her breath and jumped in bed beside her daughter. She brushed Paige's hair away from her cheek. *It hasn't been all that long since Patrick,* she thought, *and for all intents and purposes, Paige has lost her dad.* She kissed her daughter's cheek. *I mean, my God, we just moved here and haven't even gotten settled yet!* Lying back, she stared up at the ceiling. *I can't. This just isn't the right time. I won't!* But she couldn't stop the smile from spreading across her face. *Richard Giles,* she thought, *what have you become?*

Chapter 11

Abby awoke to find a new message in her email box. It was from Rick. Excited, she opened it.

> *Hi Beautiful,*
> *Thought I'd drop you a quick line to check out our connection. Actually, I was thinking (I know, that's rare) about you all night. Truthfully, I haven't thought about anything else. Attached, please find a poem I thought you'd like.*
> *Rick*

The Past

As the sun sets on another day,
for the briefest moment
close your eyes and remember.
Sometimes the memory can be selective and merciful,
other times painful and haunting.
In either case,
take all that you can
then cast the rest away.
The past is only a place where you once lived,
where hopefully you once learned.
It is never good to dwell there
for the doors have all been closed.
So open your eyes
and watch the rising of a new sun.
Enjoy even the smallest things,
but when they have passed
let them go and begin again.
Savor the present, dream for the future,
but forever keep your yesterdays behind you.

> *Dear Richard,*
> *Thank you for your sweet words. It was so nice to hear from you today. I thought about you all night, as well. I have to say, it's*

overwhelming! You leave me speechless and if you ask anyone who knows me (as an adult), that's not easy. For someone who is only in his early thirties, you have so much wisdom and insight. It's amazing! You have a gift and what makes it special is that you share it. I've been playing our wonderful conversation over in my mind. You make such good sense about my ex-husband and you've made me think. I stifle myself by my thinking sometimes. You've given me something I need, a new perspective. Your writing is beautiful and inspiring. I can't believe I know the person who wrote this poem. I am lucky. Hope to hear from you soon.

　　Abby

In the age of instant messaging, facsimile and wireless communication, they decided to resurrect the lost art of letter writing and use a string of stolen moments to get to know each other again.

　　Rick was ecstatic about the swift response, but struggled not to reply right away. He was already happier than he could remember being in a very, very long time. The last thing he wanted was to scare Abby away. Twenty minutes later, he picked up the phone and dialed her number.

　　"Hello?" Abby answered.

　　"What do you think about having dinner with me?" he asked. "I know a great little place on The Hill."

　　Abby smiled.

It had been awhile, but Abby couldn't recall being so excited getting ready for a date.

　　Paige picked up on it. "You like him?" she asked.

　　"Oh, yeah. He's unlike anyone I've ever known." As the words left her lips, she knew they were a mistake. She came out of the mirror and rested her gaze upon Paige.

　　Paige felt so much, but was struggling to express it. She felt torn about betraying her loyalty to her Dad; resentful about having to share her Mom's time, while wanting her Mom to be happy – all at the same time. She stormed out of the bathroom and into her bedroom, slamming the door behind her. She was still too young to be selfless.

　　Abby chased after her. "You want me to cancel, Babe?" she asked. "Because I will. I swear I will."

　　Paige said nothing. Inside she was screaming, but she said nothing.

　　"Okay, then." With the smile removed from her face, Abby finished getting ready.

Rick and Abby's first date was both extravagant and awkward. A black stretch limousine picked her up and whisked her off to an experience of the finest dining she'd ever known. Grilled swordfish that melted like ice cream in August was surrounded by a sweet perimeter of glazed vegetables. Rick drank tonic water with lime. She decided not to question it. He talked about work, while Abby admitted that Paige didn't like the idea she was on a date. "I understand," Rick said, but he had no idea – he'd never had to worry about anyone but himself.

Throughout a medley of piano favorites, Rick pulled at his tie. Abby was the only woman who'd ever made him nervous. That's how he knew. It's what confirmed it for him. As if it were instinctive, he began a volley of shared memories. "Those were the days," he said, "we were like union workers back then – taking our afternoon breaks on each other's front porches with tall glasses of cherry Kool-ade."

She nodded. "Sometimes I wish things were still the same today...that a caring community, not just a family, looked after its young as if they were their own."

He agreed. "When I look back, though, it still amazes me that with all the freedom we had, a strict schedule still kept life organized."

She stared off into space, picturing the simpler life.

"It wasn't all good, though," he said. "Church on Sundays meant having to suffer through an hour of some man speaking gibberish. God help us, though, if we nodded off for even a second."

She laughed. "On rainy days when everyone stayed indoors, Tracy and I played with our Barbie dolls..."

"While me and the boys hung out with G.I. Joe and Stretch Armstrong!" Rick shook his head. "Yup. Those were definitely the years...listening to the Red Sox Pennant race. The clam boils and cookouts and..."

"And the day trips during the first two weeks of July when everyone's Dad took vacation."

Together, they remembered and laughed over every detail.

After tipping the waiter for doting so shamelessly on his pretty date, Rick escorted Abby back into the limo. He'd called in a favor and landed orchestra seats for *Mama Mia*. The show was incredible. They were on their feet, dancing the entire time.

A bill that resembled a month's worth of gas and electric payments followed dessert and cappuccinos.

Abby enjoyed it all but felt somewhat uncomfortable in a world where names like Armani and Dom Perignon were common. She was more familiar with words like Wal Mart and Jif. She'd never changed, and he envied her.

On the ride home, Rick admitted, "I know I still need to grow up a little."

Abby shrugged. "I'd say it's the opposite."

He sat puzzled.

"I'd say that it's more like you need to 'grow down' and return to who you were when we were kids...no?"

He thought about it and remembered again. The sun sitting on his shoulders, weightless and warm, while the world was no more than an idea within his grasp. With a lung-full of air and a scream on the wind, the tickles of laughter and smiles were all that he needed. The freckles and dirt rings and platinum blonde hair meant the future was only a moment away. It was a magical innocence – fleeting but real, with dreams that could be hoped into life. T-shirts and skinned knees and scars of fair play proved real troubles were nowhere in sight. And tomorrow would awaken with the squeals of pure joy.

He'd been there and only needed to return to it. For a moment, Rick unknowingly stared at her crooked nose.

"Had I been born a boy, I would have learned to duck a right hook," she explained.

He felt awful. "I'm sorry. I didn't mean to…"

She grabbed his hand. "Please, Richard, never second guess how I might take something you say or do. I know where your heart is and that's all I need to know." She smiled, brilliantly. "Once you know someone's heart – really know it – the rest is an easy read. And you and I already have that part covered." She peered into his eyes. "You've always been very sensitive of my feelings, which is wonderful, but I don't want you to worry about talking to me about anything. Let loose. I want you to feel free with me." She tilted her head sideways and squeezed her grip. "I don't break, you know."

After a moment of comfortable silence, he turned to her. "So, tell me about your daughter."

And she did. Through proud and twinkling eyes, she said, "Paige is obsessed with Britney Spears and all the boy bands. She looks like me with her father's smile. She's a nine-year old Tom Boy who climbs trees, spies on adults and loves wearing camouflage. She's big into video games and types faster than anyone…without ever taking a class. And she can get around a computer faster than most adults I know." She shrugged. "At her age, hygiene has become a task. She loves to sleep in on schooldays and rise bright and early on the weekends. She's finicky at the dinner table and lazy with her chores. But when it comes time to play, she can run like a gazelle. She just got braces. She loves cream cheese on bagels. Her hero is still the pink Power Ranger. She reads Harry Potter, and her favorite movies are

Charlie's Angels and Scooby Doo, which of course, I share. She's a huge fan of Buffy the Vampire Slayer. She's tough in the light but still afraid of the dark." Abby paused to take in some air and smiled. "She's perfect."

Rick loved the randomness of Abby's description and the way her eyes lit up when she shared it.

They'd just pulled into Abby's driveway when he turned to her. "Let me take you out again this weekend." It was more of a statement than a request.

She shook her head and kissed his cheek. "I'd love to. Believe me, I would. But it's not just about what I want anymore. I still need to get Paige settled in. She's not used to…"

He placed his finger to her lips. "Okay," he said, "then when?"

She half-shrugged. "If I said next weekend, would you still be interested?"

He was taken aback, but concealed it. "I'd be interested no matter what you said."

She smiled. "Then I'll take you out next weekend."

"Great, but why don't I come get you," he said, "It's too far to drive."

She kissed his cheek again and stepped out of the limousine. "I've traveled much farther for less," she called out over her shoulder and disappeared into the shadows of her house.

Rick smiled and began replaying every second of their date. As the limo pulled away, he could still smell her presence on everything around him. He'd never felt so much passion for someone.

Paige was sprawled out on the couch, pretending to be asleep. Abby took a seat beside her and stared at her little girl. Even with her heart pounding in her ears, Paige dared not stir. Abby pulled the blanket over her and kissed her forehead. "Night, Babe," she whispered, and tiptoed out of the room. Paige slowly opened her eyes and shook her head. "Just the two of us, huh?" she muttered, and fought off the tears when she said it.

The following morning Abby awoke to find a dozen red roses on her front porch. She plunged her nose into the bouquet and inhaled deeply. She plucked the card from the ribbon and read: *Thank you for last night. I'm still smiling. Rick*

Abby hurried to her computer. As she'd hoped, his email awaited:
Abby,
I hope you enjoy the flowers. They seem such a small gesture for such a wonderful night but I wanted to make sure that you knew I was

thinking about you. As for our conversation, let me continue: I know you hate it when people tell you this (so let me join that happy list). YOU are doing a great job with your daughter! Just let go of the guilt. True love allows no room for it. Paige is incredibly blessed. For whatever reason, you're the only one who can't see it. If you expect to teach your ex-husband how to be the father you wish for your daughter, then you're just setting yourself up for disappointment. If he were that way, you'd probably still be with him. People are who they are. As far as making up for his shortcomings with Paige – just be you. Trust me, most kids should be so lucky.
I've attached another poem. I hope you don't mind but I'd like to send you a poem or a story every day.
 Rick
 PS- Remember to smile – I'm thinking of you.

Singled-Out

No commitments; crazy, free,
the envy of some friends who see
through old, distorted memories
the single life is such a tease.

Dinner for one, it's half the cost
with friends who feel that they have lost
the chance to date and sleep around
with a mate already found.

Stay up late; drink every beer,
no complaints to fill the ear.
In warmth, those friends are sound asleep,
saving money, counting sheep.

Peace and quiet, all alone,
always waiting by the phone
for friends who have a normal life
with screaming kids, a jealous wife.

This single life; a different craft
with friends who think they got the shaft.
Yet while divorced, I'm getting scared
for the grass is greener when it's shared.

Hey You,

THANK YOU for the roses. They're beautiful—and so was every moment we spent together last night. You've already cost me the loss of some serious sleep. And thanks for the compliments. You're very sweet! I feel like a kid at Christmas. Instead of running downstairs to see what's under the tree for me, I'm running to my computer to see if there is anything from you. Thanks for the beautiful poetry again. What could I possibly give that could even compare?

Abby

Once she hit *SEND*, Abby deleted the email string between she and Richard. Nothing good could come from Paige reading it.

Even with the daily emails and occasional phone calls, a week of not seeing Abby lasted an eternity for Rick. He wasn't used to waiting for anything and already sensed that a good part of his happiness now depended on her. The lack of control was humbling.

Abby missed him, too, but Paige kept her busy.

Chapter 12

Abby's weekend date was simple, inexpensive and absolutely magical.

With a full picnic basket sitting on her backseat, she picked up Rick and drove him to the beach.

The distinct sounds of hissing surf and the screech of dive-bombing seagulls floated on the salt air that filled Horseneck Beach. Short waves broke on the shore, while sharp blades of grass swayed in unison. The water's edge choked on decomposing seaweed with broken shells mixed in. Beachcombers created footprints in the sand. Like time itself, the returning surf erased any evidence of their existence, wiping them from the great blackboard of life. One shake of the giant Etch-a-Sketch and it was over. The winds whipped across the open unobstructed landscape in a raw and powerful display. On the flat horizon, like a giant red marble, the sun sat quietly and gazed into the invisible world beneath the ocean. The entire picture was mysterious, dangerous – serene.

After watching a tiny pair of sandpipers chase each other near the surf, Abby grabbed Rick's sweaty hand and headed for the sparsely vegetated dunes set back from the water. These rolling meandering mounds of sand created natural pockets, or private knolls, perfect for getting lost in. They dug a hole in the sand, contoured to fit their bottoms, and sat to watch the show. She hugged him for no reason, pulling him against her, slowly moving her hand over his smooth scalp. With the secrets of the universe being whispered on the wind, they became one with the experience. The rhythm of life, the balance – God's example of perfection was breathtaking. While they listened to the soothing music – the seagulls, wind and lapping surf on the rocks – the colors of the sunset humbled them by creating miniature rainbows before salty mists.

As the final tip of the sun disappeared, they rolled up their pants and ran for the shore. Neither of them had collected periwinkles since childhood. Foraging under the moon's light, Rick joked, "What a great place to watch submarine races."

Some things hadn't changed and she giggled because of it. "I don't know," she said. "I once heard about a boy who was attacked by a plastic blue shark not too far from here."

"Oh, yeah?" With wet feet and a giant smile, Rick rushed after her and chased her all the way back to their secret spot where she surrendered in one quick collapse.

Just as they began cuddling, two couples happened by. The first was a young pair, arm-in-arm and laughing. The second was an elderly pair, holding hands and silent. Both pairs, however, were clearly in love.

Rick turned to Abby. "Who do you think is more fortunate?" he asked.

It was her first opportunity to share her values and she capitalized. "I'd say it's dead even."

The confusion in his eyes asked her to explain.

"The old couple's relationship has already been established, lived, and their love is like money in the bank. The young couple has their future before them, filled with hope and passion and dreams to be fulfilled together. But the only thing that matters is that they're both in love right now – at this very moment. The past and the future don't mean anything. Life should be lived in the moment and when the moment is filled with love, so will the past and future be." Abby believed that spiritual things held much more value than anything in the material world and she was happy to share this belief with Rick.

For the first time since they were kids, he kissed her. This time, he didn't let her go.

She felt more passion for him than anyone she'd ever known. It wasn't easy, but she finally broke the contact between them. The heat was so intense. "Okay," she gasped. "Let's get caught up. I want to know everything I missed...everything about you."

He laughed, but she was serious. He cleared his throat. "Well, let's see: I still love amusement parks. My favorite place in the whole world, though, is on the beach at sunset...in the arms of someone who loves me." He stopped, nodded once and quickly resumed his list. "Though I like all types of music, my favorite song is *The Dance* by Garth Brooks. I love seafood and pasta and bacon and eggs any time I can get them. I would love to travel to Australia, Hawaii and Alaska...on a warm cruise ship." He stopped.

She prodded him to go on.

"My favorite color is blue. I love to read. I enjoy all types of movies. And I'm big on trying new things – just living life, I guess. My writing takes up much of my personal time, though I do all I can to share it. I'm big into having company, though I cherish quiet time, too. I'm spiritual, but not very religious. I have a dreaded sweet tooth but like to run and work out. To describe myself in a word, I'd say I'm determined. As of late, being kind is more important to me than being right or appearing strong. And I'm starting to become grateful for all my experiences, good or bad, because they've gotten me to where I am. And…" He searched her eyes. "I'd rather be here right now than anywhere else on earth."

She hugged him.

He smiled. "Now you."

"My favorite color is nearly every shade of pink and I'm a bit of a night owl when I can get away with it. If I had my way, I'd become a beach bum but the responsibilities of being a mom have taken care of that for me. I love to read, to play with my daughter and to drink hot cocoa while wearing big fat socks in front of a fire. My favorite place in the world is under a big comforter, preferably in the arms of someone who loves me." She looked into his eyes, making his heart flutter. "I have lots of favorite songs, but I like Sarah McLachlin's *Angel*, and almost anything David Corey sings works for me. I love hummus, tabouli, anything vibrantly healthy. I'm a fish-eating vegetarian and love my food to be colorful."

She stopped and looked at Rick.

His gaze was penetrating, his attention complete.

She swallowed hard. "I've always wanted to travel the world. I love lobster ravioli, but I hardly ever eat it. I like clams and calamari and I really like fruit – especially strawberries and melon. I like to watch the stars at night by a campfire and I love the occasional dinner and a movie. Chocolate is my comfort food. Anything chocolate makes me smile."

He couldn't take it anymore. As if pulled by a giant magnet, he kissed her again.

She returned the passion and got lost in his kiss. As their lips parted, she whispered, "And I think that's about it."

He chuckled and kissed her once more.

She moaned softly.

For the sake of being a gentleman, he finally pulled away. He'd never known anything more difficult.

Darkness crept in, while moonbeams danced on the water; a deep cobalt blue that shimmered and danced in the light. The sound of elephant grass dancing with the wind was as soothing as a mother's lullaby. All at once, the black sky lit up with a million twinkling stars. The same sounds, the same smells existed, but it was a whole different world to the naked eye. With no manmade light distracting them from the wonder and awe of the canvas above, they stared into the filament for hours. With crickets and crabs as their only company, the feeling of being a visitor in a different world took hold. Rick found serenity in the echo of Abby's breathing.

She was so amazing. Without spending a penny, she'd shown him the perfect date.

"What is it you want from life?" Rick asked on the ride home.

"The stars," she whispered. "I want to walk among the stars." It was the exact same answer she gave as a kid.

Rick stared at her. None of the important things had changed and he wanted nothing more than to give her the stars; to watch her dance in stardust. It was unbelievable. He'd spent his whole life in search of true love and he'd had it all along – ever since he and Abby rode their bikes down Freedom Ave. He grabbed her hand and kissed it.

Before they reached his house, he'd already thought of the opening verse to the first poem he would write for her:

Day Dreams
Bustling street or barren dune,
hazy sun or sterling moon
the time, the place – I couldn't care
my only need: that you are there...

It took an hour of kissing before they said goodnight on Rick's front stoop.

"I'd like to take it slow," Abby said. "You know I want..."

He nodded once and kissed her softly. "We have forever...if that's what it takes."

Abby drove away elated but equally exhausted. She wasn't used to the late hours. Through the yawns, she thought about Paige and dreaded her remarks about returning home so late.

Two-dozen red roses were already awaiting her when she arrived on her front porch. *He must have called on his cell phone when I nodded off,* she thought. Again, she plunged her nose into the bouquet and inhaled deeply. Plucking the card free, she read: *Thank you for such a magical night. I knew we'd have fun but I wasn't expecting perfection. I'll never forget it. With Love, Rick*

Her face burned red when she looked up to find Paige scowling at her. Abby wasn't the only one overwhelmed with emotion.

"Have fun?" Paige asked. Her tone carried the sharpness of a disappointed parent.

"I did," Abby answered, her face aglow. Again, she'd shared too much information and knew it. As if she were facing her nine-year old mother, she held her breath and felt her heart skip a beat.

"Good," Paige said, "at least one of us did." She stormed into the house, marched down the hall and slammed her bedroom door behind her.

Abby hurried in after her. "Hey, Babe," she said, "Please don't be upset. I like Richard. I do. But he's no threat to you – to us. You have to believe that." She stroked her hair. "I breathe for you, ya know."

Paige looked up from her bed, trying hard to mask her sense of relief. Her Mom's guilt was proof that she hadn't lost just yet.

"So what do you say we forget about bed times tonight, make a big bowl of popcorn and catch a late movie together?"

Paige wiped her eyes and got up.

Rick called his Grandma's house, but was happy when Bill answered.

"Do you want me to wake her?" the kind man asked with a wheeze.

"No, don't," Rick answered, his excitement fighting to break through.

"So, how are you?"

"Couldn't be better!" Rick answered and meant it. After blabbing the details of his recent dates with Abby, the conversation eventually slowed and touched on several random topics. Finally, Bill asked, "What's the story with you and your Dad, Rick?"

Rick didn't expect the inquiry and was taken aback.

Even with the obvious tension, Bill wasn't about to let it go and spoke slowly. "At the risk of overstepping my bounds, from the moment I met you both – I've always wondered what happened between the two of you?"

Rick took a deep breath and shook his head. "I suppose my Dad eventually faded off into the distance because he felt guilty about taking his family away from Freedom Ave; about not providing what he thought he should have." There was a long pause. "And the way I remember it – it didn't take me all that long to make him feel that way."

Bill cleared his raspy throat. "There's different ways to succeed," he said. "I think you might be surprised at all the people your Dad's life has touched. Money isn't the best measurement of success, you know. Sometimes the smallest things can make all the difference in the world. And from what I've heard, your Dad is a very generous man."

"I know that now," Rick confessed and then explained the start of his lifelong quest to amass monetary wealth. "Everyone hated this guy, Old Man Sedgeband, when I was a kid. Not me. Even though he was an empty shell of a human being, I secretly admired him for his financial prowess and the security it provided."

Bill cleared his throat again. "Do you know the greatest gift you could ever give your Dad – that you could give yourself?"

"What's that?"

"A second chance, Rick. Why don't you give your Dad a second chance? Life is too short and I'd say you both deserve at least that much."

Rick's answer surprised even him. "I'd say you're right. I know now that my Dad always gave his best and that it wasn't his fault my Mom got into the accident; that her hospital bills cost us everything. Maybe it's me who needs the second chance?"

"So why don't you call him and ask for it?"

Rick held down the lump in his throat. "You know, I think I'll do just that. Thanks, Bill."

"No problem, son. I'm just happy I can help. We'll see you on Sunday." As Bill placed the telephone in its cradle, Eunice buried her giant smile in the pillow and hoped that its glow didn't give her overwhelming joy away.

Rick picked up the phone again and dialed.

Jim sprung up in bed. With a quick glance at the alarm clock, he answered the phone. "Hello?"

"Hi, Dad," Rick said, "I hope it's not too late to talk."

Jim wiped the sleep from his eyes and grinned. "It's never too late, my boy."

Chapter 13

For the first time in years, Rick wondered about his father's journey and the lives that it may have touched along the way.

On the first Monday night of each month, Jim Giles gave of his time to lecture the future convicts of America. His motto was: "If I can help only one, it'll be worth it." Most weeks, though, the number one seemed larger than infinity.

After a lifetime of working for the Massachusetts Department of Correction, Jim felt the need to pass on his brutal experiences to those who needed to hear them most – troubled children. In the meantime, the precious minutes he spent trying to make a difference in their lives helped to cleanse his soul. He was never sure who received more.

Jim pulled into the parking lot of the Straight Ahead Program, a Christian-based Ministry for children confined to lockup within the Department of Youth Services, or DYS, and stared at the eerie building. Surrounded by concertina wire and steel fence, the brick fortress was built in the late 1800's. Black bars, mesh and grilles covered the filthy windows, while shadows moved behind them. These dark glimpses were the little people who blamed their entire existence on everyone but themselves. There were some tough cases, young boys who'd been abused and neglected – products of drugs and alcohol, domestic violence, oppressive poverty, welfare-systems that fostered low-esteem. Most could blame the world and be justified. Jim understood that for the nightmare they were headed to, their outsourcing of blame wasn't going to help. The only chance they had now was to shoulder their circumstances and start making healthier choices.

Each month, he sat in the lot and watched as the boys played a violent game of basketball and beat on each other like they owed child support. Every one of them cursed and acted tough, doing everything Jim would have done had he been thrown into the same hellish environment. It was important to remember that. Most nights, it was the only good reason not to drive away. They were a pack of little punks, the whole lot of them. But, they were scared little punks and they needed help.

The lecture always started in prayer and was followed by two hours of harsh reality. Jim did everything he could to paint an accurate picture of life behind the walls. He detailed rapes and murders, anything to scare them into re-thinking their futures. At the same time, he also did everything he could to show them that they were still loved.

From the first brutal word that left his lips, he threw his booming voice and grabbed their full attention. "I'm not here to share war stories, or to scare you," Jim began. "I'm here to tell you the truth about prison." Like a searchlight, he scanned his young audience and roared, "I'm here because I care enough to tell you that it's not too late. No matter what others have told you; no matter what you may believe yourself – there's hope. All of this doesn't matter, though, unless you begin to believe in yourself."

He gestured around the room with a wave of his hand. "You can avoid all this by taking responsibility for your life and by starting to make the right choices. YOU are the one who can decide not to graduate from this Junior Varsity Team and go to prison." He shook his head for effect. "But first, no more excuses about your uncle's abuse, or your mother's drug problems. It's time to stop acting like victims. It's time to hold ourselves accountable for what happens in our own lives." He peered into their small, hardened faces. "Now, how many men do I have in here?"

All hands shot up.

"Then it's time to start acting like men!" he barked.

In silence, 24 young criminals looked at him with equal amounts of suspicion and contempt. *And why not*, he thought. Long before he ever arrived, those who were entrusted with their safety and nurturing betrayed them in the most unspeakable ways.

"How your nightmare begins is this," Jim explained, "One day, the judge gets sick of seeing your face and hands you a three-to-five bid to serve at MCI-Cedar Junction, Walpole. And I'll tell you now, it's a lot tougher to get out than it is to get in."

They looked confused. For the time being, he allowed it.

"Upon your arrival, you'll be shuffled into a concrete room and asked to step onto a blue, one-foot by one-foot square located on the floor. You'll be ordered to strip, but I guarantee you won't be fast enough. Four or five officers will take you to the floor and complete the search. This roughing-up is a sort of initiation, or more accurately, a message that when you screw up you can be brought back to the room for a 'tune-up.'" He nodded. "From the very moment you arrive, and in every sense of the word, you will be tested."

After allowing his words to sink in, he went on. "Upon arriving on the block, the wolves, or fellow inmates, will size up the new prey – YOU!

Once again, you'll be tested. More than likely, a larger convict will approach and demand that you take off your shoes, or some other article of clothing and give it to him. As I said, it's all about choices, and this is a tough one. If you hand it over, then tomorrow it's your backside. But if you decide to save face and throw hands, I promise that you'll lose no matter what. In prison, strength is found in numbers. Even if you're on top, which is very unlikely given your lack of combat skills and experience as an 18-year old, other inmates will jump in and finish it. By some strange occurrence, if you happen to maim or scar your bully, you will be charged with an assault & battery, or even mayhem – which carries a sentence of 20 mandatory years. All because someone wanted your sneakers? As I said, it's a lot harder to get out than it is to get in. The chances of avoiding confrontation inside are slim to none. There's a good chance that you'll earn more time while trying to stay alive, though. It's not fair, is it?"

With mouths half hung in shock, they each nodded.

"But it's not about fair anymore, is it? Remember this: Because you didn't make the right choices on the street, you're world now exists at the wrong place…wrong time…every time!

"So, it's time to stop playing the victim, and understand that there are consequences for your actions. It's time to take RESPONSIBILITY for everything you do. At 18 years old, you'll find many people who will have compassion for you and all the horror stories that got you into DYS. Upon entering the adult system, though, that same folder will get closed and most hearts will become hardened toward you. I guarantee it. It's a matter of self-preservation. In prison, kindness is always mistaken as weakness, and there's no room for it. You'll never find it.

"You will have enemies on both sides. There are the officers who you will undoubtedly despise, though – ironically enough – they're charged with your protection. They will tell you when to eat, sleep and go to the bathroom. They will say 'NO' for nearly every request you ask of them. All the while, they will be pressuring you into working for them as an informant. Trust me, at your age the majority of you will flip. Can you imagine a more dreadful existence?"

No one answered, but Jim could see. It was starting to sink in.

"Worse yet, at 18 you are as close to a female as the inmate population has seen in a very long time. Truth is, the vast majority of the population are lifers with nothing to lose by raping you, or snapping your neck. One of their favorite sayings is: 'It don't count in prison!' Does anyone know what that means?"

A hand was raised. Jim called on it. The boy snickered, "It means a dude's not gay if he makes you his wife."

Everyone laughed.

Jim's face remained stoic. He nodded. "You're absolutely right."

The laughter ceased.

"And there's two ways it happens. The first is called seduction... when an older con promises protection for your sexual favors." He paused for effect and shook his disgusted head. "The second way is by gang rape."

His audience looked sick.

He capitalized. "Unfortunately, with the amount of overcrowding and understaffing inside, such crimes aren't usually detected until the damage has been done."

He paused again to let them absorb this. Peering into their eyes, he lowered his voice. "As I said, I'm not here to scare you. I'm just here to explain your reality if you do decide to take the next step into adult incarceration."

A handful of them nodded.

He continued by explaining the prison hierarchy and the different crimes that got inmates convicted. He detailed all the players found behind the wall and their daily games. From conmen and thugs to the pimps and the queens who fill their pockets, he never once candy-coated a word.

"Okay, those on the bottom, YOU, must unite with others to survive. Many inmates say, 'I came in alone, I'll do my time alone and I'll leave alone.' That's bull! When on the bottom, you become the drug runner, or mule; the one who evens the score, or collects the bookie's winnings. If a hit goes down against another group, it'll be you who's ordered to carry it out. You become anything that could land someone more time if caught. I mean, think about it: Why risk more time when you can force someone weaker to do your dirty work – while you slide into the shadows and laugh at some kid's poor luck?"

Those with tough exteriors looked up for the challenge.

Jim went for the heart. "In the meantime, your people on the streets will build walls within themselves because no one can live in two worlds at one time. It's hard to keep grieving someone who is gone but hasn't died."

Heads were hung. Jim couldn't tell if he was losing their attention. "But prison's not about being a fair world, is it? It's about wrong place...wrong time...every time, right?"

For the first time, they all agreed.

Jim went on to tell them about the two major crimes that landed men in prison: stupidity and laziness. He spoke of suicides. He detailed the most gruesome fights and the weapons used in each. He talked about the frightening racism shown between groups. He explained AIDS and the high percentages of becoming infected when living in a community where one in every five has it. For the adventurous at heart, he also joked about two attempted escapes. "One was of a dumb man who dug his way out from his second floor cell, only to find himself in a first floor cell."

They laughed.

Without losing his smile, he then described another who tried to escape, but hung up in concertina wire. "Every time he moved," Jim said, "the tiny razors bit into his flesh until he nearly bled to death."

The laughter ceased.

He spoke of drugs and the ingenious ways it got inside. He then told them about the young runners, men one year older than they who didn't return with the drugs and got beheaded or castrated for their lack of success.

Throughout his spiel, Jim attempted to be one of them by cursing and using street slang. To separate himself, as well as maintain order and control, he also yelled at them. It was a narrow passage to get through. And there was limited time to use humor, story telling – anything to make an impression. He needed to get into their hearts, the only place where he could possibly make a difference. There was so little time, though. For what they'd been through, the walls were so thick and high that getting through was nothing shy of a miracle. For the ones he could reach, there were only a few precious moments he could stay before he was exiled, perhaps forever.

He concluded, "If you do end up in prison, you will undoubtedly be much different upon your release and these changes cannot be good. Only two emotions dwell in prison: fear and rage, and you will spend years becoming intimate with both. It's called 'being institutionalized.'

"And for those of you who haven't figured it out yet, there is no pride in having done time. It's dead time. Just ask the nameless men who still wear numbers on their grave markings on Potter's Hill. No one talks about crying at night in his cell. Instead, they create war stories and brag. It's bull! If you want to impress people, go jump out of an airplane for your country, or save people from burning buildings. Get up every morning and go to work to support your family. Now, that's being a man. Those are the real heroes – the true tough guys.

"And now, after hearing all this I want somebody to tell me what the good news is?"

Not one of them raised a hand.

Jim smiled. "The good news is that you never have to go there. NOT ONE OF YOU EVER HAS TO GO THERE! It's really up to you and the choices you make from this day forward."

When he wrapped up, there was applause.

Month after month, the same faces returned to hear his same spiel. And, month after month he gave it, hoping that he might offer something that would save them the hell he knew they faced. *If I can save only one*, he thought.

At the parking lot, he looked back. Through the grimy, barred windows, he could vaguely make out the shadows of several of his students beating the life out of another. "We'll try again next month," he whispered, and drove away.

Chapter 14

For Bill and Eunice, each month that passed felt like a day spent in the arms of angels.

"The little whispers I had in my heart for so long were heard the day we met," Eunice said, "And I just knew God's plan would be great for us."

Right then Bill decided to have an affair with his new wife. It didn't take much convincing for Eunice to run away with him.

According to the brochures, it was hokey. It was tacky. It was the perfect getaway.

They drove all the way to the Pocono's in Pennsylvania, honeymoon capital of the east. Bill decided to stay away from a room at the Cleopatra Towers with its seven-foot champagne glass hot tub.

Eunice agreed. "I don't think we're insured enough to risk the heights," she said.

Upon arrival, an obnoxious sign, reading *YOU HAVE JUST ENTERED THE LAND OF LOVE* greeted them. Bill wheeled the car over a tiny creek bridge and entered the romantic playground for fun loving adults.

After skipping through the minefields left by a flock of gift-giving geese, they checked into the Lakeside Villa at Paradise Stream. Bordering a swamp where paddleboats and rowboats cut through the mosquitoes in search of the elusive thousand-dollar fish, their little bungalow was perfect.

With the excitement of discovery, Eunice opened the door and stepped in. The room featured a bright red, heart-shaped hot tub, a circular, King-sized bed with a mirror bolted to the ceiling and a sunken living room with fireplace. With a giant smile, Bill filled the mini bar with beer and wine, and watched as Eunice made herself at home. Her love was everything to him; a feeling, a choice; a thought – everything that was good. Her love was his religion.

Eunice chuckled over the complimentary gifts: one fire log, a large bottle of raspberry sherbet bubble bath and a tiny bottle of champagne. "Looks like they're expecting us to have fun," she said.

It was a week to remember: Breakfast in bed, carriage rides at dusk and bonfires at twilight. There was fine dining in the Huntress Room, foo foo drinks in the Red Apple Lounge and midnight snacks in the Jungle Room Café – each experience a complete delight.

Games included indoor and outdoor archery, mini golf, billiards, ping-pong and air hockey. There was a beautiful pool, with a Jacuzzi and gazebo bar beside it. There was also shuffleboard, a bocce court and nature trails for Eunice's morning hikes.

The competition between Bill and Eunice was fierce. He dominated her in shuffleboard. She killed him in air hockey. Together, however, they passed on the daily competitions with other couples – especially the karaoke.

The weekly itinerary was jam-packed with fun.

Monday was themed *Romance & Comedy*. After playing an exhausting round of mini-golf, they went for a swim and then sipped frozen *Passion Potions* in frosted souvenir glasses. The afternoon found them testing their knowledge at movie video trivia in the Red Apple lounge. Eunice was unbeatable. Bill couldn't take his eyes off her.

After cocktail hour, they were seated with four other couples enjoying a night of formal dining. He ordered Roast Prime Rib of Beef. She opted for the Stuffed Salmon with Crabmeat. While they awaited their dinners, five couples who'd never set eyes on each other before shared forced conversation. Bill decided to have fun with it.

Everyone but he and Eunice were honeymooning; idealistic, young couples excited to be together. The men spoke of their jobs, the women of their weddings. Everyone agreed. They couldn't remember a thing about their wedding – and "for all that money spent."

Bill finally introduced he and Eunice to everyone. "We come here every year to celebrate our divorce," he announced. "And it's been great!"

Nervous glances were exchanged across the table. Eunice fought back the tickle in her throat.

Bill stifled a cough and nodded. "And our new spouses have been very understanding about it. I gotta tell you…spending time together here has been better than any experience we had while we were married." One of the couples laughed, but the rest of them didn't know what to think. Bill never cracked a grin. Two slices of banana cream pie later, he and Eunice left the others to gossip in hushed tones.

The scheduled comedy began at 8:30 sharp and the *R-Rated Newlywed Game Show* had Eunice nearly wetting her pants.

Mardi-Gras Tuesday confirmed that the mornings were going to be rough. They didn't get up and out until after ten.

Just outside the resort, they went horseback riding at Mountain Creek

Riding Stables. Eunice mounted a small gelding named Barnaby, while Bill rode Hannibal Lecter, the backbiter. A scenic ride through the lovely Pocono woodlands revealed several feeding deer and a trail of wooden signs that labeled everything from trees to the homes of hidden animals.

Bill and Eunice declined to take part in the *Honeymooner's Scavenger Hunt* and instead lounged by the pool to get some color. It was time well spent, talking and laughing. As Bill jumped in for one last dip, he yelled, "What's this warm spot in the pool?"

Other folks looked over.

"I think someone just peed right here!"

While Eunice shook her embarrassed head, a woman beside her burst out laughing.

At dinner, while noisemakers, horns and Mardi Gras beads were handed out for the upcoming festivities, they indulged in a gluttonous buffet.

The masquerade party directly followed. Bill and Eunice peaked their heads in and decided on a quiet night alone.

Tropical Wednesday hosted another breakfast in bed, with an afternoon movie that had close to a hundred couples cuddling. Halfway through, Bill suffered such a terrible coughing attack that he had to excuse himself twice until it passed. Eunice was concerned, but he waved away her worries. He was feeling worse than lousy.

Dinner promised a T-Bone steak for him, while she opted for the lemon basil chicken. At the table, Bill explained, "The first night we took a hot tub, my ex-wife here misread the instructions on the bubble bath and poured in two full caps instead of one."

Eunice laughed. "I never saw so many bubbles in my whole life," she said, "the entire floor was soaked."

Everyone chuckled, adding nods of understanding.

Bill shrugged. "I figured it's not our house, so what the hell!"

Everyone laughed again.

The night rocked to the sounds of calypso music. Once again, Bill and Eunice selected to be anti-social. A late night swim under a warm rain shower seemed much too romantic to pass up. With island music playing in the background – people laughing and having a great time – they held each other in the pool and danced. It was everybody else who was missing out.

Thursday was *Roman Italian & Horror Movie Night*.

After a day spent in the throws of ecstasy, the night came quick.

Choosing Chicken Parmesan over Tortellini for dinner, a talented fire juggler bridged perfectly into the scary movie *The Others* that was shown on the lawn. By the final scene, it started to rain. It was fine. They'd already had enough.

Just as they started to doze off, Eunice leaned into her husband's ear. "Meet me in my dreams tonight?" she whispered.

Without opening his eyes, Bill smiled. "You are always in my dreams, my love, day or night."

On Friday, they ate breakfast with the rest of the world and ventured back on the highway to count down a hundred exits through the state of Connecticut – all of it on a belly full of chili cheese fries.

Though he felt nauseous, Bill looked over at his love. A full week with her had proven his newest belief: That the greatest purpose of any relationship was to bring out the best in someone and share everything— experiences, wisdom, family and friends. All the love Eunice knew was now his, as well – compounded. It was amazing. He'd finally become the best man he could be. He grabbed her hand and kissed it.

"What's that for?" she asked.

"Just a small thank you for such a wonderful adventure."

She kissed his hand back.

On their front porch, Eunice found a bouquet of fresh sunflowers tied in purple ribbon awaiting their return. She turned and kissed her husband. "You really are something else," she said. "God, do I love you."

Bill smiled wide and followed her into the house. His energy was dropping to an all-time low.

It was late when the telephone rang out. Bill looked to his left. Eunice, the master puppeteer, was already out cold. He quickly picked up. It was Rick.

"How are the Pocono's these days?" Rick asked.

"Don't really know," Bill said, stifling a cough. "I could spend a week in hell with your Grandma and still have the time of my life."

Eunice concealed her mischievous grin.

"What's up?" Bill asked.

"I guess I just needed to talk." There was a pause. "I'm still trying to find the right balance, a way around this Catch 22."

"How so?" Bill asked again, freeing the cough that gnawed at his throat.

"I know it might sound crazy, but how does someone know when they've made enough money that they no longer need to be led by it? I mean, when did you know you had enough?"

Bill grinned. His young pupil was still struggling to escape the rat race and return to himself. "It's more like when did I know that I had nothing, you mean?"

Rick said nothing.

"The moment I met the love of my life, that's when. What good is money if it stops you from being happy, Rick? If it stops you from being who you truly are?"

Eunice stirred.

"Well, it looks like I'm about to turn the same corner," Rick said. "Oh?"

"It's that woman Abby I told you about. We haven't seen each other since we were kids, but she's so amazing."

"Wonderful!" Bill replied, and turned his face away from the receiver to hack up something green and grotesque.

Rick beamed. "Honestly, Bill, I can't thank you enough. I wish there were a way..."

"From the moment I laid eyes on your beautiful grandmother, I've really wanted to write her a poem," he whispered. "Can you help?"

Eunice secretly smiled at the sentiment.

"The rhythm is in the syllables," Rick explained, "it's all about the beat..."

It was amazing how a few short months could change the world.

"Are you afraid to die?" Bill asked one day.

"No," Eunice answered, "I wasn't afraid to come in. I'm certainly not afraid to return home." She thought for a moment. "I suppose I'm more afraid of being alone."

He shook his head. "Impossible," he said. "Angels are always with us. Just because you can't see some things doesn't mean they're not there. We always have company – it's impossible to ever be alone."

Eunice searched her husband's eyes and believed. "And you?" she asked. "Are you afraid to die?"

He shook his head again. "Who would have thought that a retired widower would have learned everything he ever needed to know at the end of his journey?"

Eunice started to speak, but was stopped by Bill's index finger pressed gently against her lips.

"I spent most of my life in the office, achieving success," he said. "I missed the lives of my children, my grandchildren. This last year, though, for whatever reason I was blessed with the precious opportunity to invest all my energy and love into another human being – into you – and to reunite with my family. And I really believe that it might be enough to redeem my soul in the eyes of the Lord."

Eunice choked back the tears.

"In this past year, I've proven myself more human than what I was in my entire lifetime and it's the greatest gift anyone could have ever given me. Another person has finally taken priority over material objects, intangible goals and my need to accumulate material wealth. But you've redeemed all that."

She held him.

"You gave me the sweetest gift, Eunice, a saving grace, and my entire existence has had purpose because of you. Had it not been for you, everything I've ever done and achieved would have added up to nothing. You're my ticket into heaven." He choked out the last few words and then spit something into his handkerchief.

The tears rolled down her cheeks.

"I'm a wealthy man, yet..." He grabbed for his wallet. When he opened it, there was no cash – only a photo of he and Eunice.

She kissed his cheek.

"How much money do I have in the bank?" he asked.

"I don't know."

He grinned. "I don't know either, and it used to be the most important thing to me in my whole life. Now it means less to me than watching a chipmunk feed its young, or a rainbow bridge the gap between two clouds."

She hugged him tight. He'd finally learned.

By their first wedding anniversary, Bill Stryker had taken ill with lung cancer. Her birthday gift of his quitting smoking had come a few years too late.

While Bill joked, "I smoked two packs of menthols every day and inhaled enough fiberglass to make a fleet of Corvettes," the doctor told Eunice, "I know this is difficult, Mrs. Stryker, but I've known Bill since we were kids. For a man of 74 years, he's lived a wonderful life...especially since you came along."

She knew the old medicine man was right, but it still didn't help. She and Bill had only been given several brief seasons together. And in that short time, Bill Stryker had become the air that kept her alive.

"I'll allow him to rest comfortably at home," the doctor said. "But if he gets any worse..."

Eunice promised that she'd look after her love.

Eunice and Bill sat in silence, content to be in each other's company. As Bill worked on his poem, Eunice pretended not to peek.

She gave him a penny. "For your thoughts," she said.

With a smile, he reached into the nightstand, pulled out two pennies and handed them to her. "For your heart," he said before placing the oxygen mask back onto his face.

She sat beside him and gave him a kiss, all-the-while sneaking a good look at his work:

A Whisper Away
Sweaty palms and quivering knees,
the air is all but lost;
to spend one second in your arms
I'd gladly pay the cost
  of lifetimes spent in moments,
a glance in trade for words-
no matter what the skeptics say
I've never been so sure
  of what my heart is feeling
and what my spirit knows;
that every breath I'm blessed to take
my love for you still grows
  into this thing I cherish
I take the final plunge,
but never have I felt so…

Bill stared at the ceiling, searching his heart for the perfect words, when Eunice asked, "Where is the one place in the world you wished you'd visited?"

"Well, my dear, that's a tough one. As long as I was with you I don't think the location would matter much."

She kissed him. "I know, but where?"

He thought for a moment and grinned. "A shack on a deserted beach with no telephones would be one place. Long walks on a moonlit beach, hand in hand, stopping frequently for one of our intense kisses. Of course we would have to venture into town, so you could shop and I could buy you a new dress. Lunch on a veranda hovering over a busy street with someone strumming a guitar singing Jimmy Buffett tunes as we sip margaritas. With our shopping bags full and a tequila buzz, we could venture back to our love shack for some more quiet time. A week of that would be incredible." He paused to take in some air and kiss her hand.

"Perfect," she said with a nod.

But he wasn't done. "A romantic trip to Paris, the city of love, would also be my choice – probably my top choice," he said. "A long plane ride to climb inside each others heads and talk about everything and nothing at all, followed by check-in at a luxurious hotel with a balcony overlooking the city. There would be lots of sightseeing, shopping and wine tasting by day. But the nights, my love, would be all about us – just us. After a week of seeing all the sights but one, you take my hand and suggest we have one more stop to make before we venture home." He stopped for a moment to breathe. "With plastic cups filled with wine, we climb to the top of the Eiffel Tower where we can see it all. With the breathtaking views before us, under a perfect sky, the mood would be set perfectly. As we toast to an incredible vacation, I'd look deep into your eyes and say all the things you love to hear." He looked at her. "Yeah, Paris is definitely my top pick. I always wanted to see Paris before I died."

"Okay," she whispered.

The very next day, Eunice Stryker gave her dying husband Paris.

Bill was wheeled into their darkened dining room. Curious, he looked back at his visiting nurse when Eunice lit a candle that illuminated the room. His wife was wearing a pretty, flowered dress, her hair twisted back in a tight French braid; her tearful eyes smiling. As the nurse disappeared, Bill scanned the room and choked back the lump in his swollen throat. The entire place had been transformed by love.

Giant posters of the Eiffel Tower, the Louvre, the Notre Dame Cathedral and the Arc de Triomphe papered the walls. A hidden stereo played selected favorites by Maurice Chevalier. He and Eunice were seated at a small café table, with French bread and a small wheel of cheese before them. Even a bottle of French wine was chilling nicely. "When did you..." he began to ask when a flirtatious waitress adorned in a traditional French costume entered and poured him a glass of wine.

"Bienvenue. I'm Louise," she announced, "and I will be your server for this eve, Oui?"

"Oui," Bill answered, and chuckled. He grabbed Eunice's hand across the table. "Merci," he said, "merci beaucoup."

She rose and kissed his hand.

They started with brochette jurassienne as an appetizer, pieces of cheese wrapped in ham and fried on a skewer. It was absolutely delicious. Next came two steaming bowls of bouillabaisse, a stew-like soup with conger eel, scorpion fish, gurnet, saffron, fennel, garlic and bitter orange peel, served with garlic mayonnaise. It was equally incredible. For the main course, Eunice had insured her husband would enjoy a variety of dishes: Diots au vin blanc, pork sausages poached in white wine; crêpes, an imaginative range of savory, sweet pancakes; filet mignon de porc normande, a pork tenderloin cooked with apples and onions in cider and served with caramelised apple rings; truffade, mashed potatoes with cheese through it that is then fried with bacon and garlic; and various fish dishes that ignited the palate. It was a banquet, a feast prepared for a king, and Bill indulged as much as his health would allow. Dessert consisted of a tray of imported chocolate truffles, delicate pastries and rich coffee. The doting waitress offered Bill a shot of Cognac for his nightcap. For once, he didn't feel up to it.

And then they danced to Edith Piaf's classic, *La Vie en Rose*. With Bill in his wheelchair and Eunice on her knees, they swayed to the music and clung to each other tightly, knowing this would be their last waltz. They danced and whispered sweet nothings in each other's ears and cried.

It was amazing how love could be so damn beautiful and so damn cruel, all at the same time.

Chapter 15

Carmen Wright was a petite, neurotic housewife, with blonde hair, blue eyes and a figure that time had punished. She'd sacrificed much of her looks for her two children and wasn't pleased with the price of motherhood. Once an envied prom queen, she now reminisced about her brief time in the sun. She endured each day in a mutually miserable marriage, but was unwilling to make a move. "I have a headache," was her signature quote, and she either spent her waking hours sulking at the mirror, or sleeping on the couch. According to her husband, Grant, "She liked to work from twelve to one, with an hour off for lunch."

Grant wasn't a bad dad when he was around, but he was rarely around. Long ago, he'd chosen the discreet hobby of infidelity and was quite active at it. This attitude, of course, left little time for his children. Unfortunately, he was also unwilling to end his marriage and spare his kids the years of pain he'd endured as a child. Somewhere along the way he'd learned to become more considerate of his own feelings than anyone else's.

To most of the world, theirs was a traditional family; he, Carmen and the kids. From the welcome sign and lawn ornaments in the front of the house to the tree fort out back, it was the perfect picture of happy, middle class America. Behind closed doors, though, there was nothing but screaming kids who didn't eat right and parents who argued all the time. While he was out cheating, Carmen was either in therapy, or dabbling in script drugs and alcohol. All the while, the kids were left to fend for themselves.

He couldn't help it. Carmen didn't really like ice cream, while he'd never tasted a flavor that he didn't absolutely fall in love with.

It didn't take long for the old-school Romeo to strike again. Although he'd learned that most women wouldn't fall for his polished sales pitch, there was more than enough naïve prey just waiting to be hunted. And through the years, he'd developed the keen eye of a seasoned hunter, successfully searching out those who were starving for love.

Her name was Vicki and she was a friend of a friend, the best kind. Grant pressed the accelerator to the floor and barreled toward the finish line.

Grant smiled and worked the computer keys like a concert pianist.

He preferred penning actual letters. Email seemed so impersonal. Using his workplace for a return address, he wrote:

> *Dearest Vicki,*
>
> *From the moment I first saw you, I felt an attraction that I've never known before. Though I think you're beautiful, this chemistry I feel for you reaches far beyond physical. I honestly think it's a spiritual connection that you and I share. There are times I've looked at you and swore that you saw everything inside of me.*
>
> *I am very drawn to you when I look into your eyes. I feel tremendous passion for you. When I'm near you, it's my heart that controls me – not my mind. I think deeper forces than the mind can consciously process our attraction for each other. I don't know what the future holds, but I do know that I don't want to destroy our chance at fate.*
>
> *Through the sunshine and the pain, I've followed my heart my whole life. I hope it doesn't burn me now.*
>
> *You're so beautiful. I could kiss you for hours and never stop. All I want is the opportunity to turn your world upside down.*
>
> *I'll be thinking of you tonight, and every night after.*
>
> *With Love,*
>
> *Me*

Two days later, Grant received a letter at work. It was from Vicki:

> *Grant,*
>
> *I think you are incredibly sexy, irresistible, funny and smart. The sound of your voice completely melts me. Trust that I feel everything you do, and that's what makes 'us' so amazing.*
>
> *I have seen more than everything in your eyes, and it kind of freaks me out. In case you haven't noticed, I don't spend too much time looking into your eyes when we talk. I just can't. I feel that what we have together is what many couples aspire for, but never achieve. I really believe this.*
>
> *I also try to do what I feel rather than what I think. Some people might call that foolish, or reckless behavior. I say life's too short for anything else, especially regret. I've come to the realization that I don't want to have any regrets the day I die. I don't want to feel like I should have done something, or worse, deal with the 'what ifs...'*
>
> *I'm ready for you and wish you were here right now.*
>
> *Please try to believe in us the way I do – because I believe with all my heart.*
>
> *I can't wait to kiss you again.*
>
> *I've had a chance to see how well my determination and persistence pays off, and I believe that if I want something bad enough, no matter what*

it is... I can make it happen. The day may come that I become determined to be your wife, and it may come sooner than you think. Think of me always...
   Vicki

Grant dropped the letter on his desk and sighed. The wife comment was disturbing. It was time to get all he could from her and get out.

They went to the park. While Vicki sat on a bench and watched, he chased her two kids around and – while tiring them out – made them scream for their lives. Through it all, though, Grant and Vicki's eyes searched each other out. Every time they met, the excitement built. Without a word, they shared a year's worth of thoughts and feelings, all-the-while engaged in an intense foreplay that had both of them hoping for the sun to go down a little more quickly. Soaked in sweat, Grant stole a kiss from her each time he passed. Their smiles eventually turned to laughter, and before long Vicki announced that it was time to go for dinner. Tired and dirty, they ordered the kids favorite; pepperoni pizza, and went back to Vicki's place to have a picnic on the back deck.

Vicki bathed, while Grant sneaked a peak and a kiss. They watched a movie with the kids, and when they'd finally begun to yawn Vicki put them to bed. While she and Grant waited for the little ones to fall asleep, they returned to the deck and made out like two teenagers. They never made it to the bedroom.

Grant awoke in the morning with Vicki's head on his chest. A pang of fear ripped through his heart. He'd been out all night and would have to provide a believable alibi for Carmen. *To hell with it*, he thought, and went back to sleep.

Just as he started to snore, Vicki leaned over for a sweet kiss. "I really care for you," she whispered, and then told him what she was hoping for the future – "our future."

A squeal traveled from across the hall. "Mama, the sun's out." Grant was saved. He hurried to get dressed.

"No, you can't have Oreos for breakfast," Vicki argued with her kids. While she checked their homework and got them ready for school, Grant prepared to leave. Vicki spotted him at the door, and took a quick break from the chaos to give him another kiss. "Be careful," she said, "and hurry back. It's absolutely beautiful how you and I are so much in synch. Please don't ever question my words, or feelings for you, okay?" Her kisses were soft and wet and incredibly intense.

Even still, Grant jumped in his car and never looked back.

Vicki left a message with his answering service. "Hey You, Although I was nervous at first, I felt so comfortable with you. I just wish it didn't fly by so quickly. I will also mention that your kisses felt so incredible – your lips, your tongue. You smelled so good, too, and it felt wonderful to be in your arms. It felt right, everything felt right. I thought of you all morning long and can't wait for you to be next to me again. I have a good job, nice house...it's all good. But there's something missing. One big giant piece of the puzzle is just missing. I now know what it is, or what I want. I want you, Grant. I truly believe with all my heart that it's meant to be. I also believe it'll be absolutely amazing. I'm crawling out of my skin with ways to make you smile, and I fall deeper for you every day. I can feel your energy and could spend the rest of my life trying to figure out why your eyes shine when you smile at me. Call me later. I need to hear your voice again today. I miss you."

Grant took awhile to respond. He didn't know whether to end it now, or keep going. Her kisses were so perfect. He called her house and left a message. "The more we talk, the more I feel like I just met you. I'm starting to think we could do anything with each other. I need to kiss you for the entire time we're together – for two minutes, or two hours – and I'm leaning toward the latter." Grant hung up the phone and thought about how quickly their tryst had progressed. He shook his head. The game was already won. It was over. He'd let her know in a few days.

It was Tuesday night. Rick was already at the pool table when Grant arrived. "Sorry, I'm late," he said, "I had to stop off at the men's room and the strangest thing happened."

Rick looked up for an explanation.

Grant smiled. "I walked in and saw a wallet lying on the floor. There was no one else in there, so I picked it up and rifled through it. It was like hitting the lottery! The damn thing was stuffed with a short stack of twenty-dollar bills. Talk about a dilemma, though! I checked the license and found out that I actually know the guy who lost it." He paused for effect. "So I finally asked myself, 'If it were me who lost my wallet, what would I want the person who found it to do?' After some careful thought, I finally decided that I'd want me to learn a lesson, so I've decided to keep the cash."

Rick burst into laughter. "You're so full of it," he said.

Grant chuckled, grabbed a pool stick and rolled it on the table to check for crookedness. "Oh, I went by the old neighborhood this past weekend and saw Old Man Sedgeband standing out on his stoop," Grant said. "I can't believe he's still around. And he hasn't changed a bit...what a survivor."

Rick nodded. "And that's about all, too."

Grant looked at his friend.

"He might have survived every one of them, but that man never lived a day of his life," Rick said. "And just so you know, another old friend will be joining us in a few minutes."

"Who?" Grant asked, and racked their first game of the night.

Before Rick could open his smiling mouth, Abby stepped into the light of the pool table. "Hey there, boys."

Grant's jaw touched his chest. "As I live and breathe, it's Abby Gerwitz," Grant said. He and Abby hugged.

"Abby Soares," she corrected him, "but you certainly haven't changed, Grant Wright."

"Wow! You look incredible," he added.

Rick quickly jumped in "You might want to turn down the suction, Pal. My eardrums feel like they're about to implode."

They picked up right where they left off and the conversation was playful. "So, Rick said you got married and divorced. What happened?" Grant asked.

"My ex is a self-absorbed womanizer who can't keep his hands to himself."

Grant looked at Rick and smiled. He turned back to Abby. "I told you when we were kids that you should have chosen me."

"I did, Grant." She nodded. "Trust me, I did. The only difference was the name."

For a moment, there was silence.

"It's not too late, you know..." Grant said.

"For what?" she asked.

"For me to take you to heaven."

In spite of herself, Abby chuckled. "In your dreams!"

The night was glorious. They reminisced about the carefree days on Freedom Ave: Old Man Sedgeband and R&S Variety, the spooky Chouinard place, hanging out on each other's porches, the beach, Lincoln Park. Hours ticked by like seconds, and the laughter never stopped. They'd been blessed to grow up together and knew it. It was getting late when Grant brought up the pressed pennies down at the railroad tracks. Rick and Abby exchanged a glance. "As I remember..." Grant teased Rick, "that's the day you were cursed."

Abby was ready to defend her love when Rick stood. "Buddy, when we put those pennies on the tracks, what did you wish for?"

Grant looked at Abby and grinned. "To never settle down...to sleep with as many women as possible." He had no idea what he'd wished for, but he couldn't remember a time when he wanted anything different.

Abby shook her head.

"I guess it came true," Rick said.

Alas, Grant was silenced. Something had actually reached the desolate chamber of his heart.

Three hugs later, they called it a night.

Chapter 16

It seemed like forever since Abby kept a daily journal, but these days she couldn't coax her fingers to write fast enough. There was so much she felt; so much she needed to express. The truth of it made her glow. It seemed like forever since she'd been this happy; this hopeful. She wrote:

Once upon a time, there was a prince, a very handsome prince in a devilish kind of way, with a glimmer in his eye. The prince was in search of his heart's companion, only to have spent much time searching in vain. Not unhappy, but growing in anticipation as time went by, he was filled with hope and the desire to share his thoughts and heart with someone special.

In another land, not too far away, lived a princess. She was filled with kindness, with a heart still pure. She, too, was looking for the time when she could lay her head down to sleep with comfort in her heart and her love by her side. She'd traveled challenging paths with the best intentions and spent much time listening to her mind say what was right, proper, and good. Sadly, she felt age growing inside her otherwise youthful spirit.

One day, by chance, the prince and the princess crossed paths. It felt like the lights were suddenly switched on when the two looked at each other. Inspired, they began to walk the same path and discuss where their lives had taken them, and what could be – should Fate intervene and Faith persevere.

Before they knew it, they discovered that the path they had walked had closed off behind them. There was no more past, only a lovely garden behind them and an open expanse of horizon before them. Hands held, hearts full, the prince and the princess heard their hearts speak and joyously looked toward the future together.

She put down the pen and reread the journal entry. *Is it really possible?* she wondered, and emailed him.

Richard,

Let's have dinner tonight – my house. Paige is sleeping over a friend's.

Me

And through ongoing email, the impersonal means of communication brought them closer than any two people could get.

135

Hey You,

Dinner was AWESOME! What a great cook you are! I noticed last night that there was a tone, though, that makes you sound unsure of me? I've played out our dinner in my head (especially saying good night). Over dessert, you said that I must intimidate people. I REALLY hope that doesn't mean you?I honestly want to get to know you again...all of you.
Sir Rick
PS- Keep smiling. The world is a prettier place when you do.

It was a long six days before they saw each other again.

On Saturday night, they drove two towns over to the only Drive-In movie theater still open. For eight bucks, they made out and talked, and then made out and talked until the double feature was done, the lights went up and all the neighboring cars had pulled away. It was a beautiful experience, but at the same time unbelievably frustrating for them both.

As if reading her mind, he told her, "We can wait until you're ready."

She kissed him for his patience and understanding.

As they prepared to leave, Abby wiped the fog from her window and smiled. They'd forgotten to hang the ancient, bulky speaker.

Hi Sweetie,

Thank you for such a wonderful evening. The movie was good (haha). I could have laid on your chest all night. I'll check my email at lunch, so don't be a stranger.
Abby

Hi,

I agree. Last night WAS wonderful! You're a great listener. I was thinking that I'd like to be a great listener, too. So the next time I can see you (which I'm really looking forward to), I intend to shut my mouth and let you run with it. I'm curious about you – your mind and especially your heart. Hey, and like I said, your new job is like a bus stop – you just have to wait a little while longer until the bus shows up. I hope you're smiling today. As I said, your job is only temporary, a preparation for other things you're striving to do. Just take comfort in that thought and smile. The bus is on its way.
Rick

While Paige was struggling with not seeing her dad, Rick was struggling with the random and infrequent moments spent with Abby. Between them,

Abby felt the pull. She never imagined that finding the proper balance would seem so impossible.

> *Mr. Giles,*
> *What another incredible night! Thank you. Your words are comforting and foster serenity. I already can't wait to see you again. Write me if you get a chance. I'm eager to hear from you. And I agree. It really is the little things that make all the difference.*
> *Abby xoxoxo*

> *Hey*
> *Can't wait to see you, too. I hope you like the poem I've attached. Call me crazy, but I've suddenly been inspired.*
> *Me xoxox*

Beauty
She radiates with the light of a thousand candles,
while her movements have the energy of a lightning storm.
The sweetest aroma lures even the strong,
though it is the scent of confidence that takes the kill.
With the giggle of an innocent child,
her tone is soft and gentle, almost heavenly.
She expects nothing,
but her silence demands the best.
Her forgiving heart beats in the ears of all men,
yet it is her untamed spirit that screams out loudest.
Like a beacon in the darkest night, her comfort is safety.
Rarely revealing her deepest thoughts,
her words remain simple, for she is a mystery.
Her tender touch can be soothing or sensual,
as she is unconditional love –
both maternal and passionate.
In a word, she is Beauty...
and you should see her on the outside.

> *Richard,*
> *Oh, my God! The poem is beautiful and so are you. (Whoever you wrote it for is one lucky lady.) THANK YOU! I'll cherish it forever.*
> *Abby xoxo*

Rick called her. "I know how tough it's been, having to split your time between Paige and me," he said, "So what do you think about combining the two and letting me take you both out this Sunday when I return from Canada?"

There was a long pause. "I don't know, Richard. Every summer, my friends and I go to Turtle Rock Farm to pick out Christmas trees. It's early, I know, but we have a bonfire at night and cook out and just make a day of it."

"Then how 'bout you let me tag along, so I can meet some of your friends at the same time?"

There was the same pause. "I'd love for you to come with me...I would. But Paige..."

"Let's just give it a try, Ab. I'll be on my best behavior. I promise. What do you say?"

"Okay," she finally said, "I'll have a talk with Paige tonight."

Just as they hung up, Rick jumped on the computer.

Abby,

I don't want to scare you, but you need to know: Everything is perfect when I'm with you. You make me nervous—and no one makes me nervous. And like I said, I'm more than okay with just talking. I really do want to get to know everything about you – your loves and dreams...

Rick oooxxx

Dearest Richard,

You always know exactly what to say, exactly what I am feeling. To me, you're perfect. Please know that I always want to be with you...but that I also need to ease Paige into this. It hasn't been all that long since her dad left the picture.

Me xxoxx

PS- I am really going to miss you while you're up in Canada. Have a great trip!

Abby made two cups of hot chocolate and asked Paige out to the front porch. "Babe," she said, "let me tell you about Richard Giles..."

Paige took a deep breath and fought desperately not to roll her eyes completely out of her head.

The following day, Rick sat at the hotel's computer terminal and smiled.

Abby,

It's a beautiful morning in Canada and though you may not see it, you are with me... and we're having a great time ...missing you.

Rick xo

PS- I haven't stopped thinking about you.

After a full night of tossing and turning, Rick headed south to Abby.

Hidden away in the sticks, Turtle Rock Farm wasn't the easiest place to find. Rick checked his watch. "Damn it!" He was late getting back from Canada and cursed himself for not leaving even earlier.

He parked his car and jumped out to stretch his cramped legs. He couldn't wait to see Abby's face.

It was a quaint farm with all the charm of age-old nostalgia. He stepped across the wood shavings toward the mouth of the big, red barn. Inside, a pair of swallows swooped from the rafters and made their escape. Rick ducked and then laughed, embarrassed by his over-reaction. He scanned the barn. There were no humans walking about, though there was plenty of life. The first pen housed two snorting pigs, one of them a massive sow, with a rooster perched upon the back rail. A young Billy goat, restrained by a long rope, performed gymnastics in the next stall. Rick reached out his hand to pet the cute animal when the goat's angry eyes warned him against it. He jumped back, and for the second time felt the fool. He scanned the area and let out a sigh. No one had been watching.

Through a band of brooding chickens and past the indifferent gaze of a silver-haired mutt, Rick made it to the back corrals where a stunning chestnut mare awaited his attention. As Rick patted her neck, he breathed deeply and smiled. Even through the stink of manure, he felt overjoyed. As he raked his fingers through the horse's thick mane, he spotted movement just beyond a small cluster of trees behind the barn. Through squinted eyes, he could make out a small band of people who were boarding the rear of a hayride trailer. The last to get on looked like Abby. He was sure of it, and rushed out after her.

The old green tractor was already steaming forward when Rick made it through the trees and shortened the distance between them. Just as he was starting to pant, Abby glanced back and saw him. As if it were Christmas, her eyes lit up and made Rick lose his already struggling breath. "Stop," she called out to the driver. "Stop. We've forgotten someone!"

As the tractor's brakes let out a squeal, Paige looked back and released her own moan of disapproval. She couldn't help it. All at once, her head was shaking and her eyes were rolling. *Why did he have to come and ruin everything?* she wondered.

Rick jumped into the back, almost into Abby's arms. They both laughed. Though they tried to restrain themselves, they sneaked a kiss before everyone. Paige thought she was going to be sick.

"Sorry I'm late," Rick whispered.

She gazed hard into his eyes. "You're just in time."

As the driver ground his way back into first gear, Abby called Paige over. "Come here, Babe," she said. "There's someone I want you to meet." Rick smiled and calmed himself for the big meeting. To everyone's surprise, Paige acted as if she'd never heard the request. She never budged. It was a terrible moment. Abby's embarrassed eyes stared at Paige; Paige's furious eyes glared back. Shaking her head, Abby finally turned to Rick. "I'm so sorry. Honestly, she's never acted like this."

"I understand," Rick said, and though he wanted to take Abby's hand he didn't. For the first time since they'd reunited, the bond between them seemed so inappropriate; so wrong.

"I'm so sorry," Abby repeated.

As the ride came to an end, Abby grabbed Paige's hand and dragged her off a distance, their heated words not trailing far behind them. Left with a group of people he'd only just met, Rick felt terrible, though not for himself. The conflict that his very presence caused had to be hard on both Abby and her daughter.

When the girls emerged from the battlefield, both wore painfully false smiles. Paige marched straight toward Rick and recited her coerced apology. "Mr. Giles, I'm sorry for the way I acted." Her eyes, however, told a very different story.

"It's fine," he said. "But call me Rick, okay?"

Before Paige marched off to face the rest of the sour day, she nodded. It was clear, though. It was going to be a very long time before she ever called him anything. Paige didn't hide her emotions all that well.

Rick approached Abby, smiling. She looked shame-faced. "Come on, now," he said, "it's okay, really it is. I guess we both should have expected it. Your daughter's obviously got a lot of mixed feelings right now."

Abby nodded, more from gratitude than empathy.

"Maybe I should just go…" Rick started.

"No!" Abby blurted and the conviction in her response could have been heard for miles. She stepped in closer and lowered her tone. "I know it isn't easy for Paige, but I can't let her decide this. Besides, I want you here, okay?"

Rick nodded and decided to stay.

Paige looked on with contempt. *I already hate him*, she thought.

Even through three games of volleyball, a beautiful picnic and a bonfire that could have warmed the coldest heart, Paige wore her scowl. Rick hung in there, though – even if his presence was used more as a teaching tool than the new guy just trying to fit in.

The following morning, Abby awoke with the sun and jumped on the computer:

> *Richard,*
> *When I saw you running toward me at the tree farm, I thought I was going to cry. Thank you for sharing such a beautiful day with me and my friends. And sorry about Paige's terrible behavior. It's still being addressed.*
> *Abby xxxxxxx*
> *PS- This weekend made me realize how lonely life is without you.*

> *Babe,*
> *Trust that I feel the same. In fact, I can't remember my life without you. Just imagining it makes me feel sick.*
> *Me ooooooo*
> *PS- And don't worry about Paige. She'll come around in time. Either that, or I've lost my touch altogether.* ☺

The email courtship continued for months, and it was the first time Rick ever gave thanks for technology. With life as hectic as it was, the instant messaging allowed them time together that they would have never had. Each time Rick heard "YOU'VE GOT MAIL," he was reborn. He'd finally discovered the love of a woman he thought he'd never find. And much of what he'd learned about the adult Abby was read from a computer monitor. Although she preferred that they wait to consummate their love, with Abby by his side life was still a constant state of excitement and wonder. He wasn't sure if she was trying to preserve the innocence they'd always shared, or if it was in consideration of Paige. He suspected it was a combination of the two. What he did know, however, was that a fire burned intensely between them; friction's heat generated from both sides. At this stage in life, some would have considered him a hopeless romantic. He liked to think of himself as more of a hopeful one. Getting Paige's approval, however, was the key.

Not everything in life was heavenly, though.

It was a Saturday morning. Rick stepped into Abby's living room to find her arguing with someone on the phone. "Over my dead body!" she finally screamed and slammed the phone into its cradle.

"You okay?" he asked.

She shook her head. "It was Patrick. He's playing his games again." Her eyes became wet with frustration.

Rick hurried to comfort her.

Abby's ex-husband Patrick was threatening to take sole custody of Paige. This, of course, was ludicrous. He had a better chance of surviving a day of skydiving without a parachute. Still, it was a legitimate threat and one that Abby was forced to deal with. She just didn't have the energy for all the fighting any more. She felt ill from it.

Even the thought of Patrick Soares taking custody of their ten-year old reached beyond criminal. His fatherhood failures were countless. Dating as far back as he and Abby's separation, he'd taken a painfully casual role in Paige's life. Weeks would pass when he wouldn't even phone his little girl, never mind visit with her. This sporadic interest in Paige changed only when he became involved in a new romantic relationship, one in which his daughter was able to fit nicely into the family portrait. Like the chameleon he was, he quickly took on the appearance of the "caring dad."

Due to Patrick's history of failed relationships, this reality proved dangerous. Without the family picture, there was no need for Paige. He'd proven that he could easily cast her aside when her presence didn't benefit his lifestyle. It didn't take a mathematician to solve the equation. Paige's interaction with her father was contingent upon the success of his newest relationship. This was a difficult plight for any girl who used her relationship with her dad as a lifetime template for interacting with other men.

His inconsistent style of fathering, easily defined as mentally and emotionally abusive, was the greatest potential danger that Paige faced in her pre-adolescent years. He was the poorest representation of good fathering imaginable. While the vast majority of men placed their children before themselves, Patrick and a handful like him made a bad name for dads everywhere.

One week, per Patrick's orders, Paige called him each consecutive day. He never answered, and he never returned her calls. On the weekend, though, when he called to say that he wouldn't be seeing her, he reprimanded Paige for not calling him and shifted the blame from himself onto his young daughter.

There was also a history of failures in other areas of Patrick's life: A felonious past involving run-ins with the law; his documented drinking history (much of it in the presence of his daughter); his lack of school and church involvement, and the list went on. Even with the honest testimony of loved ones and friends, he refused to take responsibility for a single stitch of the twisted web he wove.

Besides his complaints over the Department of Revenue increasing his child support, he claimed that Abby interfered with his visitation. In actuality, it was he who didn't take an active role. It was he who seldom showed. In one entire month, he visited with Paige for one entire hour. Everything else was more important. Still, he complained it was Abby. His entire existence rotated around false appearances.

After not hearing from him for weeks, Patrick called one Sunday and told Abby, "Some things have got to change!" A brief conversation revealed that he wanted to sign off on Paige as "a clean break;" that he couldn't go on and be happy with his new wife while strapped to the past. He then blamed Abby for this decision, adding, "Paige can make up her own mind when she's 18." He concluded that he'd break the news to Paige himself. Abby didn't argue.

But Patrick didn't break the news. In fact, he changed his mind, and sent a letter through his attorney stating that he "will be pursuing sole custody: In the interim, Abby should cease and desist from interfering in his visitation."

After all he'd done, he still had the gall to threaten to take Paige from her mother. The idea of sole custody was insane, but it was still a possibility.

Rick struggled not to interfere in their domestic strife. On the other hand, he wanted to be there for Abby. With Patrick's threats of physical violence, he knew something had to be done.

By Saturday afternoon, his answer showed up on Abby's front lawn. It was Patrick, drunk and prepared for battle. With Paige nowhere around, Rick hurried out to meet him. On his way, he pictured Mrs. Parson's disappointed face. He shook it off. Even Mrs. Parsons would understand this one.

Patrick was belligerent, but he wasn't expecting to face a man. Rick leaned into his ear. "It takes more than a sperm donor to be called dad," he said. "With all the men who would die to be with their kids, you're a disgrace."

Patrick swayed back and forth, but said nothing.

"How 'bout you try to break my nose now?" Rick said.

Again, the coward refused to respond.

"Don't worry about Paige," Rick finished, "she's fine." It wasn't the complete truth, but Patrick didn't have to know that.

Chapter 17

It wasn't long before Bill Stryker was admitted into the hospital.

He gave Eunice gift certificates to the ice cream parlor for enough black raspberry to treat a good-sized island. "Before they close up shop for the season," he explained.

She hugged him.

"I know you love black raspberry, but I won't be upset if you try a new flavor," he said. "Maybe life's too sweet not to?"

She smiled at his sincerity, but shook her head. "No," she said, "I've had enough ice cream for this lifetime." Life felt dark and cold for Eunice as she sat by her husband's deathbed.

Bill pulled off the oxygen mask. "I can still feel…"

She placed her finger to his dry lips. "Don't talk, my love," she said. "Save your strength now."

Even through the tremendous pain, his eyes sparkled at her. "I can still feel the warmth of your love on my face," he whispered. "For me, the sun will always rise and set on you."

"I love you so much," Eunice whimpered, "the thought of being without you…"

"You're not without me. Nothing could be more impossible. I'm just going home first." He kissed her. "Say your prayers, have sweet dreams and keep my name on your heart, okay?"

"Forever," she promised, and knelt by his side to weep.

"Don't cry," he said. "You'll always be my sunshine, and I know that as much as I've ever known anything." He searched her eyes. "Together forever, right?"

She nodded. "I can't say good-bye."

"Good," he said, "because there is no good-bye. Now go home and get some rest. I'll see you in the morning."

She kissed him with every ounce of the love she felt for him. "So long, my love," she whispered in his ear, "I'll see you in the morning."

The disease's appetite became voracious. It didn't take long.

Bill warned his family not to sit in the rocking chair that sat in the corner.

"Why?" Eunice asked.

"Mama comes to visit me now."

"Do you see her?" she asked, "Do you talk to her?" Everyone was curious whether the claim was the result of delirium, or other things unseen.

He shook his head. "I feel her presence. I'd know her in a crowded room...before I ever set eyes on her." A tired grin completed his explanation.

They believed. And while the family churned through their emotions, he lay there in his unbearable pain and smiled at things they couldn't see.

While Bill rewound his life and played it out, Eunice told him about the *whispers on the wind.* "We wait for great signs from the Lord; tornadoes and hurricanes and thunder. All the while, the Lord holds us safely in His bosom and whispers in our ear. We're too busy kicking and screaming to ever hear Him, though. If we could just learn to be still for a moment – that moment may be all we'll ever need to find the answers we seek; the peace He intended for us."

"I understand now," Bill said, "It's all in God's time, and if it's intended to happen then it'll happen, for sure." He shook his head. "To think back now...every moment I focused on what I thought was important, life was happening all around me, peripherally."

It was a beautiful experience the afternoon Bill passed over. He'd been suffering terribly and in the final moments of his life, he made an inexplicable peace with his own departure.

When he was ready to go, he awoke and scanned the room with eyes that were filled with love. As his lungs filled with fluid, the nurse hurried in to administer more morphine. She was stopped. It was already too late and everyone knew it. A circle formed around his bed; loved ones who shrouded him like angels. The room was enveloped in love, filled with a peaceful presence. There was nothing human or mortal about it. It was spiritual, inexplicable.

To everyone's surprise, his youngest daughter, Emma, begged him to stay; screamed for it, but her selfishness was overlooked. "We just started to share our lives again," she cried, "Please don't leave us now, Daddy!" But this experience was bigger than any one person in the room. Bill's other daughter, Isabella, kissed his emaciated face. "It's okay, Daddy," she told him, "Go in peace. We'll be together again soon."

In a weak, barely coherent voice, Bill called for Eunice.

She kneeled at his side and kissed him.

"Anything I haven't said, you have found in my eyes...yes?"

"Yes," Eunice whispered. "But I do have one question."

He searched her eyes.

"Will you finish it for me?" she asked.

"What?"

"The poem," she said, and then added a grin. "A Whisper Away?"

He returned the grin. "Yes – when I see you again."

Three precious moments later, he smiled a big smile and took a deep breath. He looked toward the ceiling and his smile grew wider. He took two more deep breaths, whispered, "Mama," and the tone on the heart monitor turned to one, cruel note.

Eunice could feel his presence brush against her as he ran into his mother's eternal arms. His entire family felt him leave and each of them cried for having been left behind.

In the end, Bill Stryker gave a wonderful gift: Death did not have to be darkness. It could be experienced in the light of love. It could be beautiful.

Besides a yacht-load of money, his greatest and final gift to his children was a video he'd made for each of them.

To Isabella, he admitted how sorry he was for everything he missed. "If I could live my life over, it would be as a poor man," he explained, "So I could enjoy your love; your company, your life. The money was a curse." He apologized for having failed her. "I should have been at every one of your dance recitals. Please forgive me for that."

Isabella began to cry.

"Though I missed your college graduation, I need you to know how proud I am of you – of the strong woman and the loving mother you've become."

Isabella wailed and convulsed, while the anger and the hurt and the rage poured out of her.

"I pray that you learn from my mistakes, Bella," he said. "Make sure that you capitalize on every second with my grandchildren; that you tell them each day that they're loved." He shook his head one last time. "And use the money to make your lives easier, not as an excuse to make everything more important than family."

To Emma, he confessed to the years of neglect; to the times he should have been there for her and wasn't. He stared straight at his baby girl and pleaded, "Please forgive me, Em. I was a stupid, stupid man. I never realized that I had everything – just by looking into the loving faces of you and your sister." He began to weep on screen.

Emma joined her father and couldn't stop. The rage she'd always felt was completely gone – replaced by a love that was deep and eternal. In that one moment in time, he was forgiven. And in that one moment, she and her sister were finally healed.

"I'll always love you," he said. "And know that I'll be looking after you."

"I love you, too, Daddy," she cried. "We all do."

As Eunice climbed the steps to her porch, a strange feeling caused her to pause. In the stillness, the wind chimes began to sing out. "Oh, God," she cried, and dropped to her old, brittle knees. She knew. Her soul mate had come to visit her one last time. She could feel him. Tears poured from her eyes. She stared at the wind chimes. "Leave the light on for me, Bill," she whimpered. The chimes went still.

With Abby by his side, Rick picked up his dad – and his terrier, Ray – at the bus station. While the old man collected his bags from the belly of the bus, Rick surprised himself and nearly jumped into his father's arms.

Jim dropped the bags and locked onto an extended embrace.

"Welcome home," Rick said.

"Same to you," Jim whispered.

Abby thought that her smile might actually break her face.

"I'm sorry I haven't called, Pop," Rick said.

His dad shook his head. "I suppose it's just a bad habit you got from me." He pushed him away to look into his son's eyes. "What do you say we both make a conscious effort to change that once and for all?"

As if he were ten years old, Rick tightened his grip and hugged his father without shame or regret. The dog looked up at them and whimpered for some of the attention.

As they walked back to the car, Jim spotted Abby and smiled.

"Remember Abby?" Rick asked, while taking his rightful place by her side.

"Of course I do." he answered, and kissed her on the cheek. "I always knew it."

Neither Rick nor Abby questioned the comment.

On the ride home, Jim questioned Abby about her life.

She explained her marriage.

"Sounds like you picked your dad," Jim said.

The man's candidness never ceased to take Abby aback. But he was right. It had taken years for her to realize that she didn't have to be treated unkindly. At least as an adult, the choice was hers. Her daughter, however, didn't have a choice, so she risked the great unknown as a single parent. Abby met his eyes. "True, but thankfully I grew up. And I'm going to make sure that my daughter doesn't follow the same example."

Jim nodded his approval.

"And you?" Abby asked. "Anyone special?"

He chuckled. "There was only one love in my life and I suppose I'll be seeing her again before too long." Peace and contentment radiated from his smile. "Nowadays, I'm devoted to helping young people who need me more." He nodded. "I work to feed my belly, but volunteer to feed my soul."

Abby searched his face. The man seemed truly happy.

Jim patted Rick's back. "God also gave me a beautiful son with whom I can share my life again, and for that I'm eternally grateful."

Rick wore his father's smile.

As they unloaded luggage from Rick's trunk, Jim turned to his son and whispered, "She really cares about you, you know."

"How do you know?"

"Because she looks at you the same way your mother looked at me." He put his arm on Rick's shoulder. "And trust me, son. It's a gaze that's inescapable."

When Rick and Abby arrived for the funeral, Rick introduced his new girlfriend. "Grandma, do you remember Abby?"

The old lady beamed. As destroyed as she was over losing her love, Eunice rushed past Rick, grabbed Abby's face and kissed it. "Welcome home, Girl," she said.

Abby felt completely embraced. With Grandma, family wasn't only a birth rite contingent upon a name or blood type. Family was chosen. There were no lines that needed to be crossed with Grandma. Abby was one of them, the woman's granddaughter, and always had been.

Eunice looked at Rick and then at Abby, and nodded. "You've both been caught," she said, "and there's no better path to take." Grandma was like a flashlight in the dark. Nothing could hide, certainly not the truth.

Abby turned to Rick. His face was glowing red.

While Grandma grabbed Abby's hand and headed for the kitchen, Rick took a small tour of his grandmother's house and realized he had inherited her sense of adventure and love of novelty. Even with all his success and money, it wasn't like he'd traveled all that much, or lived so well. It was she who was responsible for broadening his perspective of the world. She'd read to him and encouraged him to read. She'd taken him to see foreign films. She'd even cooked foreign foods – Thai and Indian – long before anyone else had tried them.

As he studied one trinket after the next, Rick noticed that the house was silent. For as long as he could recall, music played in every scene of his Grandma's life, defining her every mood. The soundtrack to her life was an eclectic collection of rhythms and harmonies and beats – diverse, rich, full. But now that she grieved Bill's death, there was no song that could capture her sorrow – no harmony to soothe her aching soul. He began to understand the depth of her pain and decided right then, *Life's too damned short!* While his girlfriend and Grandma spoke in private, he silently confirmed his commitment to Abby and her daughter.

Eunice poured two cups of tea and joined Abby at the kitchen table. Without warning, the old lady opened her soul. "I've had two husbands and loved them both. Strange as it may sound, they were timed perfectly in my life. Leonard, Richard's grandfather, showed up in the spring of my life. He was a good man, a great provider and a wonderful father for my son. He was easy going and kind, and I loved him dearly. Bill, on the other hand, arrived in the winter of my life, and even at his age he brought with him spontaneity, wonder and awe." She stacked her hands, right above left. "I'm looking forward to sharing both of their company, and I have a strange feeling that they're already getting along famously." She fought back the tears. "I have a poem waiting for me, you know."

Abby smiled. "Good for you," she said. Grandma's was not a wasted life. She'd made the most of her time.

"With Bill," Eunice went on, "life was whimsical and romantic; with Lenny, conservative. Either way, a deep love was felt." She paused and searched Abby's eyes. "As long as it serves both people, the conditions of love don't matter. My first marriage was exactly what I wanted; exactly what I needed at that point in my life, and had Lenny lived I'd still be happy with him. The love was no less real because there wasn't a great romance. In my experience, being best friends is most important. In fact, I think that liking a person and sharing a mutual respect is more important than anything else."

Abby nodded in agreement.

Eunice smiled. "But you and Richard have been blessed with the complete package." She nodded. "It's rare."

Abby's mouth hung open.

"I've learned that love has no age limit, no timetable – that Cupid works on a random schedule," Eunice said. "Living in each moment to the fullest, now that's a life worth living. And once love finds you the way it has, all you can do is count your blessings."

Abby couldn't have agreed more, but it wasn't just her anymore. "If only Paige didn't have such strong reservations," she said and was surprised that she'd said it.

Eunice got up and placed her teacup in the sink. As she passed Abby at the table, she placed her hand on her shoulder. "Love can thaw any heart," she whispered, "don't you ever doubt that." She smiled. "And don't waste any more time looking for something you already have."

Abby remained at the table, pondering the blunt woman's wisdom.

Eunice stopped at the door and spun on her heels. "And I'd like to start seeing you and Paige for Sunday dinner." Without a reply, she stepped out of the room.

Reverend Bousquet offered a beautiful parable at Bill's funeral. He said "A little squaw girl was very upset over the recent passing of her beloved Grandmother, and was having a difficult time understanding this new concept of death and its permanence. Dumbfounded, she approached her father, the tribal Chief, and tearfully asked, 'Father, what do people mean when they say Grandma died?'

"The wise man dropped to his knees and pulled his child to him. In a gentle tone, he explained, 'Many harvest moons ago, in this same village, Mother Earth breathed life into your grandmother's face and started her on her journey. On the very moment she awakened, the spirits of our ancestors opened her hand and offered her what we are all given at our journey's start; a handful of seeds equal to the number of buffalo on the open plains. Each day, like us all, she was required to drop one seed along her path. On the morning that she held the last seed in her hand, she looked back on her journey to discover that there was now a forest where the barren plains once lay. Knowing it was she who planted it all, she smiled, dropped her last seed and joined our ancestors to make room for another.'

"The little girl stared at her father and asked, 'But where is this forest?'

"The proud Chief swept his hand across the village. 'This is the great forest your grandmother has planted. You will find her spirit among its trees.' He was gesturing toward all the people that stood before he and his little girl.

"The girl glowed with delight. She finally understood. Because of her grandmother's life, much of the other life in the village existed.'"

The story was so wonderfully appropriate, the entire congregation wept.

Rick hadn't been there the afternoon Bill passed away and he never got the chance to tell his friend he loved him. As he wept in the pew, though, a feeling of serenity washed over him; a familiar comfort that could only be instilled by the kind man who'd so generously helped him find his way back home. Bill knew Rick's heart well enough. He knew Rick's gratitude. Rick looked toward the ceiling. *Thank you for helping me to remember who I am, Bill,* he thought, *And if you get a chance, tell my Mom I send my love.* Tears streamed down his face. He would miss their telephone conversations something terrible.

Rick felt someone squeeze his hand. He looked up at Abby and wiped his eyes. With Bill's help, he'd finally made it home...or so he thought.

As they shuffled out of the narrow pew, Abby looked back at Richard and it hit her. She and Richard were destined to love each other long after both their names were carved in granite.

Gray clouds sprinkled powdered sugar. An aesthetic dusting quickly turned into a thick white skin. Amid the howling winds and drifting snow, the weatherman's voice turned from friendly to concerned. Static, green blotches on his map promised a long night. Eunice pulled back the curtains. The car in her driveway was already covered and the street could have been located in Alaska. From a small, frozen square of glass, she scanned the neighborhood. Tree limbs sagged. Telephone lines threatened to snap. The mailbox had nearly disappeared, and the pretty falling snowflakes now looked like dangerously thrown snowballs. The scrape of the occasional snowplow, tearing corners from her lawn, sounded like fingernails across a chalkboard. Eunice could picture the patches of tar being peeled off the street, each pass of the truck creating potholes big enough to swim in. In New England, winters weren't so much about living as they were about basic survival. Each was a test of endurance. The older one got, the more clothes they layered on to combat it. Eunice shook her head, stepped out of the window and turned up the heat on the thermostat. Turning off the light, she went to bed.

The weather turned even angrier and began to hail, hurricane winds firing them at her bedroom window. In the distance, Eunice could make out the faint sound of wind chimes singing away. She smiled. "Goodnight, Bill," she whispered, and then hurried to meet him in her dreams.

Like all life's seasons, the pain of winter eventually thawed into the new hopes of spring. For the first time in months, Eunice passed the threshold of the front door and braved the memories of the porch. The rising sun was sitting flat on the horizon when she spotted it. Tears swelled in her eyes. Beneath she and Bill's bedroom window, a bunch of sunflowers were beginning to sprout. Shaking off a shiver, she hurried to them. Not even death could stop Bill from sending flowers. A small white envelope, wrapped in a plastic bag and tied in purple ribbon, was half stuck out of the ground. She bent slowly and willed her gnarled fingers to grab it. The card read: *I can still feel the warmth of your love on my face. Together forever, okay?*

Tears streamed down her wrinkled face. These, however, were not the tears of sorrow, or even joy. They were tears of love – eternal love. Bill had been right. She was never alone.

Chapter 18

Paige was an explorer just like her Mom, except the great outdoors didn't interest her in the least. She preferred to spend her free time sitting in front of a PC, surfing the web.

Abby stepped into the living room and caught Paige staring into the computer screen once again, hypnotized by the constant hum. "Go outside and play," she insisted.

As if she were busy sculpting the future, Paige barely acknowledged the request. "Okay, okay," she said. As her Mom left the room, Paige's eyes returned to the glare of the screen and a smile returned to her face. She toggled back to the small instant message screen and typed: *My Mom's in love with this guy Richard and I can't see why. He's nothing like my father.*

Paige never knew Captain Kangaroo, but was entertained by a goofy, purple dinosaur. E.T. was old, Ricky Martin was hot and Jewel was cool. Thanks to some litigious atheist, the pledge of allegiance and school prayer were no longer recited, or welcome in her morning routine. Raised in a world of automation, everything was remote controlled, computerized, or had some smart chip built into it. By the time she was eight, she could program a VCR. Technology wasn't frightening. It was just an aspect of life that you needed to keep up with, or you'd be left in the dust. For her, anything less than a Master's Degree would land her at the bottom of every hiring list.

The 1990's were a different time: Paige never played solitaire with a real deck of cards. She wanted a cell phone more than anything. She'd once sold Girl Scout Cookies via email. She chatted several times a day with a stranger from Uruguay, but hardly spoke to the other children in the neighborhood. And she only had one photo of her Mom; a screen saver on her computer.

In her generation, everything was easier – everything but dealing with parents who hated each other and a new guy who wouldn't leave her mother alone.

Abby kept close watch. The patience and love Rick showed her skeptical daughter bordered on saintly. Rick tried again and again, and continued to show love even when Paige didn't reciprocate.

To help thaw the thick layer of ice between them, Abby suggested that Rick give a presentation on writing poetry to a class of 23 sixth graders. *Maybe if she can see who he is for herself?* she thought.

Knowing that Paige really didn't want him there, he told her, "I promise I won't embarrass you."

Why couldn't you be a rapper instead of a stupid poet? Paige thought.

Rick stood behind a narrow lectern and nervously announced, "My name's Rick Giles." The words felt like they'd been sifted through cotton and he squirmed to get comfortable. "Sitting under the dim light of a desk lamp, the artist gazes down at a blank white-lined canvas. Searching his vocabulary for the exact phrase, the perfect opener, he begins to reveal his soul for all. With a loving hand, each word is delicately brushed into sequence, one after the next. After immeasurable hours of meticulous effort, the vivid details of the picture come to life. At last, he can smile, knowing that his portrait is complete. Although it will take more than a mere glance, the masterpiece must be appreciated through the mind's eye where the reader will be swept away by their unlimited imaginations, fond memories of the past and the journey which the artist has chosen to guide."

He looked up. They obviously hadn't expected the quick recital and were taken aback. He smiled. "I've been writing for many years now. In fact, even Paige's Mom, my best friend, doesn't know that I wrote my first poem in the fourth grade. And now I'm working on a collection of poetry that I hope to share with the world someday." He scanned his audience.

Paige's eyes were locked onto her desk, while the other children were even less impressed.

Rick swallowed hard and jumped right into the lesson. "Okay, what is poetry?" When there was no response, he answered, "It's a type of communication. In many literary circles it is considered the purest form of expression. For me, it's a place where I can take one idea, one feeling, and describe it in detail." He paused. "Do you guys know why most people don't like poetry?"

"Because it's hard to understand," a small voice called from the back.

Rick was grateful. "That's right! It's not easily understood unless dissected and analyzed. This is true because the poet conceals or hides the poem's meaning in a web of woven words." He grinned wide. "But I have good news…that's not my style."

Again, there was little reaction.

"Does poetry make money, bring fame or fortune?" he asked. When no one volunteered, he answered, "Hardly! Very few poets make money. But that's not what matters. Later in life, you'll find that besides needing it to pay bills, money's worth nothing but trouble. Trust me, you'll look back and value what you've accomplished so much more." As the words left his lips, he was more surprised than the kids. "For me, it'll be my writing and of course...my family."

Paige looked up and blushed.

Keeping to his promise, Rick never broke stride. "Not one of these things has brought in any kind of money. Yet, they're the things in my life that I value most. Most poets who make money do so posthumously – which means after they're dead."

Everyone laughed.

Rick shrugged. "Then why write it?" Before they even had a chance, he said, "There are thousands of reasons: To share ideas, to give back, to make somebody happy, to live on forever, to feel better yourself...to let people know that no one is ever alone. Many people wish to live on forever by becoming the voice of their generation." He paused. "Mostly, it connects the writer to other people. By taking the pictures he has in his head and placing them into the minds of others, there is a magical connection."

They looked confused.

"It's exciting to some people that their thoughts and ideas will live on long after they do. Ironically, most poetry is personal. It's based on feelings, whereas the poet is inspired to write his feelings down and capture them; feelings that change and may be different from one moment to the next. Knowing that, I'm not sure how much immortal value is placed on most pieces that are written."

They were now completely lost.

Rick almost laughed at the truth of it. "The reason I write poetry is to make a difference in the world, an impact, so when I complain about the world I can also say that I'm doing something about it. I write it to give back what others have given me. Writing poetry allows me to stand up and speak out. And even if only one person listens and finds that their life is better because of my writing, it was worth it."

He continued. "There are four major purposes for poetry: It tells a story. It presents a picture. It expresses an emotional experience. And it reflects on life." Searching their faces, he inquired, "Where can poetry be found?"

A freckled face girl wearing pig tails raised her hand. Rick called on her. "In Hallmark cards?"

"Excellent! And in the Bible, and in music, and pretty much everywhere else you can imagine." He reached beneath the podium and pressed *play* on the portable CD player. Accompanied by a techno beat, the musical group LFO sang their melodic rap, rhyming nicely as they sang.

The kids were ecstatic, and Rick sighed heavily. The teacher, however, didn't look as thrilled. Rick waited a few minutes before replacing LFO with Don McClain, and served the teacher a healthy slice of *American Pie*. The teacher nodded her approval. Rick now had them all.

He pressed *stop*, and asked, "What's the difference between good writing and great writing?"

Still, there was no response, but something was different. This time the reason the kids didn't answer was because they didn't know the answer, not because they didn't care. They were now sitting up straight.

He cut to the chase. "Good writers make people think, while great writers make their readers feel. Poetry should stimulate the imagination, touch the heart, bring strength, inspiration, laughter, and even tears." He shrugged. "So how do you get started?"

"At the beginning," the class clown answered.

While the other students laughed, Rick agreed. "You're absolutely right. Everything starts with an idea. I know a little more about poetry than you, but not much, believe me. The difference is – I practice, which is the only way to get good at anything." He scanned the room and noticed that Paige was no longer staring at her desk, but at him. He shot her a quick smile that only she could catch and kept going. "There are two major types of poetry. What are they?"

"Rhyming!" an anxious voice screamed out.

Rick went with the momentum. "Right. And also non-rhyming, or what we call prose."

They nodded.

He passed out a set of handouts. It was his poetry, both verse and prose. He intended to read each and ask their meanings. He needed to prove that poetry didn't have to be something that was mind numbing. "I wrote a poem that was inspired by an experience I had when I was your age. Do you guys want to hear it?"

"Yes!" the class sang in chorus.

He recited the first poem in Paige's direction.

"Roller Coaster

We stood in line afraid as hell
and heard those riding scream and yell.
The line grew long, no turning back.
We took off down the twisted track.

Holding on with all our might
we climbed a hill, no earth in sight
and at the top we held our breath,
then took a plunge that met with death.

Hairs on end and knuckles white,
we screamed like children with delight.
Accepting that without control,
we placed our faith: We'd come back whole.
So up and down, through loops and screws,
our hands reached for a sky so blue
and in our hearts the truth beat clear…
trust releases joy from fear."

Paige wondered whether her Mom was a part of that experience. Rick's mischievous smile confirmed her suspicions.

"The next poem is an example of prose," Rick said, "and it was written for my friend Danny's wedding. I was the best man and recited it as my toast. I framed a copy as part of my gift. He and his wife, Carol, still have it hanging on the wall in their living room." He cleared his throat.

Paige half-grinned. She had noticed it at Danny and Carol's house.

"Unity

There is a moth which flutters in the stomach,
searching for that light of love...
for which it is so desperately attracted.
Once discovered,
a greater gift cannot be found.
Alas, two hearts beat to the rhythm of one
beginning life's unpredictable waltz.
Together, taking the hand of the Lord,
they shall be led.
Forever placing each other before themselves,
their spirits glide across a ray of sunlight.
At times, the rain drowns out that gentle harmony,
causing one to stumble, the other fall.
Yet, with understanding and simple forgiveness,
the music never stops.
Throughout the song, constant joy proves unrealistic,
but whether each step is smooth or awkward

complete unity is all they will ever need.
As partners, their unconditional love
shall dance into eternity..."

They were hooked, so he alternated a few more between prose and verse. When he was done, he looked up to find Paige smiling at him. He felt like leaping. Even the smallest victories were cause for celebration. This one was huge. He swallowed hard, grinned back and completed his recital.

"A Walk in the Clouds

I walked amongst the clouds today
and then I took a seat
to try to understand the world
that spun beneath my feet.

It was the grandest picture
my eyes had ever seen.
I couldn't make out colors
except for blue and green.

And yet I could see people,
a whole race on the run.
To tell the truth, from where I sat
they clearly moved as one.

With fear, they searched for answers
they thought were on the ground.
And though they spoke in different tongues
they made the sweetest sound.

They had the wrong perspective,
with no way they could know:
There are no individuals,
but just parts of a whole.

And so I made a wish for them
that someday they would see:
Only when they really love
is when they're really free.

I'll dance amongst the stars tonight,
while others search in vain.
For just above their point of view
there's no such thing as pain."

The applause shocked him. He shut off the lights. "Get comfortable, close your eyes and take some deep breaths. This is supposed to be fun, not work."

Once the giggles subsided, they did as they were told.

"Now picture your favorite, safest, most comfortable place in the whole world. Take your time, but once you have it, open your eyes."

All eyes gradually returned to him. Paige's seesawed between hateful resentment and a secret growing admiration.

"Now, using what you've just experienced with all five senses, write this place down, describing it in prose and take your reader where you wish them to go."

"What if I can't?" a young boy asked.

"Can't?" Rick asked. "Now there's a word that should either be stricken from your vocabulary, or understood as nothing more than a challenge. You CAN DO ANYTHING that you put your mind to...ANYTHING!" He drew in a deep breath. "As long as you can speak, you can write. Rather than opening your mouth, use a pen. The words won't just drift off with the wind and become lost forever. Instead, you can write them down and stick them in a book where they'll live on forever."

The students were given fifteen minutes to play with their vocabularies and paint their pictures. Rick strolled through the classroom, checking on their progress, inspiring each with compliments as he passed each desk.

"Okay," he said, "next, I want you to close your eyes again and imagine an event that you've attended; a circus, an amusement park, whatever, and describe how it makes you feel. And, I want you to do it in free verse, or rhyming."

After this assignment was complete, he asked for two topics that he could tackle. The kids agreed. "The beach and keeping secrets."

"Great," he said. "So while you're finishing both your assignments at home, I'll be doing mine. And once we've all finished, perhaps your teacher, Ms. Willis, wouldn't mind putting them all together to create an anthology?"

The kind woman nodded and the kids were sincerely excited. They were now working on their first collection of poetry. They were going to have their own book.

As he gathered his things, he decided to leave them with one last nugget of wisdom. "Poetry cannot be taught," he said, "only inspired."

"Thank you," they sang in chorus.

"No," he replied. "Thank you...for inspiring me. You've reminded me of the many reasons that I write and I'll never forget you for it." He looked at Paige and smiled.

She wore the most mischievous grin. It was her mother's. And although it passed when their eyes met, it was definitely a glimpse of what could be.

As Rick walked out the door, Paige turned to her friend Carissa and whispered, "He's gonna destroy my life."

One week later, Rick sent his contributions to Ms. Willis' anthology:

A Secret

I asked the wisest man I know,
"The secret to life's joy?"
He grinned and said, "Remember...
you knew as just a boy.
The secret is not found in wealth
or successes that you chase.
Nor will you be content with fame,
applause that you might face.
It does not hide in titles,
or approvals from this world
and less than true euphoria
is gained from lovely girls.
As children share, I say to you:
Be kind each day you live...
for joy is just the offspring
of the souls who choose to give.

Low Tide At Dusk

Encased in a liquid-blue sky,
the sun flawlessly marks time.
Cotton-candy clouds race by,
while beams of orange and red
discover their final escape
and race to the icy water.

162

The sleeping sea, like a patient, old man,
hums a soothing tune.
Rocking in, then farther outward,
he cleanses himself, depositing
his filth on the surf's foamy edge.
Putrid smells of dead fish and crabs lure
flocks of seagulls for the bountiful feast.
Above broken shells,
they lazily spread their wings
and enjoy a free ride on the ruffling winds.
Landing on a carpet of bleached-white sand,
they forage at the sea's outer-reach.
Rocks, blanketed in seaweed, jut out,
as long blades of pale golden grass
sway in unison.
At this foundation of the world;
this cornerstone of eternity,
a salty mist is cast, creating a rainbow
before a burst of sunlight
and in the distance, that sun grows weary.
Slowly falling off, the stiff horizon
produces mystical shadows;
mere stains of the past,
while the moon is summoned,
as if turning on God's night light-
quelling the fears of the dark.
And once again, the sea begins to claim
the ancient boundaries that are his own.

In the end, while Paige was given her first memory of just she and Rick, he learned that he was more like his father than he'd ever imagined.

Chapter 19

Jim's volunteer work eventually overlapped the world of residential treatment for wayward children. It was more despicable than any state-run lock-up he'd ever visited. The privately run, church-backed residential homes brought in $80,000 per year for each child. Needless to say, there was a lot to lose if a child miraculously became "cured." Jim never knew one of the cash cows to return to its home pasture.

In this warehouse for throwaway kids, as witnessed through Jim's experienced eyes, each child's road out of hell was a sorrowful one. There were just so many that ended up on the fringes of society where they were seldom seen or heard.

It didn't look promising. After the failed foster care and intervening attempts by child psychologists and law enforcement officials, the silent cries of children who had become lost within our society remained. The real question became: *Is the public interested, or would they prefer to remain blissfully ignorant?* The probable answer looked just as bleak.

Scott was 14 years old when Jim met him. Trapped between boyhood and manhood, he was filled with a rage that caused his eyes to glitter. He'd been viciously molested by his uncle each time his mother was either too high to see anything, or out turning a dollar as a prostitute. With more tattoos than teeth, she earned more than most would have guessed. And while she was out peddling the family's goods, Uncle Raymond was home using Scott as an ashtray, a punching bag and worst of all – his own whore. The rusted wheels of justice ground slow. Long after permanent damage had been done, the Department of Children, Youth and Families, or DCYF, removed Scott from the house and placed him into the care of foster parents. The background investigation was brief.

Without actually being raped, Scott was abused and neglected in every sense of the words: mentally, emotionally, spiritually, and physically. His new parental guides felt it their responsibility to instill respect through strict discipline. In essence, they decided to feel good about themselves by playing savior in the poor boy's life. With a heavy hand, they strove to teach him the hard lessons of life. They longed to teach him all he'd missed and were zealous in their conquest. By this point, Scott didn't need lessons. He needed hugs. A test of wills commenced and Scott's pride would allow nothing less than a complete beating each time. As the fanatical hard liners set the rules, leaving no possibility for even the timid to abide, Scott's tormented spirit clashed violently with their rigid ways. As a result, he paid dearly.

"Things just aren't working," the foster parents eventually reported to the state officials. "We tried to provide a loving, nurturing home for Scott, but we're afraid he's beyond repair." Rolled eyes and heavy sighs escorted him off to the rear of another musty van. He'd failed more adults and could see the disappointment etched in their faces. No one bothered to look for the purple welts on his back.

The second foster family proved no better. Though they didn't "mess with him," to Scott's surprise sometimes he wished they had. Instead, they hardly noticed him. It was as if he wasn't even there. His purpose was clear. He helped pay the bills. This severe neglect lasted only as long as Scott would allow. When he couldn't take anymore, he took off into the streets and was reported a runaway. The shaking heads continued. "Maybe he is beyond repair?" the state officials questioned. One court trip later, he was placed into residential treatment where his "issues" could be effectively addressed and his attitude readjusted.

He received this tragic sentence, not because he failed, but because every adult he'd ever met had failed him – and miserably. He was now condemned to live with the young sex offenders, the drug pushers and the predators of his age group. He was now asked to find normalcy in a world where it didn't exist.

By the time Jim met him, Scott had some serious trust issues. He was done taking the abuse. As they say, he was at the point when the hunted had become the hunter. The only empowerment he'd ever observed was through pain afflicted on another. For the sake of self-preservation, he made the switch. He now preyed upon those he could. Without knowing his history, anyone would have despised him. Scott was vulgar, vicious and vile. He was everything you never wanted to witness in a child. "Bad wiring," some said. "Product of his environment," others claimed. Either way, Scott wore the labels and he suffered the consequences as such. He was to blame and he was to be punished. Jim, however, saw it another way.

It was a rainy Friday afternoon when Scott verbally pushed a counselor beyond return. He'd refused to go to group therapy. When the counselor, Bob, grabbed him by the shoulder, Scott threw the man into a wall.

Scott was publicly reprimanded. Unable to lose face, he threatened physical injury on the nervous, over-reactive Bob. Jim watched on in horror, afraid for him the way a mother is when she's running late to pick up a child who is waiting alone. It was clear from the start: Although Scott had no right to push a staff member, Bob had placed his hands on the boy first – advocating the brutal theory: *Do as I say and not as I do.* Counselor Bob was more worried about himself than the child who needed positive attention so much more.

Scott's behavior could never stand. He was ordered to report to the time-out room to process. He refused. Again, he was grabbed. "NO!" he screamed, and again he pulled back violently. Eventually, he headed off to his room and suited up for battle. He put on his watch cap, took off his shirt and stood at his door, feet squared and fists clenched tight. He was ready for combat.

The showdown lasted nearly an hour. No one budged. Staff didn't want to restrain him. He was only a kid. And Scott didn't want to jump. He wasn't stupid. So, there they stood, two feet – and one whole world – apart.

Jim could see the pain in Scott's face. The boy was dying inside. Rather than let go of the tears, though, he hissed and waited for the worse. What could they do to him that hadn't already been done anyway? Nothing!

The staff ended up jumping first and bundled him. Helplessly, Jim watched on as Scott fought, bucked and convulsed, squealing like a wild animal facing its death. Several adults pinned the boy, while others sat on his limbs to restrain him. It was awful. He was carried face down to the time out room and locked in.

Jim's time in the unit had expired and he started for the door. Among the heavy breathing, however, he heard Bob, the insulted councilor, cursing Scott's name. Jim stopped dead in his tracks.

"What's that?" he asked.

"That kid's an animal," Bob panted. "There's no helping him."

"Have you even tried?" Jim asked. From the look on the staff's faces, he had just overstayed his welcome.

"Screw him," Bob said.

"So, what you're saying is that you can't handle him, right? I mean, if you think about it, you're no different from the people who helped get him here."

Bob looked angry. They all did.

"Because you're failing him, too," Jim added.

Every staff member stood silent. Jim turned again for the door. As he grabbed the knob, he shrugged. "You folks still have time to help him." There was a long pause. "I mean...if he were your son, what would you want someone to do?"

After two years of volunteering his time, Jim was seriously starting to question his impact and considered calling it quits. But it wasn't to be. The mailman delivered a package that would change his heart forever.

He opened the thick envelope. Eric Denson, the night counselor at the Howland Detention Center, D.Y.S., had hosted an essay contest. The assignment: *Write one to two pages explaining how Jim Giles's presentation on adult incarceration has impacted your life.* He sent Jim copies of the end results. Through surprised, misty eyes, he read one wonderful example after the next:

...My fists were clenched tight of fear from Jim's horrific real life stories about life in state prison. He told stories about people getting raped, killed, and getting the crap kicked out of them and it made me scared to go to prison. Jim also taught us that we still have time to change our lives around...

...Jim's stories really made me think of all the stupid things I've done in my life. I hate the pain I've put on my family and friends. I'd like to thank Jim for inspiring me to change and believe in the power of hope.

There were 26 essays altogether, and each proved another lesson in hope. He finally got to the contest winner's touching piece. It was written by a loud-mouthed, 12 year-old named Raul. There were two ink stamps on the copy. One read: *I'm PROUD of YOU!* The other: *If you can DREAM IT, you can DO IT.* It read:

Well I never thought about jail like that until Jim came in. I always thought of jail totally different then what he said. I never thought that they had people with aids. After that group I started feeling sad just thinking about what my brother must of went through. All the things that I heard from Jim weren't so nice. He got to my head so good that it made me think twice about life. It made me think how my future is gonna end. Following my brothers path like I'm doing or get my shit straight. Jim whenever he comes back he will have my full attention again, cause this guy knows what he's doing. When he first walked in I thought that he was just another guy talking about things he knew nothing about. But he proved me wrong. He totaly blew my mind. Every body always told me about jail but I didn't care. I didn't think about it like Jim made me think about. I believed every word that came out of his mouth. He's worked there for a long time. I always told people that I'm not scared to go to jail. After this with Jim it realy had me thinking. I don't want to go be some place where I'm always watching my back, always worried about who wants to mess with me. I wouldn't make it in there. Always thinking about something. And if it comes down to a fight, you'll realy be in trouble cause you could get extra years in there. And me in the hole for two-three months, I'll go nuts. I don't wanna have that type of future. I have a loving family who is there for me. I got a little brother to look out for, and right now I'm not setting a good example for him. My older brother didn't set a good example for me and look what I'm doing. The same thing he was doing. He used to call home and regret that he chilled with his boys instead of listing to my mothers advice. But now its to late for him to chang. To me I think this group is realy helpful. It realy made me think twice about life. I already told my mother that I would not end up like him. I don't want to call my mother some day in the future when it is to late to turn back. That's why I have to make a chang in my life now that I'm young. Thanks Jim. The end.

Jim drew in a couple deep breaths, picked up the telephone and dialed. Eric Denson answered. "Eric, it's Jim Giles. I just wanted to thank you for sending along copies of those essays. I just got done reading them."

"You're very welcome, Jim."

"So…what did Raul win for placing first in the contest?"

There was a pause. Eric spoke softly. "From the look of his essay, I'd say his adult freedom."

Jim choked back the ball in his throat. "Let's hope."

Chapter 20

Weeks melted into months. It was Friday afternoon and the weekend was packed with hopeful plans.

Through the heat of the blurred road, Rick drove down the highway at 30 MPH. The air was as thick as pea soup, the humidity causing those around him to lose it. Not Rick. He was glad to be alive. He kept the radio off and his eyes on the winding road ahead. Traffic was syrupy, with most drivers frustrated and visibly angry over the crawl. Not Rick. He was thankful for the time to escape into his own world where everything was perfect.

He pictured Abby looking at him with eyes that could penetrate steel. Her grin made his knees knock, his heart skip a beat. He looked inward to realize he'd momentarily stopped breathing. He chuckled to himself and imagined diving back into Abby's eyes. Even to a blind man, she was the most beautiful creature on earth. She smelled as sweet as French toast and giggled like a cherub found in childhood dreams. Moreover, she loved him and was not shy about showing it. She was his reward for everything he'd done right in his life. She was heaven on earth and he felt blessed for every second he spent in her company.

He couldn't help it. He picked up his cell phone and dialed. "Hi, Babe."

"Oh, hi." Abby was clearly frustrated.

"What's the matter?" he asked.

"Nothing."

"Nothing? There's obviously something wrong. What is it?"

"Paige and I have been at each other's throats all day."

"About what?"

"Oh, I don't know, Richard…" She didn't intend to be sarcastic, but it was hard to believe that he was that oblivious to her every day reality. "Me, you…her dad."

Rick was quiet.

"Listen, Richard," she said, "I didn't mean to snap at you like that. I'm really looking forward to the weekend, but I need to go for now and spend some time with my daughter." There was a pause. "As much as she infuriates me at times, she can be right. There's a lot going on for her right now and I need to make sure that I'm there."

"Okay," Rick muttered, unsure of what else to say.

"I'll see you in the morning," she said and hung up.

Rick folded the phone and threw it onto the passenger's side seat. "Wow," he said aloud, "I didn't expect that."

Though it began on an awkward note, Saturday morning's whale watch eventually became everything it promised to be. Rick and Abby counted 13 humpbacks, while Paige remained silent and unusually clingy. On the ride home, they stopped for ice cream. Abby ordered coffee. Rick started laughing.

"What?" she asked.

"Coffee's my flavor, too."

"I'm not surprised."

While Rick handed Paige a double scoop of chocolate chip, Abby whispered, "You really are a wonderful man, Richard Giles," and stole a secret kiss.

"I don't know about that," he said, "but whenever I'm near you, I certainly feel that way."

Hearing this, Paige rolled her eyes and got back in the car.

Abby and Rick exchanged a glance and bottled their laughter.

For the rest of the ride, Rick tried talking with Paige. "So, did you like the whale watch?"

"Yep."

"We could try deep-sea fishing someday if you want to. That's a lot of fun, too."

"Yep."

Each question was met with a one-syllable answer. Abby was aggravated, but really couldn't say anything. Paige was more disinterested than rude. It didn't take long for Rick to conclude the cold interview.

He turned his attention to Abby and they talked about things of little significance. It didn't matter. Most times each knew what the other was thinking anyway. Perhaps it was more of a feeling, or connection – as if all people were parts of a whole and their pieces fit side-by-side. Rick had loved before, but he couldn't say it was just love that he felt for Abby. It was more than that. She was the only woman who'd ever walked the earth for him, and he worshipped her every step.

Paige stepped on the court for the final basketball game of the summer season. She scanned the bleachers for her dad. He wasn't there. He hadn't made a single game.

It was a tough two halves. Everything she shot, she missed. Her team's defense was weak. They got killed. As she moped off the court with her head hung low, Rick approached. "Great game!" he said.

She glared at him. "Yeah, right. I didn't even score."

"Yeah, but you took your shots and that's all that matters, right?"

As he walked away, Paige scanned the bleachers again and snickered. Her father couldn't make one game, while Rick hadn't stopped cheering at every one of them. It was bizarre.

Paige was sent to Danny and Carol's the following night, and she couldn't have been more pleased. "Thank God!" she mumbled. The new love connection was turning her stomach.

Per Rick's request, Abby donned an elegant dress and waited to be picked up. Rick was right on time. There was an old promise to keep.

As if she were Cinderella, herself, Abby stepped into a massive ballroom that looked very much like the one they'd peered into when they were kids. Goosebumps covered her body, while teardrops blurred her vision. It was a dream out of a long-forgotten time. "How did you know?" she asked, "I never said anything that day."

He smiled. "Maybe not in words, but your eyes screamed it. And I promised myself that if we ever got the chance…"

Abby jumped into his arms and kissed him.

They danced all night. By the last song, Abby leaned into his ear. "Explain to me how a man can sweep a woman off her feet two times in one lifetime?"

He kissed her and continued dancing long after the music had stopped.

The ride home was driven at a leisurely pace. The night was just too magical to come to an end. Abby rested her head on his shoulder.

"What a coincidence it was to see you at the party," Rick said.

She looked at him. "I don't believe in coincidences, Richard. Everything happens for a reason – even the smallest things – and that's why I bless the hardest, most painful day of my life."

He looked into her eyes.

"…because it helped lead me back to you."

He kissed her. "So you think we both had to go through everything we went through to be together?"

"Maybe it takes two broken hearts to make a whole one?" she said with a shrug and melted in his embrace.

That night, for the first time since childhood, Rick and Abby loved like they'd never been hurt. With honor intact, they cuddled and held each other close. As they lay in the arms of their soul mates, another set of verbal ping-pong commenced. "Tell me more about yourself?" Rick asked.

"Well, I've never put my hand inside a turkey or a chicken, and probably won't eat meat...except maybe a piece of General Tso's chicken once in a while because it's a million miles removed from meat. But if we host Christmas or Thanksgiving, someone else can bring the bird, right?"

He nodded.

"Or I can cook lasagna." She grinned. "Eggplant can be fun."

He kissed her.

"I love the children's book, *The Giving Tree*, and I'm a total sucker for anything to do with the ocean – especially sailing under the stars. I love collecting rare coins with Paige, as much as I hate sitting in traffic. I drink too much coffee, don't travel nearly enough and really enjoy singing out of tune. I'm always looking for ways to enrich other people's lives, including my own. I worship my daughter. And I wear PJ's to bed because they're my favorite clothes...unless I'm feeling totally in love and safe where clothes don't matter."

He moved closer to her.

"Let's see...I enjoy a good political debate and feel that everyone should be involved in one cause or another. I'm fascinated with the criminal justice system and would loved to have worked for the courts if I'd had the political connections." She finally stopped babbling and kissed him. "Enough," she said. "Now, your turn."

He smiled. "I hope that you make crazy love to me every day in your mind...until the day we can fulfill our every fantasy."

She grabbed his face. "Do you even know how totally in love and safe I feel when I'm with you; how happy I am that my heart never lied to me when I fell in love with you all those years ago?" She kissed him once and then – for the first time – stood to undress before him.

Rick swallowed hard. She was so beautiful. He rose to meet her.

Abby had always wanted her lover to have the guts to be himself completely with her; to be rough and romantic all at the same time. He would tell her that he had to be with her; that he just couldn't wait any longer, and he'd mean every word of it. They would spend just enough time romancing each other, building up the tension – playfully, innocently, powerfully, passionately. He would help her finish removing her clothes, and allow her to disrobe him. There would be a complete, sensuous exploration of one another, telling each other what turns them on; meeting every whim and desire, all night, all day; however long it took until they were both completely satiated – then some more after that. There would be a complete freedom between them – no holding back.

Rick had always imagined that he and his perfect lover would be connected in every way. She would know his wants and needs as well as he knew them, and she would trust him with her body and soul. As they met, her eyes would be hungry for him, causing his breathing to quicken. A sweet kiss would turn wet and passionate. Pressing against each other, their aroused bodies would dance to the silence until one article of clothing after the other dropped to the floor. With everything out in the open, his mouth would taste every inch of her body, lingering longer where her moans requested it. It would be impossible to remember where the foreplay ended and the lovemaking began. Moving to a rhythm that suited them both, their bodies would become one, and the rest of the world would simply go away. Hours would feel like minutes, as they offered each other everything they had. Before closing their eyes, one final jolt of excitement would surge between them; the mutual thought of doing it all over again.

Both Abby and Rick got exactly what they wanted.

When Abby awoke, she found Rick staring at her. "What is it?" she asked.

"I dreamed last night that I went to hell."

"Oh, no," she said, and sat up to hug him.

"It was terrible," he said, "there was music and dancing and laughter…"

She pulled away from him and smirked. "I thought you said you were in hell?"

"I was." He kissed her. "I couldn't find you."

She punched him. "Do you always say the right thing?"

"Try me."

Without hesitation, she asked about his ex-girlfriends.

And without hesitation, he answered honestly, but with kindness. Details that would make her feel bad were conveniently forgotten in the telling. He also reminded her, "Each previous failure at love was only in preparation for you." He was sure to throw that in. She searched his eyes for the truth, but didn't need to look far. She was an avid reader and he was an open book written just for her. She hugged him for his kindness.

"Last question," she said.

"Shoot."

"What's the one thing you miss most about your first love."

"The loss of innocence," he quickly replied.

She nodded.

"But do you want to know the one thing I still love about my first love?"

She nodded, reluctantly.

"She's finally returned to me," he whispered and got dressed to make his escape before Paige returned home. Rick was learning quickly. This woman thing wasn't so hard after all. The trick to being successful in a relationship was awareness; understanding that you're not the only one with feelings. As long as he placed Abby before himself each day – and she did the same – then a happier life could not be found.

It was actually quite simple. To give Abby everything, he only had to give himself. He only had to treat her as though she were the only woman who had ever – and would ever – walk the earth. That was all.

Besides Paige's disapproval, the most difficult part of their relationship became the desire to hibernate and shut out the rest of the world.

It wasn't long before Danny called Rick. "Carol wants to head north the weekend after next to see the changing foliage. And for whatever reason she wants you and Abby to come along."

Rick chuckled. "I don't know…"

"But I do," Danny interrupted. "You're coming."

The next thing Rick heard was a dial tone.

After eating at one of the gluttonous country buffets, Rick and Abby, and Danny and Carol strolled along the shopping center to walk off the calories.

Abby and Carol lagged behind their men, happy for the privacy and the picturesque groves of multi-colored trees. Arm-in-arm, the girl's walked and spoke in hushed tones.

Danny cleared his throat. "I gotta tell you, Buddy," he said, "she's definitely the one for you."

Rick looked back at the girls and lowered his tone. "I know. Any advice on how to make it last forever?"

"The way I see it, any relationship can succeed when the sun is shining. But to be honest, I really can't imagine sharing my failures and moments of shame with anyone other than Carol. Even the pain I suffer over my sons, I share with Carol. To me, that's true love…just being there for each other when it's raining."

Rick looked back at Abby and remembered the Woolworth's bag. He grinned. Her eyes sparkled at the sight of him.

"If only Paige wasn't so difficult all the time." Rick said.

Danny glared at his friend. "Difficult or not, I wish my children were a constant in my life."

"But you don't understand, Buddy," Rick explained, "Paige is real tough."

"And I wonder why?" Danny asked. But before Rick could take a stab at it, Danny went on. "My boys have had a lot of trouble acting out because I haven't been able to be in their lives 24/7, and I'm a good guy. Can you imagine if I acted like Abby's ex-husband?" He shook his head. "Of course it's tough. Our job as parents is more important than just being a friend. Our job is to teach."

Rick started to nod when Danny hammered it home. "You have the greatest opportunity for happiness right in front of you. What I wouldn't give to add to some little girl's life…"

Rick began to nod again when Danny stopped and faced him. "It's not just about you anymore, Rick. It's about you and Abby – and especially Paige. Whatever you do, don't ever use that kid as an excuse to let your relationship with Abby fail. Maybe it's time to step up to the plate once and for all?"

Rick finished his nod, and made a silent commitment to do just that.

Two steps later, all four friends were standing in front of a small independent toy store. Danny swung open the door. The ladies stepped in first.

The store was a museum of sorts, its toys reminiscent of their childhood treasures on Freedom Ave. There were few electronic gadgets and no video games. Instead, outdated dolls and board games filled the shelves, toys that got lost in the corners of bigger franchise stores. Danny grabbed a GI Joe doll and yelled across the floor. "This is the only thing my brother and I played with when we were kids. We even had the command center!" For a man his age, there was way too much excitement in his voice. No one gave him a second look, though. Rather, they pawed through the unique inventory of Raggedy Anne dolls and Lincoln Log sets, painting mental images of a kinder time when their imaginations created reality. They joked and laughed, and each shopped privately for a time until running over to one another, anxious to share some memory that had been locked away for years.

They stayed much longer than they'd intended.

As Danny reached the counter, he found Abby checking out. For too many reasons to list, he looked over at his love Carol and felt overwhelmed with joy. She was still shopping. He decided to have one last laugh in the place.

Danny placed his goodies on the counter, winked at Abby, and then addressed the clerk. "Excuse me," he whispered and gestured toward Abby. "My wife and I don't want any problems, but…"

She caught it and braced herself. Danny was such a prankster, she didn't know what to expect.

"But do you see that woman over there?" he asked, pointing at Carol. The clerk nodded.

He leaned in even closer. "Well, I don't know what your policy is on shoplifting, but I think it's incredibly unfair that my wife and I have to pay, while that woman feels free to take whatever she wants by sneaking it into her purse."

The young clerk looked sick, but her eyes never left Carol. As she tried to quietly summons the store's manager, Carol approached the counter, completely unaware of the ongoing gag. Excited, she asked Danny and Abby, "How'd you guys make out?"

Danny acted as if he didn't even know her and was quite convincing. "Listen," he said, grabbing Abby's arm, "my wife and I don't want any problems. We just want to pay for our toys and leave, okay?"

"What?" Carol asked, stunned.

"Please," Danny squealed, "We just came in for a few things. We're not looking for trouble!"

Carol looked to her friend for an explanation. Abby was fighting desperately not to laugh. She was bent at the waist and felt like she might actually wet herself. Carol glanced up at the clerk behind the counter. The girl was terrified.

The manager approached, cautiously. "Excuse me, Miss," he said to Carol. "There's no need for a scene, but we know that you've taken some things that you may have forgotten to pay for. If you'll just remove them from your purse…"

Carol exploded. "I what?!"

Danny and Abby gathered their things and hurried hand-in-hand out of the store. When they hit the door, Danny looked over his shoulder one last time. There was terror in his eyes. It was as if he was sincerely frightened of Carol. "Thief!" he hissed, and pushed Abby out the door.

Carol finally understood.

Laughing hysterically, Danny and Abby watched the rest of the prank unfold from the safety of a window. Even Rick stood off in the shadows. His swaying silhouette was busting a gut at Carol's expense, too.

Carol tried to explain, but the manager was convinced she had stolen from him. Humbly, she opened her purse and allowed him a long look. There was nothing there.

The man apologized and offered a consolation discount. He then walked away scratching his head.

Carol stormed out of the store with her bag in hand. Danny and Abby were waiting, their faces serious again.

"So, what did you end up buying, Princess?" Danny asked his furious lover.

While Rick and Abby held each other, laughing, Carol chased Danny around the parking lot for a solid five minutes.

"But I got you the discount," he kept yelling back, winded from his desperate effort to get away.

Rick turned to Abby. "Can you imagine not sharing our lives with these crazy people?"

Abby tightened her grip on his waist. "No," she said through the laughter, "and I can't imagine not sharing my life with you, either."

Rick finally understood his father's undying love for his mother.

They kissed well past the friendly complaints of Danny and Carol.

Chapter 21

Rick had just hung a tire swing from the willow tree's thickest branch and was walking back to the house when Abby met him on the deck. It was the same swing she had in her yard when they were kids. "She'll love it," Abby said, referring to Paige.

Rick walked straight into her arms. "I was hoping you would," he teased and gave her a kiss.

It was the last day of September when Rick, Abby and Paige were forced to endure a New England hurricane together. *So much for camping in the back yard*, Paige thought. Slamming doors and boarded windows awaited the flashfloods that were promised. Emergency supplies were taken out of storage. Rick took care of the exterior of Abby's house, while she readied everything inside. As the heavy winds and battering rains threatened to huff and puff and blow the house off its foundation, they prepared to wait it out.

BANG!

The lights went out. While Paige jumped out of her skin, Rick hurried to the window. The rain lapped at the glass where everything lost its outline. Squinting, Rick saw that a telephone pole had snapped in half and fallen to the wet street in sparks. The power was out and probably would be for the night. Milk, bread, water, batteries and candles had been stockpiled. Abby had also drawn buckets of water for bathing and flushing the toilet. There was nothing more to do. The world had slowed down just enough to give everyone the chance to catch up. They were wonderfully trapped.

Abby and Rick exchanged a smile. They were thinking the same thing. *It's the perfect opportunity to get acquainted.* Abby grabbed the Monopoly game from the hall closet and settled back into the candle-lit living room. "Let's play," she said.

Paige had just passed *GO* and collected her pink $200 bill when Rick turned on the battery-operated, transistor radio. The weatherman's voice was now high-pitched. "Stay off the streets," he warned with a sense of urgency. Each of them smiled. There would be no school or work. Life was good, and if only for the moment Paige forgot about her burning animosity for Rick. They returned to the game and some lucrative real estate deals.

After hours of laughter and actual conversation, Paige pulled an afghan under her chin and closed her eyes. Abby foreclosed on the last of Rick's property and claimed a landslide victory. As the first snore announced that Paige was out for the night, Rick and Abby cuddled on the couch. It turned out to be one of the best days they'd ever enjoyed.

In the morning, the neighborhood peeked its collective head out each front door. Snapped limbs and hanging shutters were plenty proof that Mother Nature had pulled a terrible tantrum. The lawns and street resembled a war zone and the aftermath was humbling. Debris lay everywhere. Abby walked to the back deck and looked out. Trees were toppled and power lines were downed. The willow tree out back, however, still stood strong. The dangerous, rotten limb that was hanging had been cleanly amputated, but other than that she'd bent and adjusted just enough to survive. Mother Nature was a wise woman. She was merely doing her fall cleaning. Abby smiled. The tire swing was still blowing in the breeze.

Rick turned to Paige. "At least your swing made it."

But the storm was over and Paige had already returned to treating him like the invisible man. Without a word, she ignored his comment and started back toward her room.

Abby snapped. "We talked about this!" she screamed, no longer concerned that Rick was looking on. "You don't have to like him, but you will show him respect!"

Everyone froze in place.

Paige nodded once and slowly turned to Rick. "Sorry, Mr. Giles," she said and continued on to her room.

Rick stood frozen.

Frustrated and hurt, Abby collapsed onto the couch and started to cry. It was so difficult to balance it all. Paige was definitely priority one, but if she decided for them both then Abby would be destined to spend her life alone – long after Paige was grown and gone.

Rick took a seat beside her and held her hand. There was no need for words.

Through her own persistent prodding, Paige was finally allowed to spend a whole weekend at Danny and Carol's. Everyone was thrilled.

Rick and Abby never wasted a minute. Late Saturday morning, they took a leisurely walk in the park and talked. In the afternoon, they took a long ride for the season's last ice cream and talked. That night, after Rick had served a giant bowl of macaroni and cheese to Abby, they finished their after dinner cocktails at an outside café that played live acoustical music, and they talked. That was the thing. They talked about everything and nothing at all. Grandma was right: "One brief moment in love was worth more than a decade wandering aimlessly in solitude."

Equally beautiful was that conversation wasn't necessary between them. Even in the silence, Abby reminded Rick of who he was. Though some of his values might have become twisted in his pursuit of success, he'd been raised right and had all the morals needed to be genuinely good. Wealth and power was one thing, but when you got right down to it everything he'd learned as a child was everything he ever needed to know: Don't fight, use your manners, share, be kind to others, don't tattle-tale. This was Abby's first and greatest gift to him – a constant picture of himself as a child; a reminder of who he was. *I suppose no one can fool himself before another who truly knows him,* he thought.

Abby felt such passion, such intensity for Rick, that her feelings scared her as much as they brought hope and excitement. In order to experience everything, though, she knew she'd have to risk everything. She'd never been faced with such a decision. With a deep breath, she decided to jump. The rest was in the hands of God.

Together, they enjoyed the thrilling novelty of a new relationship with someone who felt as comfortable as a worn pair of slippers.

As if making up for all the years they'd missed, they engaged in another entire night of passionate lovemaking, not worrying how loud they might be. These first few times felt like an opportunity to live out the fantasies that their past lives had never allowed. But it was more than a few, short-lived opportunities. It was the start of a hot and steamy romance that didn't have to end. Fortunately, both Rick and Abby had gotten enough sleep in their previous lives. It was now time to play.

As their naked bodies lay intertwined, exhausted and grateful, Abby traced the fishhook scar on Rick's forearm with her finger. She remembered the awful day the truck had hit him and could feel a pang of anxiety from it. She studied the long scar and was surprised as her emotions shifted from sorrow to envy. Her childhood scars were invisible. Her scars ran deep and were harder to get over.

"Tell me one of your most profound memories of childhood," she whispered, "And it has to be one that doesn't include me."

He thought for a moment. "My dad once recited a poem called *A Poor Man* at my Mom's grave. It was all about loving her without ever having to spend a penny. I remember disagreeing with him at the time, thinking that there had to be more to give." He shook his head. "It took years, but I finally understand my father's quest. Today, that poem is the truest, most beautiful thing I've ever heard. To think I've spent my life pursuing wealth. It certainly wasn't from my father's teaching."

"Your dad gave you some wonderful gifts," Abby said.

Rick nodded. "He sure did. And the greatest of them was his high expectations for my life. The old man expected me to be a great man, and at an early age I adopted those same expectations for myself." He kissed Abby. "And it looks like you showed up just in time to make sure I make that happen."

She returned the kiss and realized that Rick was happy because of his Dad, while she was happy in spite of hers.

"And there's something else I should tell you," he said, "something I'm not so proud of." The need to confess had clawed at his soul for so very long.

"Oh?" she asked, and smiled as if she knew what he was going to say before he said it.

"We didn't leave Freedom Ave because my father got promoted. We moved because my mother's hospital bills broke my family and my dad couldn't afford to keep the house."

She nodded. "My Ma figured as much, and said so a few months after you left." Her nonchalant response took Rick by surprise.

He shook his head. "It's amazing how ashamed I was of that back then…how I've felt even more ashamed for hiding it all these years."

Abby kissed him. "You're forgiven," she teased. "Now get over it."

"Fair enough," he chuckled and his eyes ventured off for a moment. "Those were the days on Freedom Ave."

Abby nodded, but picturing her Ma's purple, swollen eye, she wasn't so sure she agreed.

"Now you," Rick said, "tell me something about your childhood that I don't already know?"

She didn't need time to think. There were so many. "A few months after you moved away, my dad took me to George's Hot Dogs in town for a late dinner. As usual, he was drunk and the place was packed. No sooner did we sit down to eat when some guy got thrown through the screen door, his enemy right behind him to finish the pummeling. Annihilated, my dad looked across the table at me and screamed, 'Don't tell me you're afraid?'

"I said nothing, but silently begged for his silence.

"My father then stood up and pointed around. 'Don't ever be afraid of people like these,' he screeched. All eyes were on him. 'They're all drunks,' he yelled.

"'Please, Dad,' I begged, but he didn't listen."

Rick held her tight.

"And then I watched my father get the worst beating imaginable," she said and began to share years of unshed tears.

"I'm so sorry," Rick whispered.

"But I wasn't," Abby whimpered, "and that's the point." Tears rolled down her face. The rest played out in sobs. "I knew I'd have nothing to do with my family when I got old enough to escape, and I was happy it happened. I was happy that someone bigger and stronger than my father could punish him like that." As her eyes filled, she shook her head in shame. "And then I chose the same type of father for my poor daughter." She shook her head again. "Men."

Rick pulled her head to his lips and kissed it. "Hey, not all men are like your dad or your ex-husband, you know."

"I know," she whispered, and returned the kiss to his hand. "My Grampa wasn't."

Rick kissed the teardrop from her face. "I don't remember much about him. What was he like?"

Abby's watery eyes drifted off to a better place. "Mom said my Grampa – her dad – was a tough man. To me, he walked on water.

"He had one brown eye and the other was blue – 'just like a rabbit,' he'd say. He drank shots of Mylanta to soothe the years that he'd wrestled with the bottle and lost...a family tradition. He walked slow and easy, but with purpose. He had an enormous nose and a ring of hair that surrounded his head, with the center completely bald. 'You're my best girl,' he'd say with a toothless smile and everything inside me heated up when I saw him. I loved this man unlike anyone I'd ever loved before. My Mom used to say, 'In everyone's life, there's that one special person you connect with.' For me, it was my Grampa. When I think back on it now, I believe this is true because his love for me was unconditional.

"Before our afternoon naps, I would lay on his large, round belly and be rocked to the rise and fall of his relaxed breathing, hypnotized by his distinct smell.

"He liked country music and sometimes grabbed my Grandma and spun her in circles in the kitchen. He couldn't dance for beans, but his playful spirit made it look like they glided on air.

"He was the greatest storyteller and spoke about his childhood in vivid detail. He never held back and got excited when he relayed the many pictures in his head. In my twisted childhood, he was the only real thing I could depend on. Once he even told me a poem about a pelican. 'A beautiful bird called a pelican. Its beak can hold more than its belly can. Food for a week, it would hold in its beak. And I can't see how the hell it can.' I couldn't stop laughing. Grampa was hardly the authority figure.

"He worked for the town, and they said that each morning he took whiskey and warm water in a thermos. He was 'a drunk,' but I never knew him like that. For me, he wore a halo.

"He never squealed, ever. Even at an early age, I appreciated his discretion and understood that not everyone was this way. We had our secrets: Grandma's cooking was horrendous. I sometimes acted up.

"He liked to go for long rides in the car on Sunday, and ate more vanilla ice cream than anyone I've ever known.

"Grampa was a clown. The only photo I have of him is with my hooded sweatshirt draped on his head like a real-life super hero. From the look on our smiling faces, it's easy to tell we were best of friends.

"He created the tastiest clam boil from his huge copper pot and would sit quietly sometimes, staring out the kitchen window and way beyond whatever lay in the yard. I suppose he was a dreamer and I realized young that I adopted this trait from him.

"He loved animals. When he fed his rabbits, he talked to them. When the chickens weren't laying eggs, he'd scold them like a father.

"People nicknamed him 'Fat' when he was a boy and the name stuck. He played checkers with skill, and when he was younger they said he could arm wrestle with the best of them.

"We took long walks and had longer talks, and even at my young, stupid age, he really listened to what I had to say. He was interested and it made me feel important. It made me feel the way he wanted me to – good.

"I listened to him, too, but never understood the value of his simple wisdom until later in life.

"The old Yankee wore overalls and work boots, with a cloth cap to match. He took me to R&S Variety for 'snacks' and slipped me an allowance that my dad wouldn't have appreciated. When I was small, he was there Christmas Eve, Easter morning and every other important day."

She paused to juggle the lump in her throat.

Rick stroked her arm.

"He suffered a heart attack one year, but as he said, 'the good Lord let us keep him for a spell.' Not long after, he had a massive stroke. The left side of his body was completely paralyzed. We went to see him in the hospital. Nothing before or since has bothered me more. He'd become skinny, almost transparent. When he spotted me, he tried to smile, but only half his face would allow it. I wept hard and he, himself, comforted me at my time of sorrow. When we left that day, I kissed him hard, and told him that I loved him. In his embrace, he said the same. I told my mom I couldn't see him like that again, confined to a wheelchair and withering away. Grampa was a man who strolled the yard, tending after his rabbits and chickens. He wasn't someone who smelled of rubbing alcohol. It was the first time my mom treated me like an adult and respected my wishes.

"Grampa died on a dark day in spring. At the funeral, I stayed strong in the face of family and friends. When we returned home, though, I remember changing clothes and running off into the woods to cry. I wept until it felt like an elephant was standing on my chest. I'd lost my best friend.

"Maybe a year later, I remember being dragged into town, so my Ma could do the grocery shopping for the week. Me and Dad sat in the hot Duster and listened to his God-awful country music. It was hell. Staring at the barbershop pole in the center of town, I pictured sitting on my Grampa's shoulders to watch the fourth of July parade. And I remember that my eyes filled with tears. Suddenly, I turned to find my father staring at me in the rear-view mirror. By sheer will, I pushed my feelings for my Grampa down deep – so deep that my father would never see them.

"I suppose I didn't just love my Grampa, I adored him and I still can't think about him without being emotionally moved.

"My Mom was right. Of all the people I've known in this world, Grampa has had the most profound and long-lasting impact. I just wish I could tell you why."

Rick chuckled and wrapped his arms around her.

But he was a drunk, Abby thought, *and the template my mother used for her terrible marriage.* Abby considered her mother's sacrifice and finally understood. There was no escape for an abused woman back then; no support for a single Mom. Her Ma had made the best decisions she could under the circumstances of her time. *Ma gave up her entire life for me!*

In the quiet, Rick hugged her tight.

She studied Rick's gentle face. *This man is the greatest gift I could ever give my daughter – the perfect example. With him, love is kind and generous, affectionate – not argumentative, cruel and abusive.* She initiated another round of lovemaking.

When Abby awoke, Rick was gone. On his pillow, a simple poem remained:

Family

Born into the world,
she would outgrow her youth
and adopt a family of no resemblance.
Thicker than any bloodline,
the family of her lifelong love would become her own.
Learning to view the world through her heart
and not the eyes of blindness

she would finally discover: That in the deepest darkness,
a positive light could be found.
Starting toward the dreams of tomorrow,
she would be eternally grateful for the present;
a gift of each new day.
In the end, a last name or heritage would prove
meaningless, but the love of those she called her own
would be her family.

Abby wept for his understanding, his generosity and most of all – his love. *If only all men could be as sincere*, she thought.

Chapter 22

When Vicki demanded a legitimate answer for their break-up, Grant was forced to spend a few extra days convincing her that she should bear no responsibility. "It's not you," he vowed again and again, "It's me. I'm just not ready."

She finally sent him an email. It was her first and last. *You missed out,* she wrote.

I know, he replied.

But you don't. You have no idea, she concluded and was gone forever.

Grant shook it off with a laugh. There were a million Vicki's out there.

Jodi was Grant's next victim. Even at ten years his junior, she understood more about life than he ever would.

Grant's cell phone rang. He picked up. "Yeeellow?"

"Please don't say anything until I finish, Grant," Jodi said. "Just hear me out."

"Okay," he said, while his grin threatened to consume his entire face.

"I am trying really hard to keep myself in check and not let myself get too carried away with you," she said. "As I told you before, I'm sure the day will come that it becomes much too difficult for me to hang out in the shadows. There are many things that I wish I could share with you already but I know that I can't. It's not easy, but I really am trying to keep things in perspective. I know you can't make me any promises, and I understand, but it's not easy for me. I miss you and wish that I could be with you the way I want. I'm sure it'll be worth the wait. I certainly hope I'm not putting any pressure on you. That's not my intention. On the other hand, I'm not so sure it won't get too difficult for either of us to continue. Who knows? I'm just trying to follow my heart, and believe that we will have a chance. We have to."

Grant was smooth. "There's no pressure," he replied. "Trust me, I appreciate the openness between us, and all the truth that we've shared. As I said before, one of my biggest fears is that because the timing is off right now...that something might happen that will jeopardize our future. So I hold back, knowing that the time just isn't right for us…not yet, anyway. I don't want you to feel anything that isn't true…like I'm not moving quick enough because I don't believe in us enough, or things like that. There's so much more to it than that. I don't want to ruin what could be…just because I might not be ready for it yet." His words sounded more sincere than anything he'd ever fabricated. No matter how intense or complicated the game, he was going to keep his eyes on the prize.

Several days later, his cell phone rang out again. "Yeeellow?"

It was Jodi. "I knew right away that this thing between us would become impossible for a bunch of reasons."

His mind spiraled out of control to gather the right words for the 'save.'

"The feelings between us are too strong to just be physical," she explained. "I've never cheated with anyone and pride myself on it. If the opportunity ever did arise where you and I could start to see each other again, I would never want you to question who I am, or have me do the same." She paused for air. "What's most important to me is that you and I remain good friends. Temptation is very strong, though, and also pretty dangerous. You're so sexy."

Grant sighed. "What a shame that this special connection we share will be wasted. I've given it a lot of thought, and I want you to know that I've never lied to you…and don't plan to now. Maybe it's just a matter of timing? Torn isn't even the word for this. The last thing I want is to hurt either of us."

"We've both learned that life can change dramatically," she said, "I don't see the attraction or feelings between us changing, do you?"

Grant smiled over the last-minute 'save.' "I do wish some things were different," he said, "that way certain things wouldn't be so difficult. Time will tell. I'm ready for you and wish you were here right now. As I said…the kiss…that was something I couldn't help. You're not just a woman I know, or met…you're someone I care about, even though we're not sure the timing is right for us now. But listen, I gotta run for now. We'll talk later." As he hung up, he started to whistle. She was his for the taking.

Nothing, however, could have ever prepared him for her final correspondence.

Carmen was sifting through the pile of mail when she happened upon a letter addressed to Grant. She checked the return address. It was from some strange female. Detecting the scent of perfume, she shook her drowsy head, tore open the envelope and read:

Dearest Grant,

Although it was much too brief, I truly enjoyed our time together. I loved being with you and can't begin to explain how incredible your lips felt on mine and how awesome it was to be in your arms. I'm sorry if I was too pushy with you. It's just that I want to be with you more than anything and to share everything with you. I want you to make love to me for hours under the stars until rays of sunshine take away every bit of darkness. I can't help the way that I feel for you and I have had trouble stifling my insatiable desires.

What I am not sure of is this: Where do we go from here? I wish it could be a fairytale. That you would throw everything you need into a suitcase and come to me, sweep me off my feet and promise me that we'll be okay, forever. Though you've made it clear that it won't happen that way, a girl can dream, right?

I know you are not a cheat, Grant, I do. And that is one of the many things I love about you. But I don't like to feel like I am in the backseat either. It doesn't feel good at all. I want you to be able to tell the world about us, and be happy for it. I want you to lean across the table of a crowded restaurant and plant a huge, wet kiss on me and not feel guilty about it.

Trust that I had no idea things would turn out this way when I first told you what I was feeling – no idea. I just wanted to let you know how I felt and that the sparks were flying. Now this…

I know that I'm putting pressure on you and even though that's not what I want to do, I can't seem to help it. I wish, if even for a moment, that you could climb inside of me and feel what I feel. Then and only then could you understand how real this is and how desperately I want you – all of you.

Sadly, though, I can't just have little bits and pieces of you…a phone call every day and a couple of stolen moments here and there. Like you said, with us it's all or nothing. Unfortunately, this just isn't cutting it. As much as I enjoy and look forward to hearing your voice each day, maybe it's not a good idea anymore. It really is very difficult for me and I don't want to put any unnecessary pressure on you. I really don't. Although we've said this in the past, I guess it's best if we chill out – for now. I have told you the way that I feel for you and what I want for us. That's all I can do. The rest is in your hands. I can only hope that you will think of me every day, as I will you. I hope a lot of things, Grant. Most of all I hope the day will come when everything else is behind you and we can fall in love all over again and catch up on all the things we've missed. I hope your predictions are right. I guess time will tell? Until then, you'll be in my thoughts.

I love you, Grant
Jodi

"You bastard!" Carmen hissed. But that was the life she's accepted long ago; the man she'd chose to have children with. There was no leaving. She wouldn't dare tread through life as a divorcee, broke and labeled as 'used goods.' She knew Grant cheated. *But the SOB doesn't have to wash my face in it,* she thought.

It was late Tuesday night before Grant arrived at the pool hall. He looked like he'd just lost his best friend, or worse, his reflection in the mirror.

"What's the matter," Rick asked, gesturing the waitress over to order his glum friend a beer.

"Life's starting to really get to me," Grant complained. "I know I'm wrong chasing all these women, but I can't help it." He shook his head. "I don't know…maybe if my parents had a better relationship, then…"

"WHAT?" Rick blurted, and nearly laughed at Grant's pathetic pitch; that he was the way he was because his parents cheated him out of a good rearing. "So, you're a victim then? Someone not in control of his own life?"

"My father was a dog. You knew that, tight?"

"Whatever!" Rick roared. "You've been through enough to understand what you want and don't want in life. The choices have always been yours. Damn, Grant! For once, take some responsibility. Your parents may have had a terrible marriage, but it was up to you to break the chain and not pass on the same legacy to your poor kids."

"Listen," Grant said. "I haven't changed at all. I'm the same guy. But I definitely can't say the same for you. Sometimes it's like I don't even know you anymore."

Rick shook his head. "But we're not supposed to stay the same, Buddy. We're supposed to change." He took a shot. "We're supposed to grow up."

Grant took a swing of beer. "So what am I supposed to do, then? Live the way you live? Get divorced?"

"Just tell the truth," Rick said, "be true to yourself and your wife. As long as you don't lie to people, how can you go wrong? I mean, think about it: Who could blame you for living the truth?"

Grant took the pool stick and pondered his friend's harsh reality check. Rick was right: His house was in complete disarray, chaos and sorrow. It was his childhood, revisited. An actual tear formed in the corner of his eye.

It was earlier than usual when Grant pulled the Mustang into his driveway. He stepped out of the car and watched as the *Welcome* flag waved in the wind. From the greeting sign and lawn ornaments in the front of the house to the tree fort out back, it was the perfect picture of happy, middle class

America. He snickered. Over the manicured lawn, past the pristine flowerbeds, Grant reached his front stairs to find Carmen's scowling face. She'd been drinking and she was furious.

Just as she opened her mouth to scream, a neighbor walking a small, leashed dog passed by the front of the house. Carmen smiled wide, while Grant spun around to wave. "Good evening," he called out, and the man gestured the same. As the neighbor disappeared into the distance, Grant walked past Carmen and stepped into the house. She slammed the door behind them.

"You got a 'Dear John' letter today," she screeched and threw an opened envelope into his face.

Grant recognized the perfume before he ever saw the sender's name. He took a deep breath and glared into his drunken wife's face. His life was folding in on itself again. It was going to be another long night. "Hon, let me explain…"

Chapter 23

On the morning before Rick moved in with Abby and Paige, he received his last email.

> *Love,*
> *Have I told you lately how much I love you and how much you mean to me? When I am with you, I can't get enough of you. And when I'm not, I think about you all the time. Every time the phone rings, I smile inside because I know it might be you. Well, I just wanted you to know.*
> *Abby xoxox*
> *PS- I can't wait to wake up with you every morning.*

> *Babe,*
> *I know because you make sure of that.*
> *But do you know...*
> *-that I've never felt a love for someone that I have for you*
> *-that I love you, totally, as my lover and my friend*
> *-that I will spend the rest of my days with you*
> *-that you make me happier than I've been since I was a child*
> *-that my dreams are now attainable because I have you to share them with*
> *-that you mean more than the world to me*
> *-that I love everything about you – even the bad stuff*
> *-that I never thought I'd find you (again), but I thank God every night that I did*
> *Did you know these things?*
> *If you didn't, then shame on me because I've felt them every second since we've been together.*
> *I love you, Abby. I do. And I can't wait to hold you in my arms each night.*
> *Me xoxoxooxoxoxox*

> *Richard,*
> *You really know what to say to a girl.*
> *Now you've done it. I need you...I really, really need you...all of you! Because without you, I am not me. You know, I really believed that you should never need someone – only want them. But after you, I don't believe that anymore. I need you to be the best that I can be.*

YOU MAKE ME HAPPY!
I LOVE YOU, RICHARD GILES
  Abby xoxoxoxoxox

Twenty minutes later, Abby's last email was returned – unopened. The account had been closed. Abby heard the key in the lock and the door swing open. She hurried to the kitchen to find Rick standing there, holding two suitcases and a glass bowl containing Zachary the fish. They were both smiling. She ran to kiss him. He was finally home.

From the shadows of the living room, Paige was watching. "Great," she snickered and headed for the privacy of her bedroom.

Rick didn't realize the depths of Paige's resentment until he moved in.

Before his suitcases were unpacked, Paige left her bed and peeked her head into he and Abby's bedroom. "Mom," she called out.

Abby stirred.

"I just had another bad dream and I can't get back to sleep," Paige murmured.

Abby pulled back the covers on her side of the bed and gestured for Paige to join her.

For the first few weeks, it was the same recurring nightmare – each time pushing Rick out where he was destined to sleep on the cold couch. It was the perfect metaphor for he and Paige's struggling relationship – even though she'd stopped fearing that someone would break into the house now that he was there.

Over the months, the sweet child did everything she could to sabotage Rick and Abby's loving relationship and drive a wedge between them. No matter what he tried, there were no signs of progress. Paige wouldn't speak without being spoken to. She would even do whatever she could to start an argument between Rick and her mom.

Worse, Abby and Paige's arguments were beginning to increase in both frequency and intensity. During one such match, as they debated over scheduled bed times, Rick tried to help and turned to Paige. "Why don't you just start listening to your mother?" he suggested.

Both Abby and Paige froze, and then glared at the interruption.

Rick realized that he'd overstepped his bounds, but it was too late.

"Why don't you just stop pretending to be my father?" Paige screamed. "BECAUSE YOU'RE NOT!" With a final gasp, she ran off to her room, crying.

And with the most lost and helpless look in her eyes, Abby followed her.

You're right, Rick thought. *I'm not your father. I'm the opposite.* He'd never felt so frustrated and in the way.

Before long, he'd taken his fill and couldn't make heads or tails of his situation. He decided to call Bill, but as the phone rang he realized that his mentor was no longer able to speak. Grandma picked up.

Reluctantly, Rick explained his painful dilemma.

"The girl is acting up because she's scared," the old lady said. "That's all."

"That's all?" he asked, his tone unusually firm for his grandmother.

"Richard, think about it. She just lost her dad. Then she and her Mom had to pack up and move to a strange place. And I'm sure they were just starting to get into a nice, safe routine when your handsome face showed up and decided to move in with them. Don't you think that's a lot of change for anyone – never mind a young girl?"

Rick didn't answer. It wouldn't have mattered. She wasn't looking for one. He missed Bill more than ever. The old man's words never stung this much.

"Popcorn and movie night on Friday has now been replaced with you and Abby going out. Wednesday used to be spaghetti night, but now you're coming home with Chinese food. The poor girl's feeling the same instability she felt when her parents lived together."

"So you don't think Abby should…"

The old woman was fast. "Abby allows the defiant behavior because she needs you in her life, but she also feels guilty about being a Mom who uprooted her daughter, who chose the wrong father, who let her boyfriend move in…I'm sure in her mind the list is long. Under normal circumstances, Paige is a fine girl. I'm sure of it. For now, though, it's easier for Abby to turn a blind eye to her daughter's cries for attention."

"I agree. But even if her behavior did improve, I'm not sure that little girl is ever going to care for me."

"You can never ask for someone to love you, Richard, but you can love them and open your heart to be loved in return. Love is the greatest gift God has ever given. In this case, that love must be shown as someone who is gentle and caring…someone who's not going away."

It was time to step onto a new plain of understanding. As if struck on the head with a cinder block, it finally dawned on him. *It was selfish for me to move in with them,* he thought, *but if I move out now, things will only get worse.* His greatest gift to Paige would be a sense of stability. *Consistency will be my peace offering,* he vowed to himself. *Even through the rage and confusion, I'll be the rock; the opposite of her father. I'll be myself.*

Eunice awaited a reply to ensure that he'd gotten it.

"So we'll just have to return to movie and popcorn night on Friday's, spaghetti dinners on Wednesday's and Paige will be included in every aspect of me and Abby's relationship from here on."

"You got it, Richard," she said. "Right now, Paige thinks that her mother has to choose between you and her. Just by being there through the stormy season, you can prove that her mom can have both."

Rick pondered this truth.

"You want a permanent ticket into Abby and Paige's lives," Eunice finished, "just remember these three simple rules: Be consistent, tell the truth no matter how painful, and keep your word – always."

"Thank you, Grandma. I love you."

"I know," she said. "And I love you, too. Now go be with your family."

At Rick's request, Abby cooked up a big, steaming bowl of spaghetti and the three of them sat at the dining room table.

"I think it's time to try something new around here," Rick said.

Paige stopped serving herself and looked up for an explanation.

"I think that every time we meet at this table, each of us needs to come with a topic of conversation."

Abby played along. "What do you mean?"

Rick explained. "Each of us has to describe the best thing that happened to us that day, and the worst thing."

Paige wasn't impressed, so Abby got it started. By the end, they were all laughing and sharing – and embarking on their first tradition together.

The Snowball Dance was held on the last Friday of January. It was a father/daughter dance, and Paige couldn't have been more excited. Her dad promised that he'd be there. Two hours after Rick dropped her off, Paige stared out the gymnasium window and began to cry. As usual, her dad was nowhere in sight. What she didn't realize, though, was that she wasn't alone.

Rick emerged from the shadows and approached her. Her tears were breaking his heart. "How can I help?" he asked.

"Just take me home…please."

As they prepared to leave, one of Paige's friends approached. "Bye, Paige," the young girl said. She looked up at Rick and then back at Paige. "Is this your dad?" she asked.

Paige froze.

Rick smiled and extended his hand for a shake. "No," he said, "I'm just a good friend."

Rick parked the car and stepped into the house to find Paige sitting at the kitchen table, her face a mix of sorrow and disgrace. He took a knee by her side. "You okay?" he asked.

Staring at the floor, she nodded.

He took a deep breath. "You can't make people be what you want them to be, Sweetie. They are who they are." He placed his hand on her shoulder. "You can only be who you want to be." He bent to peer into her watery eyes. "The trick is to take the best from everyone around you."

Like a toddler with fist against cheek, Paige nodded. Even though she'd never admit it, she was grateful for Rick's hand on her shoulder.

Satisfied that Rick's work was done, Abby emerged from the shadows and rushed to her little girl.

Paige continued to be tough, but Rick hung in there, doing all he could to be there for her. Abby, on the other hand, was giving her daughter everything but wings.

Another month hadn't passed before he'd taken enough of the ridiculousness. Paige was completely self-absorbed, had a real bad attitude and was incapable of being taught anything because she knew it all. In short, she was a normal, healthy ten-year old. Rick finally told her, "You want to run the show, then run it. For the entire day, whatever you say goes, okay?"

Abby didn't like it, but he needed to make his point.

With a nod, Paige agreed. The deal was sealed. Abby shook her head at the craziness. Rick was confident that it wouldn't take long.

"No school or work today," Paige immediately ordered, and they didn't go. She served candy bars for breakfast and everyone ate them. The show was just getting started.

Throughout the day, as they wrecked the house in play, they ate piles of junk food, giving every fallen crumb an extra smash into the carpet. Paige adapted to her new role well, and gladly called the shots. They did everything she wished. It was frightening.

By the time dinner rolled around, Rick had been injured while horsing around, Abby was exhausted and Paige felt deathly ill from all the sweets she'd inhaled. Collectively, they were sick and miserable. The house was a disaster, and people were starting to call, concerned. Rick insisted that they forge on.

The lack of routine was starting to make Paige feel uneasy, but she stayed strong. "Everybody goes to bed late!" Abby cringed. Rick smiled. He threw on a horror movie and made another bowl of popcorn. It was going to be a long night.

Before the first scream, Paige looked green. "Can I go to bed now?" she groaned.

Rick shrugged. "You're the one calling the shots, right?"

She stood, kissed her weary mother and turned to Rick. "Okay Rick, I surrender."

"Good," he said, "so maybe you should let your mom do her job, while you do yours?"

She nodded.

"As my Grandma always said: Love is a given. It's respect and trust that have to be earned."

She nodded again and as she walked away, Abby whispered, "I think you showed her good."

He smiled. "Well, that's great," he whispered back, "but it wasn't Paige I was trying to make my point with."

She was taken aback.

"Whatever happened to the days we grew up in, Ab?" he asked, but before she could answer, he did it himself. "It wasn't perfect back then, but at least we had manners – a simple sign of respect that no longer exists. There are no consequences today. Everyone's a victim. Both parents have to work and raise their kids in a state of guilt for not being there…and the world wonders why our children are so messed up. Even the church has failed them – the greed, the lies, the abuse. Like Grandma used to say, 'It's like the whole world's gone to pot.'"

She nodded. He was right.

"You're a great Mom," he said, "but I think it's time to stop feeling guilty because I'm around. Children are happy when their parents are happy – so start smiling."

She nodded, and with his prodding eventually smiled.

With Christmas quickly approaching, Rick knew he had the perfect opportunity to show Paige an example of selfless love, a tradition passed down by his father.

His favorite story of his father was the time that the old man dressed up as Saint Nick and single-handedly rode into a housing project to save Christmas for two underprivileged children. "There were two elves along to help," his Dad claimed, and swore that the whole thing was nothing. Rick knew better. The first night his Dad ever played Father Christmas, two unfortunate kids received much more than just food and toys: They were given a sense of awe, and confirmation of their young faith. They were gifted with a valid reason to never abandon hope, and solid proof that they were never alone. They were presented with the magic of the human will when it was convicted to place another before itself, and a memory of the simple beauty that lay beneath the ugly defensive walls of humankind. In essence, they were shown love.

Through the years, Rick's dad faced some criticism for interrupting his own holiday by doing volunteer work. "It's a night meant to be spent with family and close friends," some said. Jim chuckled. They didn't understand. Though he spent every spare moment he could with those he loved, Christmas Eve could not be any more magical than spent in the eyes of children who believed in him – in Santa. He was hardly being selfless. In fact, it was the opposite. It was the most selfish act he could have ever committed. Year after year, though, he allowed those who sighed heavy to believe he was giving up something. He only let Rick in on his secret.

Finally adopting the tradition, Rick decided to play Santa.

As fate would have it, he'd set up two stops and wanted to spend them both with Paige. Abby was more than accommodating. "I'm going along," she insisted.

On the eve of Christmas, Rick tore his father's red suit free from the dry cleaner's plastic wrap and fluffed up the wiry, white beard.

On their way, he told them about his Dad's secret love of playing the jolly fat man. He described the two children and the dilapidated housing project where it all began. "I've even kept track of the kids' progress," he said. "Jason joined the Navy and became an officer, while his sister Rachael went off to law school to become an attorney. Not bad for two kids starting off at the bottom, huh?" He just knew his Dad's love had something to do with it.

Rick, Abby and Paige's first stop was at a Grange Hall in the country. They stepped out of the van onto a path of white-stained glass. An Arctic wind howled down and tapped each of them on the shoulder. They shivered, but still paused long enough to take in the raw beauty of the evening. The trees were all dipped in white and, like folds within a sheet, the earth stretched long. While the moon showed off its halo, a million wishes sparkled in the frost. With a wolves' bite in the air, they hurried for the door.

Built in the late 1920's, the hall appeared tired. The cedar shingles were stained and curling, while the rotted gutters clearly needed replacing. The exterior of the old building had been weathered by decades of New England's relentless storms. Abby desperately hoped that the doorknob still worked.

As Paige threw open the door, Gene Autry's *Rudolph The Red-Nosed Reindeer* came pouring out. Abby turned to the fat man in the red suit and smiled. *The entire night's going to be filled with magic.* They could both feel it.

One step inside the Grange Hall and the mind's eye painted wonderful pictures of plowing tractors, almanacs and corncob pipes. Paige took notice of the old-timers sitting in the corner. Rings of smoke encircled their heads like halos, and each tipped his hat to her.

On the giant square-dance floor, a tight community of people celebrated the holiday the old-fashioned way. They strung popcorn and dried cranberries on a giant blue spruce Christmas tree. Before anyone could spot him, Rick bellowed, "HO. HO. HO!" The children came running.

Abby and Paige stood off to the side to watch. The excitement of the children was overwhelming and contagious. Paige beamed with the joy she felt for them. Abby felt blessed for the experience.

A kind looking, heavy-set woman approached and took Rick's hand, leading him to a chair that had been decorated for Santa. Though the kids never caught it, there was a bag of gifts already waiting to be handed out. Rick waved Paige over, and with Abby's gentle prodding she went to him. "Pretty girl, can you help Santa hand out the gifts?" he asked in his deep Santa voice.

With dozens of tiny eyes upon her, Paige grinned and went to work. She handed Rick a present from the bag. He read out the name and then handed it over to the excited child it belonged to. Within fifteen minutes, they handed out a bag full of wrapped presents. Toward the end, Rick caught Paige staring at him. Seated by the frozen window, she was actually smiling and it made him swallow hard. Her heart was beginning to thaw. Rick suddenly realized that with all the resentment and frustration between them, he'd failed to take notice of how much he'd grown to care for her. He returned her festive smile.

Santa and his helpers were invited to share dinner with the townsfolk – who weren't about to take *no* for an answer. Even through the matted beard, Rick enjoyed the feast of smoked ham, homemade baked beans, mashed potatoes, harvest beets, coleslaw, corn bread and Indian pudding. Just before passing out from heat exhaustion from the heavy suit, they bid their farewell.

Walking out of the Grange Hall, where dog-eared, yellowed pictures sat in frames, each preserving decades of history, the starry night ushered them back into the present. Rick hurried for the van and, under the cover of darkness, tore off his wig and beard. While Abby and Paige talked about the kids, he took in the last five minutes of air that he'd lost.

Forty miles later, he donned his wig and beard again. They were in the city at Santa's last stop of the night.

The snow-swept streets were alive with holiday magic. The

swooning of Bing Crosby and Nat King Cole kept rhythm to a wave of pedestrian traffic, while bells and horns were sounded by spirited passer-byes. Hunched against the cold, men scurried from store to store, frantically searching for the perfect gift in their last minute shopping spree. From their exchange of nods, a feeling of camaraderie was obviously felt amongst the poorly prepared. Rick, Abby and Paige stepped out of the van. With the tall buildings blocking the wind, the night felt twenty degrees warmer. Rick was in no rush to enter the muggy building. For a time, Abby and Paige were content to remain outside, as well.

Though they didn't want to leave the Currier & Ives print, the three of them stepped into the Boys Club to meet another pack of underprivileged kids.

With Paige by his side, Rick laughed from his belly, listened to wishes and handed out presents. He looked up again to catch Paige staring. He smiled, and to his surprise she returned it. He'd made progress and gotten through to her. *Will I ever make a real difference in her life?* he wondered.

Upon returning home from the incredible experience, Rick collapsed in the living room. While he wrestled the sweat-drenched outfit free, Paige proceeded to the tree. Escorted by her mother's gentle eyes, she reached under the soft pine, grabbed a neatly wrapped present and handed it to Rick. "I wanted to give this to you tonight," she said, and quickly left the room.

Rick pulled off his black boots, wiped his hands on his pants and tore through the wrapping. It was a framed essay. Through shocked eyes, he read:

The Person I Admire Most

The person I admire most is Richard Giles.
He is very funny and most of all he teaches me
a lot about life from a different angle.
He's very fluent with poetry,
so Rick hands me down the secrets in his poetry.

Rick is not just a writer; he is a wonderful man.
He inspires me to be the best I can be at everything I do.
Sometimes late at night when some kids are getting
boring bedtime stories, I'm getting real stories about Rick's life.
He shares everything with me to try to teach me.
He teaches me about sharing and everything
I need to be a good person when I grow up.

I hope that in the future I'm as honorable as he is.
Honor is one of the things he teaches me. The second
thing is love. He went into my class and taught poetry
to twenty-three kids. He also teaches me about respect
at home and I think that is pure love. The third thing
Rick teaches me is friendship... not just with me
but with everyone around him.

That's the person who I admire most.

by
Paige Soares
12/25/99

Rick wiped his eyes. He'd already made a difference in Paige's life. He just needed to remember that such truths were usually left unsaid, and normally invisible to the eye. The gift was Paige's official call for a truce.

He looked up at Abby. "I love you," he said, "both of you."

That night Paige changed the answering machine's outgoing message: "Hi, you've reached Paige, Abby and Rick. Please leave a message and we'll get right back to ya."

Chapter 24

The first few months of the new year were spent finding a common ground for everyone. And things were going well. If it weren't for the hours Paige spent waiting for her father by the living room window, it would have even been a happy time.

It was Sunday. Patrick was scheduled to arrive at 2:00 PM to take Paige to a movie and an early dinner. But he didn't show until 8:20 PM, long after Paige had paced through one sitcom after the next. Patrick never called and now stood swaying in the driveway. Abby was upset, causing Rick's breathing to quicken. With his fists instinctively clenched in preparation, the promise, *I'll never get between you and your father* echoed in his pounding head. It wasn't easy, but he left Abby and Paige to deal with the situation and headed for the porch.

"You're too late," Abby yelled, "Tonight's a school night. And besides…you've been drinking!"

"Jesus, Abby, it's always about my drinking," Patrick slurred in the cold air. "I'd say Paige is old enough to make up her own mind whether or not she wants to spend time with her dad." He looked at Paige.

Paige looked back at the porch to find Rick shaking his worried head at the situation. She then looked at her mom who was ready to cry. The whole thing was wrong.

"Come on, Paige, get in the truck and we'll go get something to eat."

With all the courage she could muster, Paige shook her head. She felt like crying. "Sorry, Dad," she said, "but you're too late." She looked him square in the face. "Let's do it next weekend instead."

Patrick cursed once under his breath, jumped in his truck and squealed out of the driveway.

Paige couldn't believe Rick. *As tough as it must have been, he kept his word*, she thought. *He stayed on the porch and didn't get involved.* It confirmed that she'd been wrong about him. Rick was a good guy who sincerely cared. It was too bad she couldn't let anyone know that she knew.

After his lifelong quest for success, for the first time, Rick felt like he could finally face Mrs. Parsons again – knowing that she would be proud. It had nothing to do with fighting. He'd finally thought about someone other than himself.

Life returned to normal after that.

The winter had been colder than hell's north acre. For what seemed forever, icicles hung from trees, glistening like diamonds in the moonlight, while a white blanket was pulled snugly over the world. Everything stayed frozen for months – the air, the sky, the woodlands. Some days the slightest breeze bit at the face. Some nights the driving sleet pounded madly against blocks of ice that had once been windows.

Just when they thought they couldn't take another moment of it, the sun took one step closer and smiled – thawing out the world. Rick, Abby and Paige looked out the window. It was a time to regroup, with the lingering memories of the previous summer and dreams of the summer to come.

"Get your eyes off that computer screen and get outside," Abby yelled.

As the screen door nearly hit Paige in the backside, Rick chuckled. "You weren't thinking that way when we were emailing each other."

She laughed. "No, but I was thinking that way when I was her age. It'll be summer before long and she'll still be stuck in the house."

Rick nodded. He remembered every moment of it as if it were yesterday: As the lazy days ticked by on Freedom Ave, the wonderful smell of fresh mowed grass lingered. There was plenty of swimming and talk of skinny-dipping lasted all summer, though the gang never went through with it. As if chased by bees, they ran through open fields past the dark, scary wood line all the way to the fishing hole. Games of Marco Polo turned their hair from dirty blonde to platinum, their skin from pale to desert tan. "Good health's found in the rays of sunlight," Grandma would say. They'd drip dry in their hidden tree fort and return home from their adventures to find a sweating pitcher of fresh-squeezed lemonade waiting. Grandma was good.

The carefree and lazy days of youth afforded the time to dream; to guess which shapes the crawling clouds created. There were no clocks or calendars. Time was marked by the rising and setting of the sun, and of course the streetlights. And not a moment of it was wasted. Rather, it was the most well spent time – ever.

Abby was right. Paige and her friends spent too much time indoors.

Rick was still daydreaming on the front porch when he spotted Paige and the neighborhood gang marching toward him; another glimpse of he and Abby's yesterdays. *Youth,* he thought, *filled with such incredible hope that they couldn't ever understand the value of it…every possibility right at their feet.*

A blonde haired boy named Brandon had come into some recent money and was gloating. "Find a penny, pick it up and all that day you'll have good luck," he sang. "…as long as it's heads up."

As they approached the porch, Paige turned to him. "Open it again and the next thing out of your mouth is teeth," she barked and stormed into the house.

Brandon tried to conceal his blush by studying his new copper coin.

Rick chuckled. "Between you and me," he whispered, "I'd say she's got a pretty big crush on you."

The boy grinned, but never replied. Paige was on her way back to the porch with a bag of chips for each of the gang.

As they headed off into the wild, Brandon looked back once. Rick threw him a thumbs-up and the secret grin returned.

Even with all the progress Rick and Paige had made on the new home front, the bond between she and her Mom was watertight. Though Abby went out of her way to maintain a mother/daughter relationship and not just a friendship with Paige, Rick had never witnessed two people closer. It was glorious and, at the same time, impenetrable. And no matter how much better things had gotten, from the moment he'd arrived he was perceived as a threat to this sacred union. It might have been unspoken by Paige, but it was clearly understood by him.

He was attentive to Paige, and tried hard to understand where she was coming from. She couldn't betray her father by showing Rick affection. Secretly, he admired her for her loyalty. Still, when he brought flowers for Abby, he brought some for Paige, as well. He let her know how special she was. Most of all, he cared enough to listen when she thought enough to confide in him. Each opportunity was precious and during those times he never left her gaze. Unfortunately, they were too few and far between to make any real progress.

It was a random Wednesday night dinner when Rick announced, "Just so you know, Abby. I'm going to ask Paige to go on a date with me Friday night."

To Rick's surprise, Paige didn't object. She looked at her Mom and smiled.

Abby acted jealous. "Where are you going?" she asked.

Before Rick could open his mouth, Paige said, "That's our business."

Abby smiled. Her little girl was finally coming around to Rick's irresistible charms.

At Paige's choosing, she and Rick ate racks of messy ribs at a local bar and grille. There was small talk over dinner, Rick waiting for her to speak first each time. At one point, she excused herself and hurried off to the ladies room. Rick quickly called the waitress over. "It's my step-daughter's birthday," he fibbed. "Is there any chance we can sing to her tonight?"

The waitress smiled. "We'll bring over the cake when you're finished," she promised. And they did.

Paige's face burned brighter than the candle – but she loved it. As Rick sang, "Happy Birthday to you," Paige thanked him with her smiling eyes.

He shrugged it off as nothing. But it was something. Her happiness was important to him, and she was starting to learn just how much. After making their way through a mountain of napkins, they headed off to Fenway Park in Boston. He needed to get her on his turf.

Everything was gray. The streets were gray. The sky was gray. Even the people were gray. Pockets of life sprung up in the filthy alleyways of a grimy world.

The train ride, or T, delivered them among the masses. From Kenmore Square, the towering lights that overlooked the field were already buzzing. Fenway Park – a landmark since 1912 – was a massive structure with walls like a prison, containing its dreams within.

Just outside the park on Yawkey Way, the street was filled with vendors, street musicians, scalpers and people who spoke with thick Boston accents. Paige scanned the growing crowd. Rick chuckled at her first impression.

Red Sox fans gathered from all walks of New England life, generations of thick-skinned northerners who'd preferred to endure seasons of close calls and pathetic long shots than entertain the idea of surrender. Fenway was a melting pot for those who still believed.

Rick was eager to brand the memory into Paige's mind. "If you're born in New England or live within its borders long enough, you have to be a Boston Red Sox fan," he explained. "And this goes for those who don't even like baseball. It's the law."

She looked at him with skepticism.

He laughed, and confirmed her suspicions.

Within the center of the herd, they walked through the gates, past the row of concession booths and then up one of the ramps that led to the field. As they approached the top, Rick's childhood came rushing back. The smells, the sounds – his senses absorbed them all. They took one more step and the world suddenly turned green: Green grass. Green seats. The Green Monster wall out in left field. Paige gasped. In one brief moment, she was introduced to decades of famous New England history, and the entire experience was burned into her imagination for all eternity. Like an old movie that had been reworked, it was the first time color was infused into their little field trip. The grass was so green it looked fake.

Rick felt like he'd just stepped out of limbo and into heaven. A slight childish squeal started from the base of his diaphragm and escaped. After all these years, it still took his breath away. He glanced over at Paige. Her eyes were as wide as hubcaps, struggling to take it all in. In the middle of Boston's concrete jungle, a bright, shiny emerald was discovered. It was awesome!

"So…what do you think?" he asked.

Paige nodded. There were no words.

Rick chuckled. It was a lot bigger than she'd expected, or he remembered for that matter– the very place where dreams of playing America's favorite pastime came true. Though he'd waited six whole months to cash in their tickets, Rick knew it was going to be worth it. The NY Yankees were pitted against the Olde Towne Team. Boston's rivalry with NY, along with their blame for the curse of the Bambino, made the atmosphere at Fenway electric.

As Paige followed him to their assigned seats, she took snapshots in her mind. The Green Monster (309 ft.) was immense, while the field was immaculate. And the way the park was set up, they would have had to be on the playing field to be any closer to the action.

Rick scanned the park and smiled. From the luxury and broadcast seats behind home plate to the enormous, hand-operated scoreboard on the legendary Green Monster, the place still gave him chills.

In center field, red-faced savages filled the infamous bleachers. Heavy drinking and the occasional affray were as guaranteed as tapping a beach ball or two. There should have been a warning sign: ONLY Red Sox fans allowed. God forbid someone wore a NY cap or jersey in the shark pit – they were open game. Hating the NY Yankees was the greatest love of Red Sox fans, a tradition as old as choking back tears during the National Anthem, or paying too much for gaudy souvenirs. The outfield bleachers were where the wave started each night and it was on those very shores that it eventually broke. Sitting in the bleachers was an entirely different experience, though. Rick wouldn't have taken Paige there if she were twenty years old.

In right field, Rick spotted the lone red seat in a sea of green that marked the very spot where Ted Williams hit the longest measured home run (450 ft.) in Fenway's illustrious history. Rick shook his head. At one time, money wasn't the only object at this home of legends. The bullpens jutted out in right field and led to the famous *Pesky* foul pole that still denied so many close calls.

From the first time his Dad introduced him to the place, he knew Fenway was special. It had that feel – like even the most impossible feat became possible on its hallowed grounds. It was a living, breathing shrine to the hopes of the fans and a cursed team's race for the pennant.

The concrete was worn from the millions that had passed before them. With the help of an ancient usher, Rick and Paige finally found their seats. It was a hard, tight fit. "I haven't missed many games," the old man boasted as he walked away and Rick felt a pang of envy. Thankful for the slight breeze, he and Paige settled in.

Without warning, the echo of the announcer ticked off the roll call and players took the field, grown men playing a boy's game. With the excitement building, the smells of stale beer and hot dogs filled the clear night. Vendors peddled everything from ice cream to hot dogs, each item requiring a second mortgage. Paige was amazed. As Rick passed his cash down the line, the hawkers threw bags of peanuts and hot dogs back at them with surprising accuracy. Fenway was pure magic where the rest of the world and all its troubles melted faster than the three-dollar ice cream bars.

From the first crack of the bat, Paige and Rick jumped to their feet and cheered. The camaraderie took Paige by surprise. Among the age-old gladiators, or fans – everyone from muscular longshoremen to 60 year-old housewives could be found. Pleasantries were briefly exchanged, but then it was down to the serious business at hand. Everyone screamed, and the occasional vulgarity was not only accepted but expected. The motto was clear: *It's us – all 32,000 of us – against them!*

Even when angry, though, everyone wore a grin. It was a different world; a wondrous world filled with history and every boy's dream of being a major league baseball player.

Beneath a full moon, the rival teams battled it out. Paige looked up to find a twinkling star, and quietly made a wish.

Rick leaned into her ear. "I hope it comes true," he whispered, his mouth full of hot dog.

She smiled at his attentiveness, a reflection of her mother's goodness sparkling in her pretty eyes.

The entire night was a roller coaster ride in the dark. As they waited for the dangerous and elusive foul ball, an occasional tune led to the chant *CHARGE*! The anxiety of a long ball from the Yankees with bases loaded had everyone at the edge of their seats. Thankfully, the Sox bullpen came through.

Ushers passed through and collected for *The Jimmy Fund*, a charity that helped kids who suffered from cancer. Rick gave generously and taught Paige a wonderful lesson without ever speaking a word. As the money hit the hat, the announcer called for a seventh inning stretch, and 32,000 people rose to do just that.

By the eighth inning, the Sox were up by two when – with two men on base – Nomar Garciaparra, their all-star shortstop, smashed one into the net above the Green Monster to put them ahead by five. The place exploded. The game was as good as done. The beloved Sox were beating up on their opponent, the evil empire. All in the world was right and good.

Rick turned to Paige and half-hugged her. To her surprise, she half returned the gesture. In the vast expanse of the park, a cozy bond was finally shared between them.

Through another inning of constant cheering, the Red Sox shut the Bronx Bombers down. It was perfect.

Rick looked at Paige and smiled. She was sure to remember this night for a very long time.

This was even more fun than the time Uncle Al put a beating on Elmo at my fifth birthday party, she thought.

In a great river of pedestrian traffic, they walked back to the T station. Among the thousands, Rick turned to Paige. "I was hoping we could talk a little tonight," he said.

She looked at him and nodded, but didn't say a word.

He took a deep breath and then the plunge. "I really love your mom, you know."

Again, she nodded, but not a peep.

"And I love you, too."

Her head flew up.

Before she could speak, he went on. "I'm not here to take your mom away from you, Paige. That's never going to happen."

Her eyes studied the pavement before them.

"Your mother's relationship with you is priority one, and it should be. It's one of the reasons I love her so much. I want you to understand, though, that I could be a positive in both of your lives. I'm not here to take anything away. I'm here to add. Your mom has a chance at happiness, we all do, but your mom relies very heavily upon your feelings and needs – before she'll ever consider her own. So, the real question is: What is it you want?"

She remained hauntingly silent.

"I'm not trying to be your father. I'm not. But I am your friend, someone here to protect you if needed, and to help guide you."

She finally looked up to meet his gaze.

He stopped walking, and as hundreds of strangers flowed around them, he blurted, "I want to ask your mom to be my wife, Paige, but I want to know that you're okay with it before I do?"

For the first time since leaving the ballpark, she grinned. "Okay," she said. The answer was simple and without detail.

"Okay then," Rick said, "and I'll need your help with the wedding plans."

She nodded, her smile growing wider.

"What do you think about giving your mother the stars?"

She smiled all the way to the train.

Chapter 25

The world was sweet with the thick smells of honeysuckle and lilac. Rick awoke Abby with a kiss. "Time to get up, sleepyhead," he whispered.

She stirred, but her moans were a feeble attempt at rebellion. Before long, one eye opened and peered at the alarm clock's red numbers. "Why so early?" she yawned.

Raw excitement begged to be freed, but Rick held it back. Instead, he grinned. "It's a surprise," he whispered.

Abby opened the other eye and saw the breakfast tray at the foot of the bed. The plate was filled with everything she loved: runny eggs, crispy bacon, two slices of toast swimming in gobs of butter and a bowl of macaroni and cheese. Steam from a ceramic mug of coffee drifted up and circled the single red rosebud that stood rigid in a tiny, crystal vase. She yawned again and opened her eyes wider. Between the rich aroma of coffee and the faint scent of early summer, she couldn't help but smile. "What's the occasion?" she asked with a cute, wrinkled brow.

Beating back the urge to yell out, he took a seat at the edge of the bed and kissed her pouty lips. "Enjoy your breakfast," he said, "and take your time getting ready. Paige is at Danny and Carol's. I'll be back in an hour." He stood and started out of the room.

Abby reached for his hand but missed. "But…"

He turned back, approaching once more and gave her another kiss. "Today's a day of celebration. See you in an hour."

While Abby nibbled her way through breakfast, curiosity ate its way through her. She swallowed the last few bites without chewing and hurried for the shower. As she let the water run warm, she realized that she had no idea what to wear. *God only knows what he has planned,* she thought. She proceeded to her closet and noticed the outfit that he'd already laid out for her: A comfortably worn pair of jeans, a thick rope turtleneck sweater and a pair of big, fluffy mittens. In spite of the growing curiosity, she chuckled. The mittens and sweater didn't make sense. It was almost June.

Within minutes, she was dressed and ready to go. Through the darkened living room, she stepped into the kitchen. A hot copper kettle held just enough coffee for one more cup. She turned to grab the sugar bowl when the bouquet of long stem roses jumped out at her. They were beautiful, eleven in all. She chuckled again. The last of the dozen sat on a tray in the bedroom. She removed the card and read: *I Love You- Now and Forever, Rick*

Time turned lethargic. She stepped out onto the screened porch, wiped the dew from the scarred rocking chair and plopped down to wait. Even with the anticipation gnawing at her insides, she took in her wondrous surroundings. The black street was barren. The buckled sidewalks patiently awaited screaming children on bicycles. Squares of front lawns glistened under dying street lamps, as birds concealed in ancient trees began the day's first harmony. The air was sweet, with a slight breeze tickling the hair on her forearms. She drew in a long breath and sighed. From the time she was a little girl, the world always seemed perfect from the front porch. Whether she was coming home to its welcomed light, or leaving from its safe embrace, those knotty floorboards and paint-chipped railings were home.

A crow squawked loud in the distance, pulling Abby back to her curiosity. In the morning mist, she almost jumped out of her skin when, on the horizon, a stretch limousine approached with the rising sun. It stopped directly in front of the house. Like a jack-in-the-box, Rick popped out of its roof. He was grinning wide, and frantically waving his arms for her to join him.

She wasn't even sure the front door was locked when the chauffer hit the gas. "What are you..?" she started, but Rick gently placed his index finger over her lips.

"Shhhh," he whispered. "Just sit back and enjoy the day." He handed her a Mimosa – half orange juice, half Champagne.

She took a sip, but couldn't help it. With puppy dog eyes, she pleaded. "Just one hint?"

He shook his head, but she could tell he was ready to burst.

Relentlessly, she forged on. "Okay, then just tell me – are we celebrating something to do with your career?"

He grinned, mischievously. "Yes, we're celebrating, but no more questions or hints, okay? You'll ruin the surprise."

She agreed, and was satisfied. *He must have gotten some big news*, she thought. The only thing that didn't make sense was her jacket sitting on the seat across from them. Like the mittens and sweater, it was just too warm.

A half hour later, the limo slowed to a halt. Rick cleared his throat and produced a blindfold. "I know this may seem strange," he said, "but I need you to trust me, okay?" As he spoke, he stuffed her mittens into her jacket pocket.

217

She giggled in delight. By now, she was ready to surrender. He helped her put on the jacket, applied the scarf, and then led her out of the car.

The air felt cool but refreshing. She held his hand tight and allowed herself to be blindly led. Neither spoke a word. She could hear the sound of her excited breathing play nicely with the whipping wind of an open field. Rick's hand was hot with sweat. He was either more excited than she figured, or he was nervous. Her curiosity grew.

They stopped and for a moment the world stopped turning. No matter what this surprise was, she had a strong feeling she'd never forget it. She drew in a deep breath. He chuckled and with a kiss, released her blindfold. There was an enormous hot air balloon displaying every color in the rainbow sitting before them. It was beautiful and she gasped when she saw it.

"The sky's the limit," he promised, and led her toward the giant ride. She needed no coaxing. Since she was a small girl, she'd always dreamed of floating among the clouds. *It must be huge news*, she thought, and took off at a run, dragging him behind.

With a grinning pilot at the helm, they slowly ascended the world. Thirty minutes later, they stood suspended above it all. Abby was so overwhelmed she could hardly speak. Rick was grateful. He had a few more surprises up his sleeve and needed her full attention.

He pulled a folded piece of paper out of his jacket and carefully handed it to her. Abby defied the cross wind and grabbed it. Taking a break from the breathless scenery below, she unfolded it. It read, simply: *Abby's Dream*. She looked up, confused.

"It's the deed to your own star," Rick explained. "I hope you don't mind, but I took the liberty of naming it."

His smiling eyes were as warm as the air that filled the balloon. With tears, she dove into them.

"The deed gives you the celestial address and the constellation in which *Abby's Dream* is located." He smiled. "I just wanted you to know that wherever you are, all you need to do is look into the night sky and know that your dream is always within reach." He shrugged, sweetly. "I mean, think about it – it has your name on it."

She threw herself into his arms. "Oh, Richard."

"And never forget," he whispered. "To me, you'll always walk among the stars."

She tried to speak past the sniffles, but Rick was so caught up in the moment he had to go on. He removed another piece of paper from his jacket, dropped to one knee and recited:

"Captured Heart

Until you…

Love was a long-abandoned fairytale;
An exhausted idea that lay panting
at the base of scar-tissue walls;
A treasure, lost to me forever.

We met…

And the legs of time turned young again,
as shared conversation chased home the moon.
Dark eyes, a pair of fortuneteller's crystals,
sparkled with beauty, a goodness within.

We laughed…

And joy was that innocence known as a child,
tickled with whispers and hopes of one trust;
Bandits, called kisses, removed all the air,
while rooms that were crowded still found us alone.

We loved…

And you were the miracle, sealing my fate;
Dark clouds were scattered and sins disappeared;
When Me became We, and I became Us
and friends became lovers, a heaven on earth.

We learned…

Love is the place that we dreamt of as home
where more stars are reached from a soul mate's embrace;
Surrender, perhaps, is the true path to peace
when the woman you breathe for has captured your heart."

He paused. "Abby, I've promised you the sky and the stars. Now…"
he choked out, "I'm promising you my heart." He produced the diamond
ring, a sparkling princess cut. "I'm asking you to spend the rest of your life

with me. Will you be my wife?"

She collapsed to meet his embrace. "Yes," she cried.

He slid the ring onto his soul mate's finger. After a long embrace and an even longer kiss, they came up for air. The balloon pilot was smiling bigger than ever. Rick returned the expression. "Thank God she said yes," he teased, "I didn't want to throw her overboard."

The man laughed. Abby joined in. Rick turned back to his love. "Abby," he said. "You are the sun upon my face, the stars that fill my nights...my everything."

As was normal lately, she was speechless.

The remainder of the ride was spent floating among the clouds, snuggled safely in each other's arms; a shared moment of heaven's peace.

Upon their descent, Abby broke the silence. "Hey," she yelled out, "that looks like your father down there, waving." She searched hard. "And Danny and Carol...and...Paige?" Her eyes flew up to meet Rick's chuckle.

"They'd better be there," he said, "it's taken Paige and I weeks to plan this day. If any one of them missed it, I'd never forgive them."

Abby's eyes filled. "Paige?"

Rick smiled. "You wouldn't believe how excited she's been about planning this whole thing. She even made some of the decisions. I promised her the same ride some other time if she took care of things on the ground."

"WELL?" Grant yelled up, asking for everyone on the ground. "What did she say?"

Everyone looked up, anxiously awaiting a response.

With a cracked voice, Abby yelled back, "SHE SAID YES!"

It was the very answer they sought. With Paige conducting her orchestra, applause guided them the rest of the way in. Descending in an aura of love and joy, the balloon finally landed to meet their families and closest friends on the ground. Rick handed the balloon pilot a generous tip. The man nodded his appreciation. Abby rushed to her daughter for a hug.

An enormous picnic – featuring a traditional pig roast – was already underway. Everyone Abby ever loved was in attendance. Each, she also found, was holding a scrolled copy of *Captured Heart* on tan parchment. It was Rick's gift to them to commemorate the occasion. She couldn't imagine a sweeter gesture. Everyone was smiling – even the pig.

Two unfamiliar women approached.

Abby searched their faces and her eyes lit up. "Trace?" she gasped.

The woman smiled wide. "Actually, it's Cheyenne now," she said and offered Abby a long hug. "And I'd like you to meet my partner,

Stephanie."

Stephanie smiled and extended her hand.

Abby dismissed it and gave her the biggest hug. "Welcome to the family."

Cheyenne pulled Abby to the side and whispered, "I always knew you and Richard would be together someday."

"Congratulations, Abby," another voice called out and Abby looked up to find Vinny standing there. He was a couple inches taller than she remembered, but other than that he hadn't changed at all.

Abby let go of one hug to lock on to another.

Vinny introduced his wife, Darlene, and then rambled on about his life and the success he'd already achieved in his law practice.

Abby smiled politely until Vinny came up for air and gave her the opportunity to excuse herself. "I hope we'll see you at the wedding?"

"We wouldn't miss it," Vinny said and scanned the crowd for his next victim.

Realizing that she was now living her dream, Abby spun to find her future husband staring at her. That big heart and clever mind of his had arranged it all. She hurried to his side, silently vowing that she'd never leave it. "A pig roast?" she asked. "No filet mignon? No chilled bottles of champagne?"

He shrugged. "It seemed…"

She jumped into his arms. "It's perfect," she said. "Thank you for this perfect day." She kissed him. "And thank you for including Paige."

He kissed her sweetly. "It is perfect, isn't it?" he agreed. "You said yes."

They ate and reminisced. They danced and spoke of the future. They celebrated and the day seemed to last three seconds.

The following morning, Rick took out an obnoxious size ad in the newspaper: *I asked Abby to marry me, and she said YES!*

Rick then called his father to invite him to the wedding. "As my best man," he added.

Jim couldn't have been more thrilled. "What do you and Abby need?" he asked, "What can I get you for a wedding gift? Cash?"

"No, Dad," Rick said, "How 'bout a poem – written and recited just for us."

"Fair enough," Jim said. "Then all I need to know is what you love about Abby?"

Rick took a deep breath and babbled on forever. At the end of the long list, he finally said, "Everything."

Jim cleared his throat. "Now I have a bit of surprise for you," he said.

"What's that?" Rick asked.

"I was wondering whether you'd mind if I brought your new foster brother, Scott, along?"

"Of course" Rick said and paused. "You're a foster parent now?"

"Sure am. The paperwork went through just last week."

"Fantastic!" Rick said. "I look forward to welcoming my new brother into the family."

Jim phoned Abby. "I have a very important question to ask you."

"Sorry," she said, "but I'm already marrying your son."

He laughed. "And I couldn't be any more pleased with his choice. In fact, it's about time! But I still need to know what you love about my stubborn boy?"

Abby never hesitated. "Everything," she said. "I love everything about him."

Rick and Abby wed at Turtle Rock Farm at sunset. It was perfect.

As Rick awaited his bride in the mouth of a plain, white gazebo decorated in bright autumn colors of red, orange, yellow and brown, he and Abby's guests were delivered by hayride tractor. Their laughter and song got louder as they inched their way down a dirt road lined with candle-lit paper bags and approached the open field. He scanned the barn and fields, and chuckled. A short time ago, he would have never dreamed of getting married in such a place. Now, he couldn't imagine getting married anywhere else.

Grandma took her respective place up front with her new grandson, Scott. For someone who didn't really know anyone yet, the boy was still wearing a smile. Dan and Carol claimed the next row beside Grant. *Carmen must have a headache*, Rick thought, and laughed when Grant gestured that his wife was ill and couldn't make it. As Cheyenne and Stephanie, and Vinny and Darlene bantered within their small group, Gary B, the guitarist, silenced them with the first notes of the night.

Arm-in-arm, Abby and Jim started down the long, white runner. Dressed in an off-white gown, adorned in tiny pearls and lace, she wore her hair up, revealing all the love in her face. She was more than beautiful. She was heaven. Behind her Mom, Paige finished the tiny wedding party. Rick caught the young girl's smiling gaze and mouthed the words, "You look beautiful."

"Thank you," she mouthed back.

Jim kissed Abby's cheek, placed her hand into Rick's and then took his respective place beside his son. Rick smiled at his dad. Jim placed his hand upon his shoulder and Rick could feel the depth of his father's love.

Before family, friends and God, Rick and Abby exchanged their vows of eternal love. "Til death do we part," they swore and meant every word. From the start, Paige began to cry. Rick glanced quickly at her. They were the tears of joy and love. His eyes filled, as well.

Beneath a giant, white tent, a family-style barbecue – including an enormous vat of macaroni and cheese – awaited their guests.

Just beside Grandma, an empty place setting was left in memory of Bill. The smiles that beamed from the wedding poses, though, more than revealed his presence. The entire Freedom Ave family was back together. Paige was glowing the brightest.

After the reverend's blessing, Jim stood and cleared his throat. To the sobs of Abby, he read:

"Everything

Into the night, I cast a wish
that my life I might share.
And when I least expected love
you answered every prayer.

I found my heart inside your eyes,
my future in your smile.
And from the day I took your hand
I've cherished every mile.

This path shall lead us to the end
through sun and freezing rain.
Without conditions, I am here
in joy and every pain.

Our love is proof that dreams come true,
I vow – in life and death:
That all I am, I give to you
with each and every breath.

From the darkness came a light
that only God could bring.
For you are not just who I love…

to me, you're everything."

Everyone was asked to open the tiny box tied in a tinier bow sitting in the plate before them. All at once, a cloud of butterflies was released into the fading watercolor sky. As they flew into the heavens, Abby grabbed Rick and kissed him long.

After everyone had licked the barbecue sauce from their fingers, Gary B began his heartfelt, acoustic rendition of Keith Whitley's classic, *When You Say Nothing At All*. Rick grabbed Abby and swayed back and forth with his new wife.

For the next dance, Rick approached Paige and extended his hand. "Will you do me the honor, Miss?"

She didn't hesitate. She grabbed his hand and followed him out to the portable dance floor.

As they danced, Abby glowed. She didn't know a better place than in Rick's arms, but even that didn't measure up to watching the two of them talking, laughing and twirling beneath a full harvest moon.

For a moment, Paige stopped laughing. "It seems strange that you and Mom would get married here – considering the way I acted toward you that day."

He stopped and peered into her innocent eyes. "Nonsense. In many ways, this farm is where you, me and your mom all began. I guess it only makes sense that we take the next step right from here."

When the song ended, Abby met Paige on the edge of the dance floor and placed both hands on her daughter's face. "I still breathe for you, ya know."

Paige smiled. "I know, Mom," she said, melting into her mother's opened arms. "I do."

For the remainder of the glorious celebration, Rick alternated dances between Paige and Abby. Eunice danced with Scott. Danny danced with Carol. Vinny danced with Darlene. Cheyenne danced with Stephanie. Grant danced with anyone he could get his hands on. And even if he wanted to, Jim couldn't have wiped the smile from his face.

Between songs, Rick grabbed Grant and stepped off to the side. "Everything okay between you and Carmen?" he asked.

Grant smiled. "You know us, Buddy. Things have never been better." He thought for a moment. "...or worse." He shrugged. "She thinks she's punishing me by making me come here solo, but don't worry about me and Carmen. We'll be together forever."

Rick shook his head. "Why did you guys ever get married?"

He shrugged again. "Because it's what we were supposed to do when we grew up, right?"

Rick shook his head again, patted his foolish friend on the shoulder and then searched out his wife for another dance.

Like rhinestones on a black velvet curtain, a billion stars lit up the sky. No one made a wish, though. On this night, it seemed that every one of them had already come true.

At the hotel room, it was late when Abby opened the last card. It was from Bill. Rick searched her face. Her tears said it all. "What?" he asked.

"Money will never be an issue again," she said and sat on the bed.

Rick picked up the card. It read: *Now that you realize you don't need it...here's my investment in your future. Sorry it couldn't be more.*

Rick glanced at the check. There were more zeroes than he'd ever seen. *Sorry it couldn't be more?* he thought. And then it hit him. Bill wasn't talking about money. He was talking about time.

Rick joined his wife on the bed for a hug.

As Abby kissed him, she whispered, "There's only one more thing that will make everything perfect."

Rick propped up on one elbow. "Name it, Mrs. Giles, and it's yours."

"I'd like to ask Grandma to move in with us."

His eyes filled and he kissed her gently for her kindness. A moment later, he kissed her more passionately and took the first step on their way to heaven.

Chapter 26

With Paige and Brandon squirming in the backseat, on a whim Rick drove Abby down memory lane – all the way back to Lincoln Park. As they pulled in to the parking lot, he was just as surprised. "Oh, my God!" they gasped and looked at each other to confirm what they'd seen.

It was essentially gone, most of it lost in a massive fire years before. With the rest auctioned off, whatever remained was completely dilapidated – mere remnants of the past. Rick grabbed Abby's hand and found a hole in the chain link fence that surrounded the perimeter. As if they were kids again, they sneaked in and took a walk. Paige and Brandon reluctantly followed.

Charred buildings barely revealed the paintings of clowns. The concrete midway was overgrown with scrub brush. The coaster; their childhood rite of passage, remained, but was no more than a skeleton of rotted wood. One good windstorm and it was sure to topple. Abby felt heartbroken. Reading this, Rick squeezed her hand. As he scanned the sorrowful wasteland, his childhood rushed back to him and for a magical moment he was back in 1978:

The Bubble Bounce was located right near the Tilt 'O Whirl and worked on the same idea. It was a square car with a fixed steering wheel in the center. It spun and twirled and claimed as many victims of sudden illness as any of them. After the second time the gang rode it, Tracy looked green and begged for mercy.

"Not a chance," Grant said.

Behind The Bubble Bounce, The Teacup Ride, with its eight-foot tall daffodil light posts, was one of the park's more tame adventures. Even though Tracy pleaded, the gang took a vote and passed it by.

The collective agreed, however, to take a brief reprieve from the spinning rides and made its way over to The Giant Slide. This waxed, yellow ribbon of grooves tickled the belly better than Abby's tire swing ever could. A long steel staircase ascended to heaven and the heavy swags of shag carpet draped over a rail were carried to the top. Once they received the operator's signal, they sat on the carpet, pushed off with both hands and shot to the bottom in a fraction of the time it took to hump the carpet up all the stairs. It was like sledding in the summer without the freezing wind and frostbite feet, and it was well worth the heavy labor.

Next was The Paratrooper Ride. With dangling legs, the kids sat beneath a lighted umbrella and watched the world swing in circles. Though the ride warned of only being intended for adults, it wasn't worth another wait in line.

Rick took a deep breath and returned to the present; to where Abby was staring off into the distance.

Abby could picture the rows of smiling families that sat in the Picnic Pavilion behind the giant roller coaster, eating clam cakes and chowder. The smells of onions frying on a grille and sweet corn boiling had the gang stop long enough to check it out.

It was an arch-roofed building with open sides, rows of long tables and a stage at its front. Though it hosted free outdoor shows of magicians, ventriloquists and animal shows, it also had a beer stand that sent men staggering through the park, red-faced and slurring their words. Without the need for discussion, the kids chose to avoid it. Abby already spent too much time with her dad.

After stuffing hot dogs and French fries into their bellies, the gang sprinted off to The Trabant; a devilish ride that used a spinning motion like a penny spun on its flat side. As if it wasn't enough that the ride spun quickly in circles, midway into the journey the platform raised and tilted. Even the most iron bellies would be tested. The gang looked at each other and wisely moved on. They could still taste lunch.

The Pirate's Den was a ride-through Caribbean experience that looked as fake as Old Man Sedgeband's smile. Abby jumped into Richard's car and secretly enjoyed the close quarters.

"Let's go win something," Richard announced as the ride came to a halt. Everyone followed.

A .22 caliber shooting gallery with targets of speeding boats and spinning ducks had the guys showing off their feathers. The rifle barrel was so bent, though, that the plush animals on the wall were older than most in the park. Only someone with a lazy eye had a fighting chance at victory.

Spill The Milk cost twenty-five cents to throw three softballs into a milk can that didn't fit them.

Beside it, gamblers could place bets on a board of numbers, while a wheel was spun to randomly pick the winner. It was the gang's first taste of gambling and even though they lost, they each felt like winners; real big shots.

At the Tigerstand, people threw baseballs at fake tigers, hoping to knock out a few teeth and win a striped kitten. Richard spent two weeks of a paperboy's wages before he won a plush kitty. "You can have it if you want," he told Abby and she accepted the gift with the same display of indifference. Grant and Vinny each shook their heads. Tracy smiled. She couldn't tell who liked who more, Richard or Abby.

At the end of the park, Richard, Abby and Tracy squirt streams of water into a row of clowns' mouths until the first balloon broke. While Tracy won herself a small polar bear, Grant and Vinny raced at the speedway with remote control cars.

"Step right up and try your luck!" heckled another carnie, and Richard threw hula-hoops until he fit one around a square block of wood. As Richard walked away, Abby chose a giant, stuffed penguin that filled her arms…

As Abby returned to reality, she found Rick waiting. He grabbed her around the waist and pulled her close. With his chin resting upon her head, they scanned the magical midway one last time. The giant roller coaster – which put courage to the test and turned fear into excitement – was the only real proof that life had once existed on this sacred ground. There were no echoes of laughter, no flashing lights, no smells of greasy delights. Instead, there was silence. Abby spun around and buried her face into Rick's neck. They now stood on the exact location where they'd fallen in love. Anyone looking on wouldn't have understood, or felt the strength of their memories. Paige and Brandon's blank faces confirmed it.

Even the Grand Ballroom was gone. Abby wiped her eyes. Somewhere along the way, Lincoln Park had become abandoned; lost in a world that held no value for places of nostalgia, or institutions that just made people feel good. It was clear. The past turned no profit, so it was discarded. Rick couldn't help but feel a pang of guilt. *No doubt*, he thought, *a businessman just like myself made the final decision to let the park go.*

For a long time, he and Abby stood in the middle of the barren, weed-choked lot and held each other tight. It was important to cherish it all, and remember – even though Paige and Brandon couldn't.

On the way home, Rick stopped by Gray's Ice Cream to see if they were open for the season yet. They were. While he and Abby each ordered sugar cones of coffee, Paige ordered a plain cone of chocolate chip. Without a thought, Brandon stepped up and said, "Make that two."

Rick smiled and ruffled the boy's platinum hair. "You're in big trouble," he told him. "Trust me."

Brandon had no idea what Rick was talking about and was much too interested in his ice cream cone to investigate it further. He looked at Paige. With a grin, she shrugged it off before discreetly giving Rick the eye.

Abby grabbed her daughter's arm and whispered, "If we could only understand what goes on in the mind of boys?"

Paige cringed. Even at her young age, the idea was frightening. She and her Mom were destined to spend many years contemplating such mysteries.

By mid-spring, both the land and hearts began to thaw. While the ground swelled with new life, it was another new beginning for everyone.

Rick decided to hang a porch swing out front for Abby and Paige. It was a beautiful gesture, a gift that would become their confessional for years to come.

It then took him two full nights to secretly carve a heart – with the names *Abby & Richard* – into the trunk of the back yard's weeping willow tree. On the third night, he added a second heart toward the bottom that overlapped and connected the first. In the middle of that second heart, he scraped the name *Paige*. Though the blisters throbbed, he was surprised it didn't take him longer to complete his masterpiece. Evidently, his hands were bigger and stronger, and the knife much sharper than the blade he'd used as a boy.

He was already on the deck admiring his work when Abby stepped into the morning with a steaming cup of tea. As she stood beside him, listening to an orchestra of birds, she noticed something unusual on the trunk of the willow tree. Even through a squint, it took a few moments before her eyes could make it out. It was their names – all of them – carved into the center of two perfect hearts. She gasped, placed her tea on the deck's rail and hurried to the tree.

Running her hand over the rough bark, she let the experience fill her soul. She turned to find Rick. He was smiling.

"Now we're home," he whispered, and they kissed.

Just then, Paige, Brandon and their neighborhood friends marched shoulder-to-shoulder toward the house. With the sun on their faces, their wide eyes betrayed their excitement. Dressed in last year's clothes, windbreaker jackets and new white sneakers, their pale faces and runny noses showed signs of newfound freedom. The neighborhood was alive and finally waking from its hibernation. Though there was still sand on the side of the road, all but the final remnants of black snow had disappeared. The gang drew closer and stepped into the soft, spongy grass. Rick's grinning face gazed upward to feel the sun's warm hands on his face.

As he looked back at Brandon, his youth came rushing back to him.

The sun sat on the boy's shoulders, weightless and warm, while the world was no more than an idea within his grasp. With a lung-full of air and a scream on the wind, the tickles of laughter and smiles were all that he needed. The freckles and dirt rings and platinum blonde hair meant the future was only a moment away. It was a magical innocence, fleeting but real – with dreams that could be hoped into life. T-shirts and skinned knees and scars of fair play proved real troubles were nowhere in sight. And tomorrow would awaken with the squeals of pure joy, while the mirror would announce he had grown.

Rick pulled Abby to him. "When I was their age, I lay in the grass and gazed into the sky. I knew exactly who I was, but wondered who I'd become. After years of searching and fumbling, with your love I've finally smartened up and returned to me – to when I was just a boy." He was choked up. "Thank you for that."

"Welcome home," she whispered, and kissed him. "Let's make a deal that we'll always try to live – and love – in the moment, and be grateful for all of our blessings."

"Deal," he said and sealed the pact with another kiss.

Abby looked up to find the kids gawking. She called Paige over. Brandon followed. As they approached, Rick teased, "Aren't you guys going to jump on the computer today?"

Paige smiled and whispered under her breath for him to stop teasing.

Brandon turned to Paige. "I thought you hated him?" he mumbled in a barely audible tone.

Paige half-grinned. "He's okay," she replied under her breath.

Abby reached into her sweater and pulled out a small handful of pennies; coins that were individually worth nothing, but when put together could add up to the treasure of a lifetime. "Why don't you guys go down to the railroad tracks and make a wish." She looked at Brandon and then searched her daughter's eyes. "Today's a gift," she whispered, "so go spend it wisely."

Paige smiled and handed a penny to Brandon. As they gathered up their friends and walked away, she explained, "We each make a wish and then place our pennies on the railroad tracks to seal them for all time…"

Filled with an overwhelming love, Rick pulled out his faded wallet and produced the pressed penny that Abby had given him that fateful day they'd said good-bye to childhood. He needed her to understand what it truly meant to him; what she'd always meant to him.

She gasped at the sight of it. "Oh, Richard."

He held up the penny. "Tell me, Abby, what did you wish for?"

She smiled, and a pair of tears caused her to blink. "You," she confessed, "I wished for you."

All these years, he thought, *she made the wish and I held it for us both. I carried our dreams in my wallet and never even knew it.* He kissed her for every moment he'd missed.

As they embraced, Abby began to sway.

"What are you doing?" he asked.

Her mouth quivered, trying to shape the right words. "I'm dancing in stardust."

Curled up under a blanket, Eunice looked up from her book to see Rick and Abby kissing, while Paige and her friends headed for the railroad tracks. Above the song *The Dance* by Garth Brooks, Bill's wind chimes sang in the gentle breeze. She smiled and returned to her book. Everything in the world was exactly how it should be.

Just then, a speeding truck skidded in front of the house before hitting the lawn and sliding sideways across most of it. While Abby and Rick rushed toward the front of the house to investigate the accident, Patrick slid out of the cab of the truck and staggered toward the porch. "I DON'T GIVE A DAMN WHAT YOU PEOPLE THINK OF ME," he screamed. "WHERE IN THE HELL IS MY DAUGHTER?"

With clenched fists, Rick took one giant step before Abby's firm hand stopped him. With surprise, he looked at her.

Her eyes were set like granite, confident and in control. "I'll take care of this," she whispered and marched out to face the belligerent drunk.

"YOU BETTER LISTEN GOOD," Patrick yelled, as she approached

"No," Abby said and stepped inches from his face. "You listen to me..."

Patrick was as shocked as Rick.

Abby's voice was calm but firm. "I don't believe in monsters anymore and if you ever come around here acting like one again, I'll make sure it's the last time you do." With each word, she took a step forward.

Patrick back-peddled and did all he could to stay on his feet.

"Understand?" she asked and took one final step.

Patrick didn't know what to say. He just stood there, his mouth hung open, his body wobbling from a mix of alcohol and shock.

"Good," she said with a nod. "So why don't we try it again next weekend – sober."

Dumbfounded, he looked up at the porch for help. Rick could only offer a smile. The drunk looked back at Abby and nodded. "Fine," he said and staggered back to his truck. A minute later, the sound of squealing tires faded into the distance.

When Abby turned to make her way back to the porch, Rick caught something different in her eyes. There was no mistaking it. It was peace.

Epilogue

By nightfall, Rick sat down at his laptop and turned it on. With a smile, his fingers pecked at the keys, creating a rhythmic beat. There was no hesitation, no second-guessing. As if they came from a higher place, the words just seemed to pass through him. He wrote:

A Gift
(for Paige)

In the morning when you rise,
wipe the nightmares from your eyes.
The present; a gift, a brand new day
to laugh and love your fears away.

When the sun has reached its crest,
take a breath, your mind will rest.
The present; a gift, a different view
to search within and find what's true.

In the evening when you pray,
ask for peace, just one more day.
The present; a gift, a real surprise
to watch the world through infant's eyes.

The present; a gift – don't let it flee
the future can wait, the past isn't free.
But stealing 'right now' is nothing like theft.
For all that you know, it's all that is left.

As the last word made its way into the verse, Rick sat back and read his work. By the third review, a smile made its way into the corners of his mouth. *We're going to be fine*, he thought, *Paige, Abby, me...we're going to be just fine.*

Read Other Works By Steven Manchester

The Unexpected Storm
The Gulf War Legacy
ISBN: 1555715427

Stealing away the last remnants of innocence, Steve and his friends witness the after-effects of 41 days of uninterrupted bombing. It is as if someone has raised the curtain to hell, lending the whole world a free show. It is literally hell on Earth.

Steven Manchester shares his true-life experiences of Operation Desert Storm, his fight to return home from the Middle East and the treatment he received from the government when he returned home. This is a true story of courage, valor, disappointment and redemption.

Jacob Evans
ISBN: 0976093308

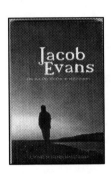

Jacob Evans is at times oddly normal, familiar yet surrealistic, falling somewhere along a continuum with Stephen King at one end and Norman Rockwell at the other. If Manchester hasn't invented a new genre, he has at least improved upon an old one.

**Harley B. Patrick, Editor,
Hellgate Press**

A very tender and remarkable piece of literature. The series of uplifting stories will touch your heart and ease your spirit. A wonderful and unique work of writing. Simply enjoyable.

- **Victor Franko, Director /Producer**
- *Nine Men's Misery*

Available at **www.stevenmanchester.com**, Amazon and Barnes & Noble or directly from Sunpiper Press.

Read Other Sunpiper Titles:

Voice of a Soldier: Operation Liberty
An Anthology of Heroism
By Margaret Marr

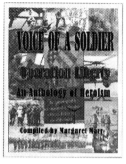

Voice of a Soldier is a conglomeration of true stories, fiction, and poetry that represent the acts of bravery, tears, laughter, love, and friendship of American soldiers from past battles to present battles. They will make you laugh, make you cry, make you proud and make you think. Most of all, it exemplifies the true inspiration of the American soldier.

Messages of Hope and Healing
By Linda Pynaker

Linda Pynaker, renowned psychic medium, healer and international speaker, has a message for anyone who grieves for a lost loved one.

You will survive one day or one moment at a time. Your loved one will rejoice as you gradually pull yourself together and reach out to life, again.

In her third book, Pynaker shares her insights of the world beyond the realm in which we live and traces the love-lines that connect us to our loved ones on the other side.

Pynaker explains in her preface, *"I wrote Messages of Hope and Healing to reassure you that your loved ones in spirit remain present in your life and to assist you in recognizing the signs. I also hope to help you to develop your own ability to communicate with the spirit world. Finally, I hope to promote universal love."*

To see other upcoming titles from Sunpiper Media Publishing, visit:

www.sunpipermedia.com/Books.html

Sunpiper Press
"Reaching Heart, Mind and Spirit"

Printed in the United States
63589LVS00001B/61-69

9 780977 005048